Between Light and Night

Rebecca Barto

To every kid desperately trying to use headphones and a tattered library book to be invisible—I see you.

New York

Part One

Chapter 1

WILLA CELADON WAITED BETWEEN the abandoned gas pumps, tapping her unlit cigarette against the flaking metal as the sun faded behind what was left of the New York skyline.

The woman didn't see her, passing underneath the dark gas station canopy with the baby in her arm, plastic flip-flops crunching on broken glass. She was singing, soft and sweet, the same as she had every night this week. The song curdled in Willa's stomach.

The mother walked easily, with no weapon on her hip as if the world hadn't changed. As if she were safe.

Willa tucked her unused cigarette behind her ear and let them pass. She didn't smoke. It was a foolish waste of rations. But sometimes the smallest token—a cigarette or a single battery or a bright red tomato—could be the difference between living and dying.

The baby smiled over her mother's shoulder, warm brown eyes filled with a light that didn't permeate the rest of the bleak world—still untouched by her future. Still, Willa could see their unwavering destiny in the woman's hollow cheeks and the lines of dirt caught in the folds of the baby's skin.

She lifted the ancient Nikon at her hip, capturing the pair with her lens before slipping behind them, breathing through her mouth to avoid the stench of body odor and sour milk. The baby babbled, pudgy fingers tangled in her mother's matted hair.

The bell jingled above the convenience store door when the mother pulled it open and Willa closed the distance quickly, dipping her hand under the woman's too-thin arm to pinch the tender skin of the baby's thigh. The little girl's face twisted, her pink lips opening in a silent O.

She stole into the store on the wake of the wail; disappearing down the nearest aisle under the cover of sorrow and the mother's soft hushes.

Willa tugged at the hem of her faded t-shirt. It was tattered but clean, and two sizes too big despite the curves she'd inherited from her dead mother. Starvation had carved into her body years ago.

She tried to make herself presentable, tying the shirt into a knot at her hip and brushing her thick hair into a braid, but by the end of the work day her jeans were ripped at the knee and her dark hair was dusted in sawdust. The only thing remotely appealing about her was the green of her eyes, just a few shades lighter than expected, and unique enough to make her dip her head.

The clerk glared at her over the rusty magazine racks and the mother's bent head, the buttons of his shirt straining to cover his protruding gut, four greasy strands of hair combed across the gleam of his forehead. The name *Stan* was stitched on his pocket in worn yellow lettering. He tapped one finger on the butt of his shotgun.

Willa made a show of looking at the nearly empty shelves. Sometimes it was almost impossible to remember what the world was like Before. She still remembered when her father would bring her by here after school for an ice cream sandwich or a cold Pepsi, the corner store bustling with tired grandmothers buying Power Ball tickets and men in stained ball caps leaning against the counter to gossip about the latest political scandal.

Stan wasn't the only one who'd changed when the Darkness came.

Willa ran her thumb through the thick dust coating the shelves. The dim light of the candles on the front counter didn't penetrate far into the belly of the store, but she didn't bother to flick on her headlamp.

She liked the dark now. Darkness hid things.

Her fingers twitched, hovering over a dented can of pinto beans. Most people shopped at the Night Market, choosing to barter instead of using cash, the slips of green paper practically useless except for burning for warmth on a cold night.

Willa contemplated the number of hours she'd have to clock at Firewood Distribution to buy it. She'd been working overtime lately, her forearms freckled with splinters. Two more shifts and the boss had promised her an extra protein ration. Her mouth watered at the thought of chicken—or at the very least, a plump pigeon.

With one eye on Stan, Willa slipped a pack of batteries into her bag. Pleasure skittered down her spine. God, she loved stealing.

On the other side of the store, the bell above the door jingled, the baby's watery sobs fading as it swung shut. Willa wondered when she had become a bad person, and if it even mattered anymore.

When the first electromagnetic pulse hit the East Coast, the government had assured people that the electrical outages were temporary. That they should all stay calm and return to their homes. That the power grid would be fixed soon.

Days had gone by. Then weeks. In the vacuum of information that followed, rumors of bombs being dropped over North Korea were whispered in the streets—retaliation for a technological war the government couldn't fight. But then more EMPs followed: San Francisco and Tokyo, Auckland and London.

Soon—much sooner than anyone could have expected—the reason didn't matter anymore.

Computers and phones stayed silent. The black eyes of traffic lights and blank screens a blind witness to growing panic. Without electricity, the modern world ground to a halt. The stench of the dead drifted down from the skyscrapers and the nights were filled with looting. Fires raged in every corner of the city.

Willa wasn't sure when temporary tragedy had given way to a new reality. It was probably the day the tanks rolled across the Brooklyn Bridge. Fifth Avenue had been lined with people, a horrible silence settling underneath the steady pound of soldier's boots.

She'd hidden in the apartment that night and a hundred endless nights after, tensing when a scream leaked beneath the door, her father sitting crosslegged across from her, cradling a gun he didn't know how to use instead of his guitar.

"Buy something or get the hell out, " Stan yelled, interrupting her morbid memories.

"Almost done!" she called, swiping a roll of tape she didn't need to steal into her bag.

Stan frowned. Even in the growing dusk, Willa could see the flames of color hovering around his body. An aura that only she could see.

His was a murky fog, muddy tendrils of color that dragged through the air when he reached for his gun. If she hadn't known better, Willa might have thought it was just a trick of the light. But she did know better.

When she was little, she'd thought everyone could see the colors. That each person's aura was just another part of them, as ordinary as the size of their nose or the complexion of their skin. She had learned the truth the hard way.

Stan picked up his shotgun as she stole a half-crushed pack of peanut butter crackers. She should stop. The justice system didn't work the same way it did before the Pulse. There was no jury of your peers, just the Department of Homeland Security and the Compound where people disappeared.

A small can of dog food caught her eye. Willa glanced up at the blind surveillance camera, before slipping it into her—

Someone stepped into her aisle.

Her heart rattled. It was dark, but she knew immediately it wasn't Stan. The figure was lean, moving toward her with the easy grace of youth.

She snapped on her headlamp. The stranger paused and held up a hand to shield his eyes.

He looked about her age. The patch above the pocket of his navy button-down read: Al's Auto Parts. The black grease staining his shirt was the same shade as his hair, which curled loosely just below his collar. Good looking in an average sort of way.

"Do you mind?" the boy said, squinting into the light. Willa lowered the beam, careful to keep his face partly illuminated. The kid didn't have any visible weapons, but she knew he was armed. Everyone carried these days.

He kept his hands up, his stance relaxed even as he moved closer. "I'm not going to hurt you."

She snorted. "I'd like to see you try."

He laughed. It was an easy sound and strange. Willa couldn't remember the last time she had heard someone laugh.

His aura rippled as he eased closer, different shades of blue that danced like a gas flame around his face. Willa tensed but didn't reach for her knife. She'd been in many dangerous situations since the Darkness—cornered in alleys by strange men or begging for food in the brittle cold. Survival had taught her to listen to the voice inside of her. The one that whispered and warned and told the truth.

The voice was silent as the boy approached. As if danger couldn't be sustained in the wake of his laughter.

He brushed by her in the narrow aisle, careful to keep his hands up. Willa eyed him warily. He'd seen her steal the can of dog food. She wondered if he understood desperation. If he had ever curled against the cold spine of despair to keep warm.

She crossed her arms when he paused in front of her, shooting a look over at Stan and then down at her. His eyes were nondescript from a distance but up close they were the bruised sky at dusk, black and blue and gray.

When he leaned closer, she didn't stop him. "It's not me you should be worried about, Robin Hood," he said, voice low. He smelled like rain and motor oil. "Stan likes to shoot people who steal from him. Even pretty girls."

She bristled. "That is none of your goddamn business—"

"Asher," he supplied helpfully.

"Well, Asher..." she said, smiling sweetly, "if you would just move the hell along, that would be fucking fantastic."

The boy shrugged. "It's your funeral."

Willa gritted her teeth. She'd had enough of stupid know-it-all boys to last an eon. "Listen—"

"No loitering!" Stan bellowed.

Willa flinched, her hand going to her bag and the stolen merchandise hidden inside. The boy raised an eyebrow at the furtive movement. She opened her mouth to tell him exactly where he could put his concern, but he just shook his head and turned away.

Willa glared at his back. She didn't have time for this.

Stan was glaring at her, balding head reflecting the candlelight. The stranger who knew her secret reached into the warm freezer for a soda. His aura glowed around his bent head like cobalt fire.

Willa adjusted her camera strap and headed to the front of the store, slapping a pack of gum onto the counter. Stan squinted at it. Willa could have sworn her bag got heavier against her hip while she waited for him to hike himself back onto his stool. It wobbled precariously. She wondered what other things Stan was selling to afford the rations it must take to support his ample girth. Drugs maybe. Or women.

"You were back there a long time," Stan grumbled, sweat dripping down one temple.

Willa's stomach turned. She handed him two dollars, hoping he wouldn't notice the slight dampness of the bills as he flattened them and added them to the cash box.

"Sorry about that, my mom sent me for Tylenol but you're all out so I got this instead. Figured she wouldn't mind."

Stan narrowed his eyes.

Shit. Stores hadn't carried pharmaceuticals for years. After the hospitals had been dismantled, medicine was controlled by the Night Markets.

She held out her palm. Stan hesitated, her coins still tight in his fist as he studied her. "You know...I've been having a lot of trouble with stealing lately," he said slowly. Willa nodded despite the fear twisting through her veins. "Maybe I should check that bag of yours. Just to be—"

An arm slid around her waist. Willa tensed, but Asher's hand settled on her hip as if it belonged there. "There you are, Robin," he said, dropping a kiss on the top of her head. Willa blinked. His body was warm.

Asher smiled easily at the clerk. "Sorry we took so long, sir. She couldn't keep her hands off me back there." He waggled his eyebrows in that stupid way boys did when bragging about a conquest.

Before she could react, Asher leaned down to kiss her, his knuckles firm underneath her chin. It was just the lightest brush of lips—casual and familiar—but her whole body jolted in response. His fingers tightened on her waist.

He pulled back, touching her nose with his finger playfully, but his eyes were a warning. She forced a tight smile. "I just can't help myself," she confessed, her breathy laugh a lie even to her own ears.

Willa could see the glimmer of amusement in Asher's eyes. The bastard was enjoying this. She bared her teeth at him.

He laughed and released her, leaning easily on the counter as he pulled a wallet out of his backpack. Stan took his hand off the gun and reached for the cash box.

Asher's fingers danced along the counter as he waited for his change as if playing an instrument that wasn't there. Colors only she could see shimmered above his knuckles. He seemed completely relaxed, chatting easily with Stan about the uptick of crime in the neighborhood while her body screamed at her to run.

Willa wondered how he did that. How he could act as if the world wasn't a minefield.

Stan handed Asher the change for the soda and her gum. Sexist, but she didn't even care. Relief started to bleed into the fear clenched around her heart—only a couple more moments and she'd be free.

The bell above the door jingled cheerfully again.

Willa didn't even have a chance to turn around before a meaty hand thudded on her shoulder. The familiar stink of aftershave and salami assaulted her. She groaned.

"Well, if it isn't the prettiest little thief on the block," Frank boomed. "I told you I'd lock you up the next time I caught you in this neighborhood. How stupid can you be, girl?"

Willa closed her eyes. Six years of hiding and running, stealing and starving, had come down to one hand on her shoulder. He shoved her forward with his forearm, his thick body pressing her against the counter while his other hand skimmed down her arms. She shuddered.

She'd heard things about Frank. Unpleasant things. She would not be surprised to discover the rumors were true.

He was a recruit in the Department of Homeland Security, the worst of the militia that had formed after the Pulse. Not a soldier really. Just another bastard with a gun, a small dick, and a heart filled with hate. The DHS was filled with guys like him.

And now they controlled the city—hell, the world as far as she knew—following every crazy mandate passed down from what was left of the US government.

"Slimy thief," Frank sneered, shoving her cheek against the sticky counter. Asher's eyes turned to flint, the cool blue flame of his aura threading with red.

"Fuck you," she spat as he patted her down, his thumb brushing the side of her breast.

"Is that really necessary?" Asher asked quietly.

Willa's eyes slid over to him. He was still relaxed, one hip propped casually against the counter, but there was something in the sharp line of his shoulders—like the cold slide of the river under a thick layer of ice.

Alarm rang through her. The idiot should shut his mouth. This was not his fight.

"She just came in here to buy a pack of gum," Asher said.

Frank snorted, his fingers dipping into her empty front pocket. Sweat followed the bent curve of her spine.

"I'm doing my job," Frank shot back, his hands drifting down her thighs, "you know, cleaning up the trash."

"Sure," Asher said with a shrug. "Or maybe you're a pervert who likes feeling up young girls with an audience watching."

Willa's head shot up at the insult. Frank swore and yanked her around.

She blinked. There was something wrong with his aura, watery brown and nearly translucent it faded in and out like a lost cable connection. His eyes were unnaturally small between his bushy eyebrows and squashed nose. It was the face of every bully she had ever known.

Frank ripped the bag from her shoulder but spoke to the idiot, "You're Asher Flint aren't you? I know your mama."

Asher stiffened.

"She wouldn't want to get mixed up with garbage like this," Frank continued, wrinkling his nose at her as if she were the one who smelled.

Willa fought the shame that clawed at her cheeks. She knew who she was—*what* she was—but it sucked to hear it out loud all the same.

Frank tipped her bag, letting the contents clatter to the floor. Her flashlight. Three tampons. Rat jerky. A faded picture of her dead mother. And nothing else.

All the things she'd stolen were gone. Willa swallowed and forced herself not to look at Asher. *How the hell—*

Frank tossed her bag to the side, cursing, and reached for the camera at her hip. Rage sliced through her fear. She punched him.

Frank grunted, almost as surprised as she was, her fist glancing off of his soft chin. He reared back, slightly off balance and she tried to duck around him, but Frank was a brawler. He came up swinging, his meaty fist catching her in the shoulder. She spun, stunned at the sharp pain, banging her forearm on the counter.

Asher caught her, pulling her against his chest as he drew a hidden knife. The blade winked in the candlelight, wickedly sharp and jagged—a direct contradiction to the laughing boy she'd just met.

Frank sneered at him and flicked open the holster at his hip with a thumb. Willa felt the moment shift from an unfortunate encounter with a dirty cop to something with a dangerous edge. His gun gleamed—government-issued, oiled and cleaned, and very loaded.

Behind her, Asher tensed, muscles coiling to attack—until Stan nestled the barrel of his shotgun into the divot in Asher's skull.

Willa sucked in a sharp breath. Asher froze. A slow, mean grin spread across Frank's face.

"Get this trash out of my store," Stan snarled.

Frank gave a tiny salute with his forefinger. "That's what I'm here for Chief."

Willa glanced up at Asher. She could see that he wanted to fight, fury bleeding through his veil of calm. His gray eyes sliced toward her. She knew what he was asking.

She shook her head. There was no way she was going to let him take the fall for her stupidity.

A muscle ticked in his jaw, but Asher dropped the knife, the metal ringing against the concrete floor like funeral bells.

Frank grinned and yanked the backpack from Asher's shoulder. A can of dog food, a roll of tape, and a package of peanut butter crackers tumbled onto the floor.

"Well, Mr. Flint, turns out you're the thief after all."

Asher shrugged despite the gun digging into his skull. "And maybe you're just an asshole who has nothing better to do than harass innocent kids to compensate for your small—"

Frank punched him in the stomach. Asher gasped, doubling over.

"Hands behind your back," the cop barked, reaching for his cuff.

And then it was over. Willa pressed a hand to her stomach as Frank dragged Asher toward the door. "I have just the cell for you, Mr. Flint. Your own little spot in hell."

Willa blinked. "But I—"

"Keep your hands clean, Robin," Asher interrupted, craning his neck around Frank's beefy arm to meet her eye.

"You idiot," Willa hissed, but Frank was already pushing open the door. The bell jangled one last time.

Willa followed them. She couldn't let this happen. Couldn't let someone she didn't know take her punishment. The world didn't work that way anymore.

She gripped the doorframe as Frank dragged Asher to the beat-up Impala parked half on the curb. Night had fallen, the tips of broken skyscrapers disappearing into blackness above their heads.

But she would die in prison. A girl her age wouldn't last a week.

There was nothing she could give Asher now, but she called out anyway, her words nearly swallowed by the night. "Willa. My name is Willa."

Asher's face was pale in the darkness as Frank fumbled with his keys, but she saw his smile. "Nice to meet you, Willa," he said, even though she knew it wasn't.

It was cold out on the sidewalk and quiet. Her hands hung loosely at her sides. Frank shoved Asher into his backseat and slammed the door.

Asher shot her a crooked smile through the car window. Willa squinted. Something bright glinted between his teeth.

It was a key. A tiny handcuff key.

Asher winked as Frank pulled away, and Willa felt something inside of her that had been dark for a long time crack open. She laughed.

Chapter 2

18 months later

WILLA GRIPPED THE STEERING wheel tighter as her battered Chevy pickup shuddered. "Darkness, not again," she swore. The engine rattled ominously above the frantic beat of the windshield wipers.

Pumping the gas helplessly, Willa leaned forward to stroke the cracked dashboard. "I didn't mean it, Gloria," she told her truck. "If you can take me the last couple miles, I swear I'll get you some filtered gas—none of that crude that Nico sells on down on 8th."

The truck responded with a loud bang and promptly stalled. Willa let Gloria drift to a stop at the curb. The headlights sputtered and then died, plunging the cab into darkness. She stared out of the rain-streaked windshield while the engine ticked quietly.

What the actual fuck? Willa pressed her forehead against the steering wheel and wished, for the hundredth time in the past seven years, for a cell phone. A vehicle that wasn't held together with duct tape and prayers would be nice, too.

Willa glanced in the rearview mirror at the cord of firewood in the bed of the truck, glad she'd taken the time to cover it in a tattered blue tarp, even though her back ached from her eight-hour shift at work.

She watched the rain pool against a clogged gutter and debated her next move. The wood in the back of the trunk was practically useless—bits of broken furniture and scraps of flooring that would undoubtedly fill the apartment with toxic smoke—but it was hers, and it would last the winter.

She glanced gratefully at the half dozen dry logs she'd stacked on the passenger seat. It was real wood, cut from the few precious trees left in Central Park or carried in from the forests upstate. They'd cost her a whole month's ration, but meat wasn't much good if she couldn't cook it.

Willa sighed as wisps of smoke drifted from Gloria's engine, the cold night air already seeping into the cab. She should be grateful even to have a truck. The original Pulse had fried electric circuits for a hundred square miles, the massive magnetic discharge erasing every computer from JFK airport to her Fitbit. Eventually, someone figured out that old cars could be brought back to life, the lack of complicated technology turning junkers into the new supercars of the road. She'd stolen Gloria—an 83' Chevy pickup—three years ago. It was the first decision she'd made on her own and still one of the best.

Willa watched the storm paint rivers down her windshield. She'd been so young when the world had changed when everything tilted and reorganized itself into something hard and unforgiving. It would be easier if she couldn't remember. If Starbucks and iPhones were just a fairytale someone had told. All that was gone now, the memories curling around the edges like old photographs in a forgotten shoebox.

The world had ground to a halt one afternoon in late September when the planes had fallen from the brilliant blue sky like dying locusts and the buzz of information in everyone's hands had gone eerily silent.

No one was prepared. The Pentagon had contingency plans for a nuclear fallout or pandemic, but an electromagnetic pulse being used as a weapon of mass destruction had been farfetched at best. The United States spent years worrying about North Korea's nuclear program, unaware the enemy had been working on a different kind of weapon. One specially designed to destroy a society that was completely reliant on technology.

The first few years had been brutal, filled with sickness and dying and endless hunger. It was better now. The remaining survivors had settled into their small lives. Or tried to.

But some people weren't survivors.

Her father lasted two years before despair took him. Willa thought of his hands the most; the callouses worn onto his fingertips from years pressed against guitar strings. They were strong hands and his music soothed the pain of that first long winter.

It turned out that his hands were the only strong thing about him. It wasn't an unusual story. People changed when the Darkness came. As life settled into its new horrible rhythm, a rolling tide of suicide and despair swept over the dwindling survivors.

Her father had faded, the cheerful yellow of his aura growing thin like fading sunlight. And then one day he'd left with his guitar and a small duffle bag and never came home. She'd been on her own for six years.

Lightening flashed in the distance, startling her from her memories. Willa straightened. She wasn't getting any closer to home sulking about the past. Muttering unpleasant things about Gloria's virtue under her breath, she wrapped her camera in a plastic bag and shoved it in her backpack before stepping out of the truck. It was like jumping into the East River.

Willa let her hood fall back to her shoulders as cold rain soaked her instantly—she might as well be trying to stay dry with tissue paper.

If it weren't for the storm she would have felt nervous leaving Gloria and the firewood, but tonight the streets were deserted. She fingered the blade in her pocket and started down the sidewalk. There were rumors that monsters haunted the city at night, nameless horrors that lurked in dark corners and stole your will with bony fingers. Creatures that snatched your soul and left you a lifeless slave. Stupid. The only monsters Willa knew wore the hard faces of men.

After ten minutes, she was soaked to the bone. After an hour, her boots squished with every step, her hair a cold curtain plastered against her neck. She passed no one. Not even a monster would brave such weather, but she moved to the center of the street just to be safe, keeping her eye on the faded double line, measuring the passing of time in the chafe of her thighs.

If it hadn't been for the white glow of light in a puddle, she might have missed the open garage.

Willa glanced up. When she was little, her father used to take her to Coney Island at night. They'd walk to the water's edge until the noise of the boardwalk was swallowed by the hush of waves. She'd stand with her feet in the ocean and watch the twinkle of the Ferris wheel as it spun.

The garage reminded her of that. Light spilled out onto the wet street, warm and inviting, a mirage in the rain. Just inside, a lone figure was bent over the engine of a rusty sedan, a lantern swinging from a hook above his head.

Willa reached for her camera, even as cold rain slithered down her collar, tucking the image inside her Nikon before crossing the street.

The mechanic was banging on the engine with a wrench, shirt pulled up, his skin a pale crescent above the waistband of his jeans. She cleared her throat, but he continued working, humming something as he worked that sounded vaguely familiar. His aura glowed across the lines of his body like a second skin, an invisible whisper of blue.

Willa hesitated and then reached forward to tap his shoulder.

The man yelped, jerking upward and banging his head on the hood with a painful clunk. Willa took a quick step back as he spun toward her, the nebula of flames around his body charring to black.

She had her knife out before he finished turning, an enormous wrench clenched in his hand. The mechanic's eyes widened—seawater blue and familiar. He froze, face twisting.

Willa lowered her knife. "It's you."

It was the boy from the convenience store. Only he wasn't a boy anymore. His face was leaner than she remembered and he'd grown a beard, trimmed close to his jaw.

Still, she should have recognized him. He was wearing the same blue work shirt, only now it was covered with so many grease stains it was nearly black and soft, like the kind of shirt you borrowed from your boyfriend after sex.

He looked good. But different, too. The hardships of the world had chipped away the lightness she'd seen that day in the store, his pale blue aura permanently shot through with black fissures.

He set the wrench on the edge of the car frame and arched an eyebrow. "Let me guess—car trouble? Either that or you can't afford to pay for a shower."

Willa resisted the urge to straighten her sodden clothes, knowing how she must look. "My truck broke down a few streets back."

He nodded, eyeing the knife she still held. "I think we've established I'm not going to hurt you. You know, since I saved your life the last time. Maybe you could put that away?"

Willa shoved the knife back into her jacket. "You're..."

"Asher," he supplied. "And you're Willa?"

Willa rubbed warmth back into her arms and tried not to shiver, glancing back at the open garage door. Asher looked at her for another beat and then nodded to himself as if deciding something. His muscles flexed as he slammed the hood shut, and Willa was suddenly painfully aware that her hair hung in limp rags around her shoulders.

Asher pulled out a battered thermos before hopping onto the car's hood, patting the spot next to him. He cracked open the thermos lid. The air filled with the smell of coffee.

Willa's mouth watered. Mother of Darkness, he had coffee.

During the first few years, it seemed that the supply of coffee beans would never run out. There was an abandoned cafe on every street corner, after all, but after eight cold winters, coffee was difficult to find.

Asher held it out to her. Willa only hesitated a moment before sliding up next to him and taking the thermos. She took a sip. It was sweetened slightly and filled with cream, so lush and decadent she groaned. "Holy shit, where did you get this?"

He laughed.

She remembered that, too. The way he laughed. But it sounded wrong as if the Darkness had tarnished it. As if something had twisted the joy inside of him.

"One of my foster moms worked at an Aldi warehouse, you know...Before," Asher said.

Willa nodded. There was no need to clarify. There were only two times that mattered now—Before and After.

"She runs the Night Market in Midtown," he continued, taking a drink.

Willa studied Asher with newfound respect. Government mandated rations were impossible to live on, so people had found another way to get what they needed. Most of the Markets were dangerous places filled with junkies and prostitutes. Anything and anyone could be sold there. But the Midtown Market was notorious for being safe and fair. She'd made the climb to the 10th floor many times.

They were silent for a moment, listening to the rain tap against the sidewalk. She should probably say something. She was responsible for the darkness that strangled his laugh and the wariness in his eyes.

Willa cleared her throat. "Thank you, for..." She waved vaguely, "you know."

"For the coffee?"

She scowled. "You know what."

Asher's shoulder brushed against hers as he shrugged. "No worries."

She knew there must have been many worries. No one went to Compound in Central Park for shits and giggles.

Willa tapped a finger against the car hood and studied the garage. There was a couch along one wall, olive green and sagging in the middle. A pillow peaked out from a nest of blankets on the floor and an old igloo cooler was sitting on a workbench next to a few dirty dishes.

"So, what happened after you were arrested?" she asked.

She tried to keep her tone casual, but it sounded like bullshit even to her. She couldn't ask the questions that pressed against the back of her teeth, like: how were those long nights in prison? The cold, lonely ones meant for me? How was it being beaten and starved for a crime you didn't commit? How *was* it?

Asher flashed her a lopsided smile that was shaped like a lie. "Well. I *almost* escaped."Willa's heart hollowed. She picked at piece of car rust with a fingernail. "That bastard Frank caught me sneaking out through the trunk—locked me up for a while. It was no big deal. A few solid meals a day did me some good."

She looked at him then, but his gaze slid off hers like ice.

There was a scar, faint but noticeable, that started at the bridge of his nose and disappeared beneath his left eyebrow. She was pretty sure it hadn't been there before.

Willa peeled her wet hair from her neck, separating the tangles with her fingers. She'd let him keep his secrets. Everyone had them, and they were practically strangers.

"So what's your story?" Asher asked after a few seconds of awkward silence.

Willa separated her hair into three sections, smoothing them as best she could before she started braiding. "Not much to tell. I was ten when it happened."

"You living with anyone?"

Willa thought about her dark empty apartment. "Not really. My mother died Before. My dad was around for a while...but he's gone now. What about you?"

Asher tapped his fingers on the hood absently. "I was bouncing around the foster care system when it Pulsed. My foster moms could have kicked me out, but they didn't. I got lucky."

She nodded, flicking her wet braid behind her. Asher took another sip of coffee. In the distance, church bells peeled quietly. Eleven tolls from the Timekeepers who keep the city in rhythm.

"Shit," Asher said, sliding off the hood. "I've got somewhere to be at midnight."

Willa straightened. Of course. This kid wasn't just waiting around to save her ass, he had his own life. She hopped down as Asher arranged his tools in the top drawer of an enormous dented red toolbox, noticing with amusement that each tool was neatly placed in a carefully drawn outline of itself.

"Sorry," he said over his shoulder. "I don't have time to fix your car tonight, but I can drop you off somewhere."

"That's okay. I can walk," Willa said hastily, trying not to shiver as she swung her bag onto her shoulder. It was raining again. She stifled a sigh.

"Don't be stupid," he tossed a dirty rag into a bin, flicking off the lantern. "It's no big deal. I'll take you home and look at your car tomorrow."

Willa squinted at the back of his head. She already owed him an enormous debt, the fact of it nagged at her like a rotten tooth. Still. She was miles from home and it would take her all night to walk back to the apartment.

There was no real decision. Willa followed him out to the sidewalk, ducking underneath the sheet of water pouring from the clogged gutters. The street was barren, but she could hear the occasional *whoosh* of a car sweeping by on the highway overpass above their heads.

Asher pulled the garage door closed with a slow rumble and then jerked his chin to the left. "My car's just around the corner."

She followed, her steps faltering when Asher bent to unlock the sleek Camaro parked in the alley next to the shop. It was in pristine condition, a gleaming twin to the shining black puddles on the pavement. The car looked ridiculously out of place as if a tiny piece of the past had driven itself to this empty corner of the city to wait for them.

Willa whistled as she reached for the handle. Asher chuckled and he slid into the driver's seat next to her. The car even smelled good. She ran a hand over the inky leather seat. "Beautiful," she said, raising her eyebrows.

"I know it's a ridiculous luxury," he confessed as the car roared to life. "But it's one of the perks of being a mechanic."

Willa hummed as they pulled away from the curb, forcing herself not to comment. Driving a car in this kind of condition was more than a luxury. It made you stand out. The roads after the Pulse were filled with old pickups and minivans, their engines cobbled together from a thousand junkers. Most people were ecstatic to have a car at all, but this Camaro was something else entirely.

Asher shifted gears and picked up speed, keeping to the middle of the road, the shining black hood gobbling up the faded yellow line. The throaty rumble of the engine vibrated under her thighs.

"Where can I drop you off?" Asher asked, his fingers drumming on the steering wheel.

Willa cracked the window, letting the cool night air catch in her hair. "Where does a car mechanic have to be at midnight?"

"I have a gig on Beacon Street. Well, *under* Beacon Street."

Asher's bag sat at her feet. For the first time, she noticed the drumsticks poking out of the top. "You don't mean the Thursday night show?"

He looked over at her, his eyes hidden by the night. "Yeah."

"Wait, *you're* the drummer for the Wraiths?"

He nodded, clearly pleased. She leaned against the door. There was no point trying to play it cool. She was impressed. Beacon Street was the most famous underground club in the city. Willa went as often as she could, which was almost never.

"Can I go with you?" she asked, trying not to sound too eager.

Asher downshifted, taking a tight corner too fast. Willa gripped the edge of the leather seat, but the car banked smoothly, drifting a little before the tires bit into the asphalt and shot forward. "Aren't you a little young?"

She could see his grin in the dark. He was teasing her, the arrogant ass. He couldn't be more than a year older than her.

In response, Willa tugged her wet t-shirt over her head and tossed it at her feet, exposing the black lace bra underneath. Asher's fingers stilled on the steering wheel as she kicked off her boots, and braced her feet on the dashboard to shimmy out of her damp jeans. They hit the floor with a wet thump.

"I have a girlfriend," he told the windshield. It was Willa's turn to smile in the dark. "Good for you."

He looked. It made her skin tingle.

She took her time pulling a change of clothes out of her bag, yanking on her spare tank top, and wiggling into her cut-offs. It was way too cold for such an outfit, but it was the one she had stored in her bag before the summer had started to melt into fall, and it would have to do. There was nothing she could do about her wet feet, so she just tucked them back into her sodden boots.

Asher's gaze was firmly back on the road, but she could see the flush on his neck. Swallowing her triumph, Willa touched the back of his hand where it firmly gripped the gear shift.

"Please?" she asked sweetly.

She sensed, rather than saw, him roll his eyes. Willa smiled, one more time, into the darkness.

Chapter 3

WILLA CLIMBED OVER ONE of the abandoned barricades that littered the city and followed Asher into the bowels of the subway. After the first riots, large gatherings had been forbidden. Groups of people tended to share their stories, and desperation was contagious, so the floundering government banned them—stealing community from an already broken world. But survivors had found a way, hiding music underground, burying their joy under tons of concrete.

Willa trailed a finger through the condensation on the concrete wall as they descended into the darkness, tracing the outline of faded graffiti. Asher paused at the bottom, the beam of his flashlight catching on the corners of the empty platform. Faint bursts of color pulsed from the mouth of the train tunnel, illuminating the small city of discarded tents that littered the floor. The distant thrum of music echoed in the cavernous space, cutting through the eerie stillness.

They stood still for a moment, listening for the scuff of feet or the metallic slide of a blade, but there was nothing. All the people who'd lived here had moved on years ago.

"I've heard some strange rumors about these tunnels," she whispered when Asher started moving again, kicking at a rat that scurried across the toe of her boot.

Asher wove around garbage and gray puddles. "What kind of rumors?"

Willa shrugged, trying not to notice the way the throbbing lights cast ghostly shadows on the wall. "Oh, just stupid ghost stories. Monsters lurking in the dark and all that."

They stopped at the edge of the subway tracks. She almost expected to see the headlights of the E train emerging from the black throat of the tunnel. She could practically feel the warm press of bodies and the murmur of commuters, an echo of her life before.

Asher leaped down onto the tracks with annoying grace and held out his hand. She ignored it, sitting down to scoot off of the platform. Her boots skidded on the loose gravel when she jumped, but she managed to keep her balance and her dignity.

He didn't comment, rubbing his empty hand on his jeans. "Do you think the stories are true?"

Willa thought about the number of times she had felt fear trickle down her spine. The times she had been walking alone and something had made her pick up speed. She didn't know if it was hysteria or wisdom, and she'd never stuck around long enough to find out.

"I think," she said, brushing off her ass, "there are enough things to worry about without adding some sort of fucking monster to the mix."

They started down the tracks, keeping the dead middle rail between them. "Probably just a bunch of kids trying to scare people away from this place," Asher agreed.

Willa wished she believed that—wished they didn't live in a world where anything horrible could be true.

Gravel crunched under their feet as they entered the subway tunnel. Willa's stomach clenched. She hated being underground, with countless tons of metal and glass and pavement pressing down on them from above.

Asher had flicked off his flashlight so they were navigating by only the dim flashes of colored lights that bounced off the curved ceiling. She wanted to ask him to turn it back on, but wasting batteries was careless, so she just shifted closer, the back of her hand brushing his.

"How long have you been a drummer?" she asked, trying to distract herself as they moved deeper.

"One of my foster families got me started in middle school. At first, I just thought it would be a cool way to get girls."

She laughed. "Did it work?"

It was so dark that the world was just shapes and shadows, but she could hear the grin in his voice. "Of course."

"So why do you do it now?" she asked, picking her way over a pile of debris.

"What do you mean?"

"You said that you *used* to do it for the girls. What, not anymore?"

For a minute she thought he wasn't going to answer, the hollow crunch of their footsteps echoing in the tunnel, but then, "Now I do it because I have to. Because it is the only time I feel normal."

He paused. She could feel his gaze in the darkness. "You?"

Willa squinted down the tunnel. She understood what he was offering. *I am alone in this world and this is how I keep from drowning. What does your life raft look like? How do you keep your head above water?*

"We should keep moving," she said and started walking again. After a moment, she felt him follow.

The steady pounding of music grew as if they were descending into the heart of a giant beast. The passage forked, and then forked again, the air cooling as they walked deeper. She shivered and refused Asher's jacket. He shook his head but didn't argue.

They turned a second corner and came to a stop. Willa swore. She'd never been to Beacon Street from this direction. She should have expected complications. Nothing was easy in this world.

A wrecked subway car obstructed most of the broken track, the half-crushed cab tilting at such a severe angle that its roof leaned against one curved wall. The crash had been violent, taking down chunks of the ceiling and ripping up part of the rail. Willa could practically hear the scream of metal and voices in the twisted wreck.

The car had come to rest on a slight bend in the tunnel, its sharp wheels suspended off the ground, cutting into the concrete on one wall. The ceiling had collapsed, creating an impenetrable barrier of gravel and rebar on that side, but there was a narrow people-sized triangle between the car and the wall just wide enough to squeeze through.

Asher clambered over the rubble and shrugged off his backpack, glancing back at her as he crammed the bag into the dark triangle with his toe. She smiled tightly back at him.

"You okay with this?" he asked, pressing his back against the tunnel wall.

"Of course."

Asher arched an eyebrow and squeezed himself into the tight space, kicking his bag forward with the side of his foot. It was so narrow his nose brushed the side of the train as he shimmied further into the crevice, narrowly missing several sharp corners of twisted metal.

It wasn't far—only about 50 feet, but it would be slow. Willa tried to ignore the fear that scaled her spine as Asher disappeared into the darkness.

She hesitated. She could see inside the train through the dirty window, cracked in one corner, the words EMERGENCY EXIT printed backward on the glass. The tipped seats were littered with soggy blankets and rusty cans. A stuffed animal lay by a small pile of bones, its eyes torn out to make a nest for a family of mice.

"Come on, Robin," Asher called, his voice hollow and already distant.

Willa scowled and shoved her bag into the space before wedging herself in next to him. She was forced to turn her head sideways, the metal train wall cool against her cheek. Her breath hitched.

Asher was a few feet away, the pulsing lights silhouetting the lean shadow of his body. She swallowed and shuffled forward, grimacing as the rough wall scraped her bare shoulders.

For a moment there was nothing but the rasp of their breath and the rhythm of the music as they inched forward. Asher's head was pinned toward her, so he was moving blindly. It was a stupid thing to do, but she was grateful, the calm in his eyes keeping her steady despite the fear clawing at her throat.

"This sucks balls," she observed.

Asher snorted. "You're the one who wanted to come."

"Well, I'm an idiot," she retorted, bending her knees a little to avoid a chunk of rubble wedged above her head. As she slid past, loose bits of rock showered her hair.

"Your goddamn band better be good," she muttered, blinking dust from her eyes. Willa couldn't help grinning at Asher's choked laughter.

Somehow, he wasn't afraid. She could see it in the aura ghosting around his face, only the ghost of black marring the edges of his indigo flames. It was a comfort, so she watched the dance of his secret fire and tried to breathe.

Kick. Shuffle. Kick. Shuffle. Kick. Shu—

Willa jerked to a halt, the strap of her tank top strained against her neck. She tugged again, unable to turn her head to see what she was caught on. Whatever it was held her firmly, sharp metal digging into her shoulder.

"Ash," she hissed, fighting tremor in her voice. "I'm stuck."

Willa wiggled forward to show him. Asher cursed, his expression half-hidden by the darkness. His hand gripped the outside edge of the train car.

He could leave her, Willa realized. It would be the easiest thing. Understandable, even. He'd already paid her debt after all. But Asher didn't hesitate before starting back to her. Her throat clenched in relief, her vision blurring.

He must have seen because he touched the skin just above her elbow, his tone soothing, "Hey, you're okay. I can get you loose."

There was dirt caught in the scruff of his beard. She could smell the coffee on his breath, sweet and familiar. He leaned closer to see where she was stuck.

She wondered if his lips were soft.

His gaze cut toward her, heat flashing in his eyes as he reached for the strap. She hoped he couldn't see her blush in the dark.

Her breath feathered his hair as he fumbled, mumbling to himself. She stared toward the triangle at the end of the tunnel, trying to ignore his cheek pressing against her neck as he worked. The pulsing lights from Beacon Street had vanished, the music temporarily silent, the blackness yawned—

Something moved out there.

Just a slither of pale against the inky night, like exposed bone. A white flicker that had no place in the darkness. Willa stiffened, fear trickling down her spine.

There was something wrong about whatever was out there—like flesh peeled from white bone. She felt it. Not out there in the damp tunnel, but inside her mind, an invisible invasion that made her bile pool in the back of her throat. Her whole body shuddered as it scraped the inside of her skull, rummaging through her consciousness.

Willa made a strangled sound, trying to warn Asher who was still working on her strap, but her tongue felt thick and useless.

"Easy," he breathed, oblivious to what she was seeing. What she was *feeling*.

The thing inside her head was black poison. She started to struggle like an animal caught in a snare. The metal cut into her shoulder. A thin stream of blood blazed a hot trail down her arm. Asher swore.

Out in the dark, the flicker tapped against the concrete wall.

Once.

Twice.

It could have been a rat scuttling along the tunnel floor. But it wasn't.

Willa bit back a shriek. She was going to die here trapped under the coffin of the earth with a nightmare inside her head—

Asher shouted and she felt the snag loosen. Willa lurched against him, pressing her forehead against his shoulder. He cupped the back of her neck. Willa felt the thing in the tunnel slip back into darkness. Felt the claws retract from her mind.

Asher murmured in her ear, quiet words that meant nothing. She wasn't sure how long they stayed like that, crouched in the darkness underneath the city, but he didn't move until she lifted her head.

He tugged her forward gently, and after a few steps, they tumbled out into the open. The lights throbbed around them as if they had never stopped, flashes of purple and red. Asher watched as she turned in frantic circles until her eyes accepted what her heart already knew. Whatever had been out here was gone.

Willa sunk to the ground, pressing her forehead against the cold center rail. After a moment's hesitation, Asher sat next to her, crossing his legs under him. She waited for him to say something. To comfort or tease her, but he was silent, so she breathed and shook until the terror bled out of her into the hard-packed dirt, leaving behind shame so bright it lit her cheeks on fire.

Plastic crinkled.

"You hungry?" Asher asked.

Reluctantly, Willa looked up to find him digging through his bag. "I've got to eat something," he continued easily. "Once we start playing, the crowd won't let me stop."

She managed to sit, stomach roiling, but when Asher held out his water, she took it, watching as he unwrapped what appeared to be a homemade granola bar—seeds and oats held together with a few precious spoons of honey.

Asher set a piece on her knee. She took a bite reluctantly and then three more. "Is this nutmeg?"

"I like to cook."

Willa was surprised to find herself smiling. It was a strange thing to say. No one liked cooking anymore. Food was fuel, each meal cobbled together from rotten scraps, old tins of mushy veggies, and meager rations.

They ate in silence. She should tell him there was something down here. Something that could slither into your mind as easy as mist. She should tell him, but she couldn't seem to find the words. There was so much horror in this world already.

"What's with the camera?" Asher asked, licking the crumbs from his fingers.

Willa glanced down at where it still hung at her hip. Her camera was hard to explain. Hard to justify how something so small could keep her clinging to life.

What does your life raft look like?

She fiddled with the lens. "I collect faces."

He folded the leftover plastic wrap into a neat square, tucking it back into his bag. "Why?"

Willa studied him—the thin scar cutting across the bridge of his nose and the gauntness in his cheeks. The boy who'd saved her.

She lifted her Nikon and shifted so that the pulsing lights cast shadows across his face. He didn't smile as he looked back at her, his haunted eyes a nebula of blue. She snapped the picture and lowered the camera, her hands still trembling slightly. "Because every survivor has a story to tell."

Chapter 4

T HERE WAS A RED door wedged into the wall of trash.

The towering barricade of garbage stretched the width and height of the tunnel, mildewed mattresses and rusty ovens stacked like stones to the curved ceiling. It was too old to smell like anything more than dampness and rust. Colorful strobing light leaked from every small crack and the whole structure trembled from the pounding music inside.

The door was strangely out of place in the center of the trash wall, like the entrance to an expensive brownstone on the Upper West Side. Two oil lamps flanked the threshold and the tarnished lion's head knocker was straight out of a children's book, as if a wintery woods and a fawn might lie just beyond.

Asher climbed up the steps fashioned from dented computer monitors and shattered flatscreen televisions. He knocked.

"Password!" a muffled voice shouted.

"Umbra," Asher responded.

Willa raised an eyebrow. He shrugged. "It means *shade* in Latin. Don't ask me who comes up with this shit. These guys think they're in a Mad Max movie or something."

The door creaked open. For a second, Willa thought it was a child who stood there silhouetted against the frantic flash of lights. The tiny girl peered out at them, wearing a red lacy bra and a pair of tight black jeans. Her bright pixie hair was violently pink.

She would have looked entirely incapable of defending a door if it weren't for the enormous Glock tucked next to her pierced belly button.

"Asher!" the pixie cried, swinging the door wide and launching herself into his arms. He caught her easily, chuckling as she wrapped her legs around his waist. She kissed him, and Willa glanced away.

Eventually, Willa cleared her throat and Asher pulled away, kissing the girl's nose. Willa rolled her eyes as the pixie took her time sliding down his body before dismounting with a wicked grin. Asher had the decency to look sheepish but kept his arm around her waist. "Tink, this is Willa. She's a....friend."

Tink saluted. "Happy to meet a friend of Asher's."

A tribal tattoo twisted around the girl's wrist. It was shiny and black, obviously new. Willa wondered where a person acquired a tattoo these days. Or pink hair dye.

"Uh, Tink?" Willa asked, following the pair through the door.

Tink laughed as she secured the three deadbolts behind them. "Asher's kinda big on nicknames."

She kept talking, but her words were swallowed by the music coming from the stage. The street entrance to the Beacon subway platform had been completely blocked off years ago, but tonight it was filled with hundreds of people pressed together on the dance floor. The soaring curve of the ceiling held the music, keeping the secret of it underground.

Before the Darkness, music had been everywhere—spilling from coffee shops and car stereos and AirPods. As if music and art were something we deserved.

Now, an event like this was sacred—music, a cathedral for the still living.

Tink tugged Asher toward the bar on the other side of the cavernous space. Willa tried to keep up, but the dance floor was a writhing mass of skin and sweat. Fingers touched her waist. Lips grazed her shoulder as she pushed through the crowd. Someone grabbed her hand and spun her—just a flash of dark skin and smiling eyes—before disappearing back into the throng. Willa laughed, the music soothing the fear that still clung to her.

They reached the bar. Tink elbowed a boy twice her size out of the way, squeezing them into a space at the counter. She draped herself around Asher and signaled for a drink. The bartender, a tall blonde with half her head shaved, poured them a drink from a clear bottle, the label worn off years ago.

The bar counter was no more than a few wooden doors set on sawhorses. Dozens of large mason jars and old wine bottles lined the shelves behind the busy bartenders, colorful liquids glinting in the strobing lights. Moonshine—fermented from potatoes or apples or whatever else could be cobbled together—was the only alcohol widely available anymore.

Tink buried her face in Asher's neck as he laughed at something the bartender said. Willa turned to watch the dance floor. She shouldn't be surprised that Asher had a girlfriend. He wasn't a knockout, but she supposed the stormy blue eyes and mysterious scar probably brought plenty of girls to his bed.

The statuesque bartender slid a glass toward her through a puddle of booze and nodded in Asher's direction. "On the house," she yelled over the deafening music.

Willa saluted Asher with the glass, which was filled with a milky liquid, and downed the shot. Rice, she guessed—like sake, only stronger. She relished the way her muscles loosened when the warmth hit her stomach, gesturing for another as the opening band finished their set and stepped off the stage.

She was reaching for the second shot when the room plunged into darkness. Her ears rung from the sudden absence of sound. There was a smattering of nervous laughter as dozens of headlamps switched on like fireflies on the dance floor.

They obviously only had enough gas for the generators to run during a set. Willa was adjusting her headlamp when Asher paused in front of her, Tink still wrapped around him like a second skin. "We're on next," he said, waving at the stage. "Our set usually lasts an hour or so. You'll be okay to wait?"

She crossed her arms. "Of course. I don't need a babysitter."

Asher's eyes flickered down her body, and she remembered her little show in the car earlier. "I'm sure you don't."

Willa felt herself flush, but she didn't hate Tink's frown as Asher led her back through the crowd. They climbed the plywood stage that had been built over the useless train track. Tink reached for an electric bass that matched her bright hair, fiddling with the amp as Asher settled behind the drum kit. He twirled the sticks between his fingers a few times before tapping out a quick practice rhythm.

Willa watched the tension bleed from his shoulders as he played. She understood. It was the same feeling she got in the tiny dark room in her apartment when she lifted a fresh photograph from the developing chemicals. The feeling that there was still a fragile shard of herself that was her own—unbroken.

A boy she didn't recognize jumped onto the stage next to Tink. He looked a few years older and was wearing ripped flannel. He fist-bumped Asher before making his way to the microphone. At the bar, a pair of younger girls giggled.

Willa rolled her eyes. The singer was cute, with a mop of shaggy brown hair and an infectious smile. The kind of boy who liked his grandma's cooking and pulled over to help a stranger change a tire.

Asher pulled his shirt over his head and tossed it behind him. The two girls at the bar squealed, and this time Willa couldn't help but agree. He was lean but his muscles flexed nicely as he twirled the drumsticks and began playing.

Willa jumped as the generator roared back to life and the dance floor burst into a rainbow of swirling lights. The shaggy-headed boy stepped up to the mic, introducing himself as Grayson before hitting the first cord. The crowd roared in response.

The song swelled on the back of Tink's guitar. Grayson's voice rose over the crowd, a familiar song Willa had heard on every street corner this summer. The crowd lifted their glasses and started to dance, their voices rising to twine with Grayson's, half-naked bodies writhing between light and night. The aura of the crowd hung over the dance floor like a prism only she could see, each colored flame mixing with the next. Willa leaned her head against the wall and let the music wash over her.

Asher met her gaze from across the room, sweat gleaming on his skin as he kept up with the rapid beat. He was still smiling but it did nothing to hide the haunted look in his eyes—the double-edged sword of taking your hope out of hiding.

Willa sank into the crowd, away from Asher's eyes, and let the music break over her as she started to dance, pressed tight against bodies she didn't know. There was nothing but skin and breath here. No empty bellies or soldiers. No shallow graves or loneliness.

She moved and let the music swallow time until she was measuring the moments by the ache in her legs and the soreness of her throat.

"You're too sexy to be dancing alone," a husky voice said in her ear.

Her eyes flew open. Willa reached for the knife strapped to her hip as she spun around, but her angry words dried up in her mouth. She'd expected some creep with greasy hair and wandering hands. Someone with empty eyes who wanted to press his expectations against her skin.

The boy grinning down at her was devastatingly handsome, from his crystal blue eyes to his crooked smile. His blond hair stuck up in a haphazard way that she suspected was far from casual and his tight black shirt showed off toned biceps. A burnt orange aura shimmered around him like a flickering flame.

Heat bloomed in her belly. He looked dangerous and delicious. She lowered her knife.

The stranger held her eyes as he slipped his hand to the small of her back, and she didn't stop him. Not when his fingertips slid beneath her shirt or when he pressed his hips flush against her own.

She knew better. Should *know* better. But when he moved, she moved with him. Their hips dipped with the swell of the song, the fly of his jeans pressing into her belly.

Willa shivered and danced. The throbbing lights were a red spiderweb against the delicate skin of her eyelids. The stranger's hands skimmed up her sides. He didn't seem to care about the forgotten knife that she held flat against his spine.

Or maybe he liked it. Either way, each song slipped seamlessly into the next. Some a frantic beat that had him spinning her across the floor with laughter caught in her throat, and others pulling them close, hips rolling.

Sweat molded his black t-shirt to his body, showing off the delicious outline of lean muscle and the holster that crisscrossed his chest, holding twin blades against his sides. She twined her arms around his neck as the music changed to a slow sensual throb. His aura darkened, fissures of scarlet bisecting the burnt orange flames.

Willa pressed her lips to the curve of his shoulder, darting her tongue out to slide across his skin. He tasted like salt. The boy murmured something. She lifted her face, and he captured her mouth, his hands straying further up the back of her shirt. Willa dimly noticed the music had faded amidst a chorus of cheers. She heard Grayson announce that the band was done for the night—that they didn't have to go home, but they couldn't stay here.

She groaned when the boy lightly scraped his teeth across her bottom lip before lifting his head. He gave her a slow smile that made her think of twisted sheets in the dark. "Caspian," he said, his voice low.

She should be embarrassed but she wasn't. She smiled up at him. "Willa."

He chuckled, tugging her through the sweaty crowd. "Want to get out of here, Willa?"

She did. Darkness, she did. But as the haze of music slipped away, the world seeped back in.

She glanced up at the stage. Asher was still behind the drum, Tink on his lap, but he was watching Willa, a question in his eyes. Over the crowd, she shook her head and he nodded. She wasn't going anywhere with a boy she didn't know, even if he did dance like sin and taste like heaven.

"My place isn't far from here," Caspian said too casually, handing her a drink, the amber liquid winking. He took a shot. Willa did the same, the alcohol burning like fire. It did nothing to quench her thirst.

She tugged at the hem of her shirt. Her bare feet had blistered inside her damp boots. Willa suddenly remembered her broken truck and empty apartment and the splinters embedded in her palms. It had been a long night. Sweat slicked her spine. Her limp braid was still littered with grave and her mascara had given up hours ago.

Willa studied the strikingly good-looking boy in front of her. Caspian could have his pick of any girl tonight. She wondered why he'd chosen her. If he could see her desperation wrapped around her like a funeral shawl.

"I'd like to get to know you, Willa," Caspian was saying, shrugging on his leather jacket.

"Really?" Willa asked, unable to keep the skepticism out of her voice.

"You're interesting." His gaze flicked down to her lips. "There's something about you...."

She snorted. "Nice line."

He flashed her a lazy smile. "I get it. You're cynical. The world is a shit hole, but I'm a nice guy. Promise."

"Oh, I'm sure you're very...nice."

Willa considered. Boys like Caspian were used to getting what they wanted. Getting *who* he wanted. She usually hated guys like that. Still. He was ridiculously hot and there *was* that saying about gift horses.

Willa plucked a sharpie off the bar, knowing she'd probably regret it later. "Why don't I give you my address? If you still think I'm interesting tomorrow morning, come by."

Caspian smiled and this time it touched his eyes. His burnt orange aura swirled around him like embers. She bent over his hand to scribble her address on his palm.

"I'll see you soon," he said with a parting wink.

Willa admired the way he filled out his jeans as he disappeared into the crowd. She'd never see him again. The harsh daylight had a way of clarifying the mistakes of the night. But it had been a lovely interlude in her otherwise dreadful life.

So she was still smiling when she spun around in the crowd, to make her way to the stage. And ran into the guy behind her.

"Watch it," he snapped, grabbing her arm.

Willa glared up at the guy. He was beautiful, in that way unusual people are beautiful, his pale skin nearly swallowed by freckles, bright red hair like a beacon.

She jerked her arm from his grip. "What's your freakin problem?"

"No problem, just watch where you're going."

Willa tried to push around him, but he blocked her, leaning alarmingly close. "Lemme give you a piece of advice—"

She stopped. "Oh, I can't fucking wait for this."

The redhead shook his head. "I know Caspian can be a bit of a distraction, but try to maintain some dignity. You were practically fucking him on the dance floor."

Willa's brows rose. "And who the hell are you?"

He smirked, his emerald eyes sharp. "Eden Samara. I'm Caspian's..." He paused as if to consider what to say. "Friend."

"Well, Caspian's friend, why the hell is it any of your business?" She looked him up and down. "Are you jealous? He *is* pretty."

Eden's eyes narrowed. "Oh, don't worry about me. I just like to warn Caspian's female conquests," he hissed. "It saves me from having to clean up the mess later."

Chapter 5

T HE STREET WAS QUIET when Asher parked the Camaro in front of Willa's building. She was asleep, cheek pressed against the passenger window, breath fogging the glass.

Asher cut the engine and silence settled beneath the ringing in his ears. His fingers twitched as if he still held his drumsticks.

Willa was curled up in a ball, his spare sweatshirt stretched to cover her bare toes. It had taken twenty minutes to persuade her to let him drive her home. As if she had other options.

She'd been nothing but trouble since the moment he'd met her. Asher rubbed the scar on the bridge of his nose, reading the uneven edge like braille. Reading the story of the baton and the cage and the darkness that had swallowed him after Frank shoved him into his cop car.

Asher leaned his head back. Willa was a survivor. He should just drop her off and drive away. She didn't need his help. Or want it.

Still. She looked small bundled up in the passenger seat like a tired kid. Her dark hair had come loose from the unruly bun she'd fashioned on top of her head, stray pieces framing her face, and sleep had stolen the sharpness from her features. Just another piece of lost flotsam.

Asher rubbed his forehead and stared out the windshield. Between the cracks of the city, the horizon was tinged with the gray light of predawn. A man appeared at the end of the street, shuffling down the sidewalk with a rusty shopping cart filled with tomatoes collard greens, and whatever other produce could be grown or stolen. A Newsie flew by on her pink bike, cap backward over her pigtails, bullhorn strapped to her back with a piece of twine.

Asher stretched, grimacing at the ache in his arms. His chest was filled with the hollowness that always haunted him after a set as if music had carved out a piece of his flesh.

Willa muttered to herself, dreaming. He wished he could let her sleep, the ferociousness in those sharp green eyes did nothing to hide her despair, but he had to be back at the garage in a few hours.

His sweatshirt had slipped, exposing the delicate curve of her shoulder. Asher wondered if girls knew how damn appealing that was as he shook her, careful to keep his fingers on fabric.

Willa woke like a soldier during battle, sitting up abruptly and glaring at him in the morning light. "You let me sleep."

"We just got here," he lied.

She threw him a knowing look, stifling a yawn as she climbed out of the car, slamming the door behind her. He did the same, locking the Camaro as he followed her to the steps.

Willa stopped abruptly. "What the hell are you doing?"

Asher suppressed the urge to roll his eyes. "Walking you up to your apartment."

"That's ridiculous. I'm fine," she said, dismissing him as she hiked her bag up her shoulder.

"I know you're fine. Jesus Willa, you don't have to prove anything."

She flicked a hand at his car, "Well then..."

"I don't leave friends on the side of the damn road."

Something shifted in Willa's eyes at the word friends. He stifled another sigh. She tapped her finger on the railing and then shrugged. "It's on the 4th floor. If you want to climb that far, it's your own funeral."

"Fair enough," he agreed as Willa rummaged around in her bag for her keys.

He waited patiently, ignoring the ache in the back of his neck. The man with the shopping cart had stopped at the corner, setting his goods out on a wobbly card table. A baby cried somewhere nearby. The smell of weak coffee mingled with the stench of the trash.

Willa struggled with the rusty lock, cursing.

The baby cried again—closer this time. Asher turned, frowning. "What was that?"

The cry came again, plaintive and soft. Willa shook her head, swinging the door open. "It's none of our business. Leave it."

Asher back down to the sidewalk. The sound was quiet but close. He nudged the pile of trash and dirty rags at the bottom of the stairs with his toe.

One of the rags moved, shifting to reveal a small face and a single dirty hand.

"Help me," the face whispered.

His stomach clenched. A child—young, maybe seven or eight, although starvation had a way of stealing years.

"Asher," Willa said from above and behind him, her voice a warning.

He crouched down. The child's dark eyes followed him, wary but resigned. "Easy there, little sprite," he soothed, brushing candy wrappers and disintegrating paper towels from her face.

The child flinched. Asher swallowed a curse, keeping his fingers gentle. There were bruises underneath the grime on the girl's skin, her hair so matted it was impossible to tell the color.

"Asher," Willa repeated, "you can't help her. She's already dead."

He knew she was right. The girl's lips were cracked and bleeding, her skin stretched tight over the sharp bones of her face. It wasn't uncommon. Starvation was a familiar bedfellow after the Pulse.

The child would be dead by morning. He had seen it a hundred times.

Asher murmured soothing words as he reached into the front pocket of his backpack for the small baggie of pills he kept there. He took out four.

He felt Willa behind him, her keys jingling softly in her hand, but he kept his attention on the child in the trash.

"I know a little girl just about your age," he told her, taking a piece of bread from another pocket in his bag. It was a few days old and burnt around the edges, but it was the softest thing he had. Asher pressed the pills into the stale dough. "She's not as pretty as you," he continued, "but I bet you'd be good friends."

He offered the girl his water bottle and she took it greedily, leaving traces of blood on the spout. Asher kept his tone gentle as he held out the bread. "This medicine will help you sleep. Maybe tomorrow, I could take you to see her, okay?"

The girl's gaze didn't waver from his. Dried tears had tracked streaks down her dirty cheeks. She wasn't a child. Not anymore. There was a bleak sort of *knowing* in her eyes that made his stomach turn.

"Thank you," she said softly and took the bread. Her hand was impossibly small, the nails caked in dirt. Somehow he kept his face neutral despite the white rage that clawed at his ribs.

He waited patiently while she ate the pieces, one small bite at a time. She grimaced, her mouth likely riddled with sores. The girl took the last sip of water and smiled shyly as she handed it back.

Oh, Darkness help him.

Asher shrugged off his jacket and tucked it around her. She pulled it up to her chin like a child being read a bedtime story.

"Does your friend have a bed?" the girl asked wistfully, nesting deeper into the pile of rubbish.

He nodded. "A soft one right by the fire. With lots of pillows and a warm blanket. She usually shares it with her brother, but I bet she'd rather have another little girl to play with instead."

The lies rolled easily from his tongue, the hopes and dreams of a different life just below the surface. If the child knew, she didn't let on, smiling as she closed her eyes. He touched her forehead, trying to ignore the heat radiating off her skin. "Sleep now, little one," he whispered. "It will be better in the morning."

The girl drifted off—a piece of trash among the trash.

· · · · ·· · · · ·

The heavy front door closed behind them, the sound final and hard in the dark foyer. A single candle guttered on a narrow table underneath a bank of empty mail slots, and the skeleton of a bike frame crumbled in one corner. Asher braced for Willa's judgment about the girl in the trash, but her expression was distant.

"This way," she said, her voice echoing in the deserted entryway as she headed for the stairwell beside the broken elevator. He kept his head down as they climbed, following the circle of Willa's flashlight. By the time they reached the fourth floor, he'd buried the dying girl with a thousand other tragic memories.

The landing door screeched, and she led him into a long hallway. Most of the apartment doors hung open, abandoned. Weak light filtered from the dirty window at the end of the corridor, highlighting the stained beige carpet. The air was musty and stale.

It looked like no one had been up here for years. Most people kept to the bottom floors when elevators became obsolete. Less trouble. But the fourth floor was smarter. Safer.

"You up here on your own?" he asked quietly.

Willa glanced over her shoulder. "Not exactly."

He'd tried to live in one of the high-rises, but something about the emptiness of dozens of floors pressing down on his head had left him itchy, so he'd moved to a brownstone in Soho.

Asher followed Willa, pausing when she rapped on a closed door. Someone on the other side tapped back—three quick beats. Willa didn't explain but simply moved on to her door.

"What was that about?"

Willa fumbled with her keys. "My only neighbor—Mr. McMurtry. Old guy. We keep an eye on each other."

Asher nodded, relieved that she wasn't up here all on her own. Something moved on the other side of the door. Asher tensed but Willa didn't seem to notice as her keys clattered to the floor. She bent to pick them up.

There was another quiet shuffle. A scratch.

Willa scooped up her keeps and reached for the doorknob.

Asher grabbed her wrist. "Don't."

Willa blinked. The door shuttered. Whoever was in her apartment was not small. Asher reached for his knife.

"Whoa there, cowboy," Willa said, laughing. "Donut is not a murderer."

Donut?

She shook off his hand and opened the door a crack. It rattled in its hinges.

"Donut, you big idiot," she growled, leaning hard on the door, but it was too late. The enormous dog barreled out of the narrow gap. Willa swore, and Asher had just enough time to get a knee up before the beast nuzzled him enthusiastically in the crotch.

"Whoa, there," he yelped, pushing aside the dog's fuzzy head. The beast slobbered on his hand in response.

Willa grabbed for Donut's collar, but the mutt managed to evade her, vibrating with silent glee as he galloped down the hallway and back. He was some sort of sheepdog, with a mop of shaggy brown fur and a lolling tongue that was too big for his mouth.

"I'm sorry," Willa called over her shoulder as she chased Donut, yelling useless commands before getting a hand on the beast's collar and hauling him into the apartment. She pointed at a tangled nest of blankets by the fireplace and Donut had the decency to look guilty as he slinked over to his bed.

Asher chuckled as the dog spun twice before settling down with a huff. Willa ignored Donut's baleful eyes as she tossed her keys on the messy kitchen island and lit the oil lamp in the center.

He hovered by the doorway. The generous loft was just starting to brighten, thanks to the bank of windows that took up one entire wall. A small container garden was growing on a narrow metal balcony outside and there was a surprisingly good view of the Manhattan skyline beyond it. The apartment featured exposed brick and a beautiful matching fireplace. Before, a place like this would have been rented for thousands. Now squatting was the same as ownership. Whatever you could keep—whatever you could *hold*—was yours.

Willa slung her bag onto a tattered leather armchair and kicked off her soggy boots before heading into the kitchen. In the living space, a cast iron pot was suspended over the cold fireplace with an elaborate system of cord and pipe, a dwindling pile of wood, and a small hatchet nearby.

He touched the quilt hanging off the edge of the couch. It was worn and soft, the stitching broken through and patched dozens of times. If the pillow and pile of books were any indication, Willa slept here, although there was a hallway by the kitchen that most likely led to a couple of bedrooms.

"Nice place," he said.

"I wasn't expecting company," she replied, opening the refrigerator. The block of ice on the bottom shelf was almost melted, filling up the rusty holding pan. He couldn't imagine how she'd gotten it up four flights of stairs by herself.

Donut lifted his fuzzy head as Willa started filling a bowl with chunks of something from a plastic container. "What's with the dog?" Asher asked, leaning his elbows on the counter.

"I know it's ridiculous," she said, smiling at the mammoth dog who bounded over, noisily scarfing down his breakfast. "It's hard enough to feed myself these days."

Donut finished in thirty seconds, padded over to Willa, and plopped his hairy butt on her foot. He looked up at her with adoring eyes as she ruffled the fur on his head.

Asher thought of the small dying child outside. Thought of his own bed, which most likely had a drunk Tink sprawled across it right now. A girl he was sleeping with to keep the darkness at bay.

"No, I get it," he said. "Why this fuzzy guy though?"

The green of her eyes softened. "Found him behind a donut shop a couple of years After. My dad had, uh, just left and I was..." She cleared her throat. "I didn't expect to keep the stupid mutt, but he followed me home. Thought he might be a good guard dog."

Donut leaned against her thigh, eyes half closed in ecstasy as Willa scratched behind his ear.

"He seems very vicious," Asher offered.

She laughed softly. "Clearly."

He couldn't help but grin back. Willa had smiled more in the past few minutes than the whole evening. It transformed her face, moving her swiftly past mildly attractive to beautiful.

Asher looked away, studiously studying the narrow brick wall behind her. It was covered in her photographs, carefully printed on shiny paper, and pinned haphazardly to the wall from the floorboards to the ceiling. He wandered closer.

The pictures were stunning, each composition carefully curated; the colors sharp and crisp in places, soft and dreamy in others. All the old photographs, the ones from Before, had faded and yellowed with age but these breathed life.

But it was the faces that drew him closer. A woman laughing with a baby on her lap, her face streaked with dirt. An old man curled on a park bench, his eyes empty and bleak. A girl dancing in the street with her thin arms lifted to the sky, eyes closed as she moved to silent music.

They told a story he had seen a thousand times. They told his own story.

He wanted to tell her how beautiful they were—wanted to tell her that the pictures broke through the darkness inside of him.

Asher touched a shot of a boy chasing a deflated ball across broken pavement. "These are very good."

She shifted next to him, her fingers circling her wrist, twisting. He'd never seen her nervous before. After a moment, she cleared her throat and said, "Why'd you help that girl, Ash? The one on the sidewalk down there."

Asher studied a shot of a woman pulling a bright red wagon down the center of 5th Avenue. The wagon was filled with the small body of a child, wrapped carefully in a blanket.

He swallowed the tightness in his throat. He wasn't the only one bearing witness.

"I helped for the same reason you take these pictures." He turned and this time she met his gaze. Her cerulean eyes glowed in the rising sunlight. "Because I know what it's like to be thrown away."

Chapter 6

WILLA WAS SOAKED BY the time she got to the fourth floor. The heavy water jug she'd picked up from the dispensary dug into her back, splashing down her collar with every step. She winced as the sling's leather straps cut into her palms. It wasn't a perfect system, but it was the best she could do.

"You got my water, girl?" Mr. McMurtry hollered from his recliner as she passed his open apartment door. Willa paused, biceps quivering. The elderly man looked up from the Bible on his lap.

She bit back a sigh. Mr. McMurtry was skeletally thin. His peppered beard contrasted with the deep brown of his wrinkled face. He frowned at her over his bifocals, his rust-colored aura weak and transparent.

Willa had never seen him leave the floor, let alone his ratty armchair, and he'd never called her by her name. Not once in the past seven years. Willa was pretty sure vitriol and the Lord kept him alive. But Mr. McMurtry was a gifted gardener, and he kept her supplied with kale and tomatoes so juicy that Willa swore he was magic. She'd asked him what his secret was once, and he'd said vodka in the soil. She was almost positive that was a lie.

They maintained a tentative peace, based mostly on Mr. McMurtry's affection for Donut, who in turn, loved the old man with a boundless enthusiasm that made her question the mutt's ability to judge character.

Normally, the situation benefited all of them, except on days like today.

Willa gritted her teeth as the straps tore into her palms. "You're next, Mr. McMurtry," she called kicking open her door and carefully backed the water jug onto the counter as Donut danced around her feet.

She inspected her palms. They burned, but when she looked, the skin was smooth and pale, without a hint of red. It wasn't a surprise. She rarely bruised and hadn't had more than a cold since the Pulse. Willa chalked it up to good genes and—

"Some time today, girl!" Mr. McMurtry bellowed from the other room.

Willa muttered and headed back to the door. The old man quoted scripture to her as she passed in the hallway. Something about the sin of sloth, but she ignored him.

The trip down the stairs was much faster, and she blinked in the sun as she stepped outside, glad to see Gloria still parked on the curb. It had been three weeks since Asher fixed her truck. She'd been working her debt off at the garage ever since. At first, it had just been sweeping floors and organizing tools, but they'd discovered she had a knack for fixing engines.

She liked putting broken things back together.

It was unusually warm for late fall. Across the street, Mrs. Gorara's twins played stickball, the crack of their broom handle bat mingling with shouts. Above her head, a woman was singing softly as she put the wash on the line. The air smelled like leaves. It made her think of hot apple cider itchy homemade costumes and glowing pumpkins on windowsills.

Willa grimaced, nudging the pile of rags at the bottom of the stairs. Happy memories were specters of the past, always unexpected and never welcome, because just beneath the happy sound of kids playing, was the relentless stench of rot and despair. She bent to pull Asher's leather jacket from the pile. Once winter came he'd be glad to have it back regardless and the little girl was long gone.

Willa didn't wonder what happened to the child. The story was well-worn. But she did think about the pain in Asher's eyes when he'd turned away from the dying girl on the street.

She was still thinking about Asher and his eyes when someone touched her shoulder. Willa whirled.

"Don't kill me!" Caspian half-laughed, hands up in surrender.

"Oh. It's you," she said breathlessly, immediately feeling stupid.

She'd given up the hope that her mysterious dance partner would show up weeks ago. Yet here he was, wearing tight jeans and looking like every girl's wet dream.

He smiled crookedly. "You looked lost in thought."

Willa tried not to glance down at her dirty jeans and tank top, lifting her grimy hair off the back of her neck.

"I didn't think I'd see you again," she said.

He leaned a hip against her truck door, his gaze skimming her body. Willa forced herself not to fidget. "You're hard to find, Willa. You didn't give me your apartment number. I've been riding by here every day for the past couple of weeks."

He nodded at the Harley parked behind her truck. For the first time, she noticed the black helmet dangling from one hand. Of course, he rode a motorcycle.

Willa propped one boot on the truck runner. "Well, here I am."

"I can see that," he responded, his eyes dropping to her lips. "How about a ride?"

She'd never been on a motorcycle, but the idea of cruising through the streets with her arms wrapped around Caspian's chest was not unappealing.

"I have to go to work..." she started, but her words faltered when Caspian stepped closer, crowding her. His hand settled lightly on her waist. It was presumptuous, and Willa tried to be annoyed, but she didn't pull away.

"Later?" he asked, leaning in. He smelled like the cold wind. She started to nod but then he was kissing her and she forgot the question.

It felt good. She pressed closer. His bottom lip teased hers, keeping the kiss light and playful before pulling away.

Willa's stomach buzzed pleasantly as he walked backward toward his bike with a lazy grin. She couldn't remember the last time she'd had sex. The information suddenly seemed very important.

"Nine o'clock?" he called, swinging a leg over the bike. She nodded and he winked. It wasn't until he roared away, taillights glowing in the distance that Willa remembered the boy's warning on the dance floor.

She wasn't stupid. She knew Caspian was dangerous. But he was dangerous in a safe way. In a Before way.

Just a cute boy on a motorcycle.

Nothing she couldn't handle.

· · · · ●· ●· ● · ·

Willa wiped her hands on the greasy rag, shoved the wrench in her back pocket, and scowled at the Jeep's engine. The thing was held together with wishes and wire. It should have been junked years ago.

Asher crossed the garage floor and stood next to her while she silently seethed. The Frankenstein engine stared back, pieced together from the corpses of other cars and a disturbing amount of duct tape. It was the first car he'd let her work on solo, and she couldn't figure out what was wrong with the damn thing.

Asher scratched the stubble on his cheek and squinted at the engine. Willa crossed her arms and waited for him to point out what she was missing. Instead, he chuckled.

Her head swung in his direction in disbelief. "What the hell is so funny?"

Tink and Grayson started to laugh from where they were lounging on the garage's sagging couch. Grayson had been there all afternoon, flipping through ripped copies of *Car and Driver* and bouncing song ideas off Asher as he worked. Tink's now-purple head dangling from the edge of the couch, bare feet propped against the wall. She was reading Willa's battered copy of Capote's *In Cold Blood*. Or she had been until the giggling started.

"Don't be mad," Asher said, holding his hands up but unable to wipe the grin from his face.

"I'm waiting," she snapped.

"One day someone is gonna fix that damn thing," Tink called. "Then you're going to be really surprised!"

Asher wiped his forehead with the back of his hand, leaving behind a streak of grease. "If someone could fix it, then they should own this whole damn garage."

"What the hell is going on?" Willa demanded.

Asher slammed the hood of the Jeep closed, ignoring the flakes of rust that rained down on the floor. "Let's just say, it's a little initiation we have for new grease monkeys. This thing is a shitstorm. Unfixable. We just like to see how long someone will work on it before they admit defeat."

Willa stared at him in disbelief. "So you are saying...that you wasted my damn time for some sort of fucking PRANK?"

Asher straightened, looking guilty.

"What the hell is wrong with you?" she fumed, throwing her dirty rag at him.

Asher swiped it out of the air as she stomped away, tossing her wrench in the meticulously organized toolbox. The laughter on the couch stopped abruptly.

This is why she didn't bother to have friends. People couldn't be trusted. She cursed under her breath, snatched her bag off the floor, and stalked toward the garage door.

Asher took two quick steps and grabbed her elbow. "Hey, don't leave. I'm sorry. I didn't think it was a big deal."

She whirled. He took a step back. "You're still getting paid," he added hopefully.

He looked truly sorry now, despite the lingering amusement in his eyes. He tucked his hands in the front pocket of his jeans. There was still an adorable streak of grease across his forehead. Willa took a deep breath. Being mad at Asher was like kicking a puppy.

"Lighten up, Celadon," Grayson hollered without looking up from his magazine. "Asher lost his shit when *he* couldn't fix that damn thing."

"We only tease the ones we love," Tink added, her foot tapping to a silent beat against the wall.

"I spent forty-eight hours tinkering," Asher offered. "I was so exhausted that I started hallucinating—couldn't screw in a bolt cause my eyes were blurry. I finally threw my wrench and quit. Loudly."

He waved at a small window near the ceiling. The glass was a spiderweb of cracks. Willa's lips twitched.

"If it makes you feel any better," Asher said quietly, so Tink and Grayson couldn't hear, "I've never seen anyone work on that piece of junk longer than you." He rubbed the back of his neck, his blue aura shot through with streaks of yellow. "Sorry?"

Willa tossed her bag back on the floor. "You are all idiots," she huffed.

Asher's shoulders sagged as she crossed the garage and flopped down on the couch next to Grayson, who offered her a piece of pigeon jerky. Willa took it, gnawing on the meat. Asher pinched Tink's ass to get her to move and squeezed between them. His thigh was warm against hers.

After a while, they fell into easy conversation about music and books and the forgotten taste of ice cream on a summer day. Safe topics that held the night at bay.

"What do you miss the most?" Tink asked after a long soliloquy about her grandmother's matzo ball soup. She was now stretched across the three of them like a log, Grayson rubbing her feet absently as he flipped through another magazine.

Willa let her head loll back on the musty couch. "Hot chocolate," she confessed. "When I was little, my mom would make the real thing on snow days. Big chunks of real chocolate melted in warm milk with a dollop of whipped cream on top—the good kind that came in the red can...do you guys remember that stuff? I would sneak into the kitchen at night and squirt it right into my mouth..." Willa trailed off as the group murmured their agreement and launched into a heated debate about the merits of the blue tub vs. the red can.

Asher's arm had ended up along the back of the couch, his fingers fiddling with the ends of her hair. Grayson lit a cigarette, the smell mingling with the ozone of impending rain. Willa swallowed, happiness crowding her throat.

She could have stayed like that forever, but eventually, night started to spill into the garage, crowding the circles of light the lanterns cast on the concrete floor.

"Time to go," Tink announced, flipping herself off of the couch. Grayson stood and stretched, scratching his belly. Willa glanced at the Jeep. She had an hour before her date with Caspian. "I think I'll stay."

Asher grinned up at her.

Willa shrugged. "What? I think I can fix it."

He just shook his head.

Chapter 7

"**M**ORE LIGHT OVER HERE," Asher said, his voice muffled. He was half inside a Buick, pulling out the carburetor. Willa, who was perched on the edge of the engine block, stretched further with the lantern and tried not to notice the way his shirt rode up as he struggled with a rusty bolt.

She'd given up on the Jeep again an hour ago. Asher hadn't even flinched when she had cursed the damn thing's mother and stalked over to help him with the sedan.

"So. Caspian," Asher said casually as he handed her the greasy carburetor.

Willa hopped off the hood to grab the new part. "What? You know him?"

Asher didn't look up from his work. "I've seen him around."

Willa arched an eyebrow at the back of his head. "Why do I think you are about to offer your unsolicited opinion?"

Asher ignored the question, calling for a socket wrench. She slapped it into his open palm. His biceps flexed as he tightened the carburetor onto the intake manifold.

Willa fiddled with a pair of pliers. The problem with having friends was they thought they were entitled to opinions about your life.

Asher drew back, propped a hip against the radiator grill, and wiped his hands with a tattered bandana. "I've seen him at the club a dozen times. He's never alone. And he's never with the same girl." He shoved the rag into his back pocket. "I just don't want you to get hurt, Robin."

"Don't call me that," she said automatically. Asher shrugged, moved around the car, and slid into the driver's seat. Willa glared at him through the passenger side window. "What's it to you anyway? I can take care of myself."

"So you've said."

He turned the key, pumping the gas until the car roared to life before nodding in satisfaction. "A guy like Caspian is only looking for one thing."

"Well, Asher Flint, as much as I appreciate your concern, did it ever occur to you that maybe I am using Caspian for that *one thing* you are referring to?"

Asher's mouth tightened. It was a nice mouth.

She looked at it a beat too long, and when her gaze flickered back up to his, Asher had gone still, his aura the deep red of a fallen sun. Something fluttered in her chest and—

"What's this all about?" a voice interrupted.

She tried to pull her eyes away, but it wasn't until Tink poked her head in the driver's window that Asher finally looked away. Willa blinked, heart racing.

He slipped out of the car, threw an arm around his girlfriend, and kissed her on the forehead. "Willa's got a date."

Tink arched an indigo eyebrow over the car roof. "A date?"

Willa hoped the flush on her neck wasn't too obvious. "We're just going for a ride."

"Is that what they're calling it these days?" Tink laughed, elbowing Asher in the ribs. "A ride?"

Asher frowned. Tink smiled up at him, but her usually vibrant pink aura was washed out.

Shit.

Willa turned away, pulling her hair into a ponytail, and securing it with the tie she kept around her wrist, before gathering her things. "I'll be fine."

Asher cleared his throat. "I'm making a trip to the Night Market tonight."

"Oh?" She swung her bag onto her shoulder, forcing herself to glance back over.

His arm was still around Tink's shoulder. As if he'd forgotten it was there. "If you want to come, you could meet me here around midnight?"

Willa shoved her hands in her pockets and considered. She knew this was Asher's lame attempt at making sure that she was okay after her date with Caspian, but she did need a few things for the winter, and for the first time in a long time, she didn't feel like visiting the Market alone.

"I'll see you back here," she agreed, sending Tink a small wave and avoiding Asher's eyes as she ducked into the street.

· · · ·●·●· · · ·

Tink had fallen asleep on the garage couch an hour ago, her guitar propped on the worn cushion next to her. She had played around with a few new songs while he tinkered with the Buick's radiator, their conversation easy and comfortable.

It was what Asher liked best about her. Like everyone, Tink had suffered her own brand of trauma after the Pulse, but it didn't seem to stick to her, as if sadness couldn't thrive in the face of her unrelenting brightness.

They'd met a few months after Frank had dumped him in the gutter outside of the Compound prison, bloody and bruised. He supposed the bastard didn't have any interest in something that was already broken.

Tink had shown up at an audition for the band he and Grayson were trying to cobble together. Her hair had been neon green, a match to the suspenders she wore over a lacy black bra, but it was her smile that had stood out—full of light and mischief—as if she held a delicious secret. It was the first thing to break through the dull haze of his grief.

Asher knew he could never love anyone again—not after what happened at the Compound. But maybe he could have someone *filled* with love.

He wiped his greasy hands on a rag and watched Tink sleep, her newly painted lavender toenails poking out from the garage's stiff blanket. He didn't want to hurt her. But the part of him capable of love had been carved out by screams a long time ago.

· · · ·●·●· · · ·

The girl slept for hours after Frank's thugs threw her into the cell with him, spine pressed against the cold bars, her long black hair trailing into a puddle. Asher had covered her with the only thing he owned—a thin scrap of blanket—but she still shivered when night began to penetrate the dirt-packed walls.

The guards had taken her shoes and her pale pink toenails peeked out from her tightly curled body. It was such a normal detail, that he couldn't sleep for seeing it. Couldn't stop seeing her delicate features and the thin gold hoops in her earlobes. Her lip was split and the knuckles tucked underneath her chin were bloody.

She was the most interesting thing to happen in months, so on the second night, he pulled her into his arms. He'd dozed, cheek pressed against the top of her head, listening to the soft rhythm of her breath. It was the first time he'd been warm in months.

At daybreak, she woke. He watched the horror slowly dawn in her dark eyes before she scrambled away, pulling the silk collar of her blouse tight around her throat. She eyed him wearily from the corner of the cell. Asher could only imagine what she saw—a filthy criminal with a scraggly beard, hal-crazed from hunger and loneliness.

There was nothing he could say to ease such a moment so he stayed quiet, gesturing to the dented tin cup by the bars. He'd eaten her dinner the past two nights—a sleeping girl didn't need a meal—but he'd left her plenty of water. He wasn't an animal. Not yet at least.

She only hesitated a moment before snatching up the cup, wincing when the metal touched her cracked lips, and drinking deeply. A simple gold cross rested in the hollow of her throat and her fingernails were painted the same soft shade as her toes.

"I won't hurt you," he said, his voice rusty. He attempted a smile. She flinched. Asher supposed it was more of a grimace than a smile.

Her gaze darted around the small cell as if she might find an escape hatch or door he hadn't noticed. Asher understood. He'd spent the first few weeks certain a loose brick or lazy guard would be his salvation, but that was only in the movies, so he let her look, angling his chin to see through the tiny barred window and the red rising sun beyond.

He had nothing but time. There was no one to talk to down here. The woman in the cell to his right was crazy, every night filled with choked screams and whispers about monsters hiding in the darkness. The murderer to his left was even less of a conversationalist.

"I'm Deliah," the girl said quietly, hugging her knees to her chest, her linen pants already turning black from the dirt floor. "I'm here because I spit in Frank's ugly face."

"This I've got to hear."

They'd talked day and night after that, watching daylight move across the cell floor like the hands of a sundial, legs stretched parallel to better share the moth-eaten blanket. It turned out Deliah had tried to rescue her little sister from Frank's wandering hands and gotten herself thrown in the Compound for her troubles.

When the evening meal arrived in a stained Tupperware—a bland mix of beans and rice he hadn't stopped hatting—he'd shared his portion, claiming to be full. Sometimes she pretended to believe him.

In the end, he'd told her everything. He told her about the good foster homes that broke his heart and the bad ones that broke his spirit. About finding happiness with his moms after the Pulse and about the pretty girl in the convenience store who'd ruined it all. Deliah had listened, inching closer every night, and told her own sad stories.

The blanket wasn't big enough for both of them but there were other things they could do to stay warm—touches stolen under the cover of night. The smell of honeysuckle perfume lingered in her silky hair for weeks, lulling him to sleep as they curled together on the hard floor.

He'd never belonged to anyone before, but he belonged to Deliah for eighty-two days.

On the eighty-third day, Frank came.

Frank wanted things. Things Deliah didn't want to give. She'd fought like a wild cat, dragging red lines across the bastard's face until Frank wanted something much darker than what he'd come for.

It had taken three guards to hold Asher down.

He'd gotten free once, rage snapping in his chest like bloody teeth, but he'd been starving for nearly a year and Frank had broken his nose with one lazy swing.

When Asher swam back into consciousness there was a knee in his back, his face pressed hard into the dirt. Until that moment, he'd thought the screams of the person you loved would be the worst sound in existence, but he had been wrong. The silence that followed was much worse.

Chapter 8

WILLA'S APARTMENT WAS ONLY a few blocks from the garage but it was fully dark by the time she arrived. She tried not to listen for the distant roar of an approaching motorcycle. She wouldn't be surprised if Caspian didn't show, but when she turned the last corner, he was stretched out on the bottom step, elbows propped behind him, face tilted to the sky.

His aura flowed around him—a beautiful current of burnt orange. Willa's hand immediately found the Nikon at her hip, silently begging him not to move as she captured the moonlight that cut across the sharp curve of his cheeks.

"It's warmer over here." Caspian's low voice drifted across the cracked sidewalk. He didn't shift his gaze from the stars, patting the step next to him. Willa crossed the street and sat, their hips brushing as she craned her neck. Through the canopy of buildings, the Milky Way splashed across the sky.

"Sometimes I can barely remember what it was like Before," Caspian murmured. "The city was loud and fast...so much noise." She could feel his breath on her cheek when he turned to look at her. "After the Pulse, I was stunned by the quiet."

Willa met his gaze. Caspian's eyes were the color of the cold stars. "Your friend—Eden—warned me that you were dangerous."

The colors around him pulsed but he smiled and leaned in. "You don't fool me, Willa Celadon." His lips brushed hers. "You like a little danger."

She smiled against his mouth, shivering when he dragged her closer. Caspian kissed the way he did everything else, reckless and bold, his lips tattooing wildfire down the side of her neck. His tongue flickered out to taste the line of her shoulder before he pulled away, grinning, his golden hair tousled. Willa grinned back. The downside of dating a guy like Caspian was that he had kissed a lot of girls. The upside was that he had kissed a lot of girls.

"Well," Willa said breathlessly.

He laughed and pulled her to her feet. She adjusted her shirt, grateful for the cool night air on her cheeks as he led her over to the bike.

"Have you been on one of these before?" he asked. Willa shook her head as he swung his leg over the bike and cranked the engine. It roared, the sound ricocheting around the empty street.

He raised an eyebrow; an invitation—or perhaps, a dare.

She climbed on. The seat was tilted forward, forcing her to mold herself against his back. Caspian patted her thigh. Willa swallowed a squeak when they rocketed into the street, arms sliding around his waist. He shifted gears, and they picked up speed.

The city was empty at this time of night, and Caspian opened it up when they hit a long straightaway. The engine roared. 60 miles per hour. 70. 80.

The speed twisted her stomach. She had the distinct feeling that this was a test, but she wasn't afraid. Hadn't been allowed to be afraid for a long time.

The wind tore at her hair, and she lifted her arms, letting her hands lift and fall with the current. The engine obliterated everything but the vibration between her legs. The stars were stationary against the inky sky even though the street was a blur of light and night.

Caspian yelled something that was lost to the wind, but she lowered her arms, letting one hand slide inside of his shirt, pressing the hard ridges of his abdomen. His muscles tightened as he downshifted, still going too fast as they approached the barbed wire fence that blocked off Central Park. She could see the gate in the distance, armed guards silhouetted against the glaring lights.

This was stupid. Stupid and reckless. If they got caught—

Caspian took a hard right, the back of the bike fishtailing wildly, her knee coming so close to the blurring asphalt she could feel the cold street through her jeans. For a split second, it seemed as if the bike would lay down, but then the back tire caught and they shot forward.

Willa's heart was in her throat. She never wanted it to end.

Eventually, Caspian slowed, taking several turns before rolling to a stop in a dark alley. She climbed off the bike first, knees wobbly. The air smelled like burnt rubber. The silence was deafening when he cut the engine.

Willa laughed as he stalked toward her, backing up until she hit the brick wall behind her. He didn't stop, pressing himself between her legs. She let him, craving the wildness as she buried her fingers in his hair, catching the sweep of his tongue. This kiss was different than the rest—greedy and desperate. She closed her eyes, liking the way her back scraped the rough brick.

His teeth grazed her earlobe and she tried to pull him closer, frustrated by the clothes between them.

"Willa," he gasped, his hands wrapping around her rib cage, lips burning across her neck. She stilled at the sound of her name, the cold night air seeping back into her skin. He was still kissing her, and sweet Darkness, she wanted him. But not like this.

Willa pressed her hand firmly into his shoulders, trying to find a shred of sanity. Caspian froze, lips pressed against her collarbone. God, he felt good.

"Caspian," she rasped.

A whisper of air appeared between them. His breath was ragged, but he kissed the corner of her mouth and pulled away.

Willa smiled and opened her eyes. And swallowed a gasp.

Caspian burned.

His familiar aura had turned golden, smoldering underneath his skin like buried embers. It traced the outline of his lips and sparked across the line of his jaw It was beautiful and horrible and strange. She'd never seen anything like it.

Willa blinked, struggling to arrange her features into a neutral expression. Only years of lying—of ignoring the things she saw with her own eyes—made it possible.

His hand was still on her waist. Willa knew what would happen if she told him her secret. He'd smile in that way you smile at a sick person, and then he would ride off on his sexy motorcycle and she would never see him again. Not until she ran into him at some club where he'd nod as they passed, whispering to his pretty date about the crazy girl he had kissed once in an alley.

So Willa looked into Caspian's face, at the color crackling across the arch of his brow, and said, "We should be getting back."

"Can I take you out again?" he asked, tucking a strand of her hair behind her ear.

He was still gorgeous, even with the blue of his eyes ringed with fire. Willa looked into his glowing face and forced her smile to touch her eyes.

· · · ● · ● · · · ·

Asher stood in the shadow of the Market building as Willa climbed off the back of Caspian's Harley. He knew he should look away when they kissed, but he watched anyway, jaw clenched.

After, Willa stood on the curb, hands tucked into her front pockets, the red glow of Caspian's taillights cutting across her face. He expected her to head toward him but she paused, eyes on the tip of her boots.

Asher straightened, pushing away from the wall. Something was wrong. If that womanizing bastard had—

He saw the moment Willa sensed his presence. Her spine stiffened and whatever truth that had been written on her face evaporated. She turned, smiling. "Hey!"

Asher blinked. The jade green of her eyes was still stunning, but there was a flatness behind them that he hated.

He didn't blame her for hiding her secrets. He had plenty of his own. So he choked back his loneliness and returned her false smile. Maybe a day would come when they wouldn't have to hide, but it wasn't today.

"You ready?" Willa asked, looking up at where the top of the building disappeared into the rolling fog.

Asher glanced away from the naked line of her neck. "Piece of cake."

That was another lie. Climbing twenty flights of stairs was never something he looked forward to despite having done it thousands of times. His legs ached just thinking about it.

Asher snapped on his headlamp as they entered the cavernous lobby. It smelled like urine and rot. Trash bags were piled behind the counter that used to welcome guests, spilling their contents onto the filthy tile. Willa shrugged her jacket off and tucked it into a nook under the stairs.

Her hair was already in a ponytail, a dozen tendrils falling around her rosy cheeks. She looked windswept and lovely. Asher swallowed. "Shall we?"

Willa gave him a little salute and they started up the stairs. They were quiet at first, saving their breath for when the climb stole it. On the sixth floor, a couple passed them on the way down. Asher didn't have to look too long at the short skirt and haggard eyes to know the girl was selling herself. It looked like she'd been keeping alive with her body for a long time. He slipped a granola bar into her bag as they passed.

They climbed three more flights before he couldn't contain his curiosity any longer and asked, "How was the golden boy?"

"What do you mean?" Willa managed between gasps of breath.

"Was he a douche?"

She laughed. "Well, he's a good kisser, if that's what you want to know."

Asher scowled. That was not what he wanted to know.

At the 16th-floor landing, Asher stopped, leaning on the railing to catch his breath. Willa slumped against the opposite wall. He dug in his bag for water, taking a drink before tossing it to her. "Do you think you'll see him again?" His voice echoed in the hollow staircase.

Willa lifted her collar to wipe the sweat from her face, the hem of her shirt hiking up. Her stomach looked soft, and he wondered what she would do if he crawled over and pressed his lips against her skin. If she would gasp and thread her fingers through his hair.

"What's with you and Tink?" Willa asked, interrupting his thoughts.

Asher met her eyes. It felt like a dangerous question. "What about her?"

Willa's gaze glanced off his and settled somewhere in the dark. Her hair had come loose during the climb, tumbling around her shoulders. "Well, you two have been dating for a while, but it doesn't seem serious. I guess I was just curious..."

Her cheeks were flushed, and Asher wondered if it was the stairs or the unspoken words that slid underneath the polite conversation they were pretending to have. "Tink and I have an arrangement."

Willa arched an eyebrow. "And she's on board with it?"

"It doesn't matter. We agreed a long time ago."

Willa frowned. "That doesn't sound like you."

She was right. He decided to change the subject. "How was the motorcycle ride?"

Willa tossed the water bottle back to him. "Fun. It's nice to feel free for a minute—even if it's a lie."

He pulled a switchblade from his pocket, twirling it between his fingers. "A couple times a year I take the Camaro upstate late at night. The highways are empty, so I can go as fast as she'll take me. I drive until I forget."

Willa huffed. "And what does Asher Flint need to forget?"

The spinning blade nicked his palm as the handle settled back into his grip. It was an innocent question. He sometimes forgot all the things Willa didn't know about him.

Asher thought about Deliah's delicate fingernails caked with blood and the gnawing emptiness of starvation. If he'd never gone to the Compound, he'd have never known the feel of her soft laughter against the crook of his neck. Would never have known the pitch of her screams.

His days of living in a cage were behind him, but Willa was the reason he had been there.

He wasn't sure why he had sacrificed himself for her that day. It had been stupid and reckless. Willa had been no one, and he had given her everything.

"Asher?"

He forced himself to unclench his fists. Willa had not asked for his help that day or any day. The consequences of his choice were not her burden to carry.

"Where did you get the scar?" she asked, as if reading the dark spiral of his thoughts.

Asher touched the jagged line across his nose. He could still feel the rough outline of where Frank's ring had cut his face. He stood abruptly. "Let's just say that I got it in a fight that I couldn't win."

Willa scrambled to her feet. "Asher," she said, her voice a question.

He shook his head and started up the steps. After a moment, she followed, but the last few floors were filled with silence and secrets.

Chapter 9

W ILLA CLUTCHED HER KNIFE down by her side as she followed Asher into the Night Market. It wasn't the sort of place that rewarded weakness, so she made eye contact with the enormous bouncer guarding the heavy steel door. He was an ethnicity she couldn't place, the warm tone of his skin accented by the tattoo arching from the crest of his wide forehead to the tip of his chin. He sneered at her.

She was always frisked when she came here—on the way in *and* the way out. Not for weapons—everyone was armed—but rather to prevent stealing. The Night Market had its own way of dealing with thieves, but punishment was always swift.

Which had never stopped her before.

She hid a grin when the bouncer stepped aside, nodding at Asher before going back to crossing his arms.

As if reading her thoughts, Asher stopped and pointed at her. "No stealing." Willa widened her eyes in mock innocence. "I mean it. This is my mom's place."

"Fine."

He shook his head before starting through the crowd. Willa crinkled her nose at his back and followed, slipping her knife back into its holster.

The 20th floor must have been an office Before, filled with cubicles and copy machines, but now the dividing walls had been stripped away and wires hung from the ceiling in thick useless ropes. People filled in the space between the market stalls, spilling into the main artery that ran down the center of the floor. The stench of unwashed bodies mingled with the smell of cooking meat and flames. There was an aura for every shade and color, but most of them were thin and dingy, like murky dishwater.

A cool breeze ruffled her hair. The windows lining the perimeter of the floor had all been shattered, and through the crowd, she could see glimpses of the silent city below and the stars beyond.

Lanterns dangled from several stalls, creating crevices of dark and light that hid the scantily dressed men and women lurking in the shadows. A gang of wild children raced by; rags and dirty faces doing nothing to hide their sly eyes and quick fingers. Willa squeezed her bag against her side.

It should have been loud with so many people jostling and bartering, but a hush hovered in the air. Willa wondered if humanity was just waiting for the final tragedy. Holding their breath as if the Darkness was just a prelude to some greater disaster—to a horror that they couldn't even imagine.

She kept her head down as they made their way through the crowd, but Asher paused every few feet to exchange words with the merchants and even some of the wretched souls hiding in the shadows. She saw smiles mirrored back to him; his aura a clear blue flame in the dark.

Willa scanned each stall they passed. One held a dizzying assortment of tools and weapons. Another, batteries and broken appliances, their insides exposed like the innards of a corpse.

She let her fingers dance over a small set of throwing knives. The weasel-faced man running the stall eyed her suspiciously as she tested the blade with the pad of her thumb. She let her other hand linger on a moldy box of bullets, just out of his eyesight, glancing shyly up at the merchant, an innocent expression she'd practiced a hundred times.

She put down the knife, and slipped the box of bullets into her bag with her left hand, keeping her steps unhurried as she moved to the next stall. No angry voice rang out. Willa ducked her head so Asher wouldn't see her smile.

They passed a stall where pigeons were being roasted over an open fire, the fat spitting and hissing. The smell of cooking meat made her mouth water, but she ignored the rumble of her stomach. Hunger was a constant companion. She barely noticed anymore.

Asher paused to speak to a thin girl with long dirty hair standing in the shadows. The girl, who couldn't have been more than fourteen, eagerly pressed her body against his. He shifted to keep space between them, hands on her shoulders. The young girl's eyes shined when Asher slipped her an apple.

Willa looked down at the table in front of her. The merchant was selling pantry items; dented cans of soup, sugar, tough flatbread, and bags of small hard potatoes. Willa tapped a finger against the potatoes. They would last into the winter, but she didn't want to think about the long nights huddled in front of a dwindling fire with nothing but boiled potatoes to fill her belly.

Her hand settled on a small ziplock of powdered hot chocolate filled with tiny marshmallows. Willa rummaged in her bag and pulled out a tea cloth wrapped around a vibrant red tomato; the last of the summer. She held it up. The man running the stall shrugged, but she hadn't missed the way his eyes lit up. After a bit of bartering, she was tucking the hot chocolate into her bag.

Asher was still talking to the young street girl, his dark head bent close to hers, so Willa wandered across the bustling aisle to a medicinal stall. Dried herbs hung from the metal bracings and the table was lined with orange prescription bottles. A piece of cardboard was propped against it, the name Mother Ezra scratched in a nearly illegible marker.

An old woman crouched inside the stall, tending a fire burning in the center of an old truck tire. Her gray hair hid her face as she stirred a heavy cast-iron pot, the smell of rotting leaves and ancient spices hanging around her.

Willa grimaced. Just another crazy lady trying to cash in on people's fears. People would pay anything to save a friend or stop an illness.

Mother Ezra looked up, her gaze cutting through the crowd. Willa sucked in a startled breath. The old woman's aura was a bright silver mist, like the pictures of Mary she'd seen in the yellowing pages of Mr. McMurtry's Bible as if she was touched by divinity.

The old woman gestured, and Willa found herself stumbling closer. She wore a long gray dress like a nun's habit, the hem stained with mud, a ratty shawl wrapped around hunched shoulders. She ladled something into a small chipped tea cup and rose slowly to her feet.

Willa fiddled with one of the orange prescription bottles, unsure of why she was waiting and waiting all the same. In another lifetime, a woman named Miranda Bell had taken oxycontin. Now her medicine was laid out with a hundred other stolen bottles.

She slipped Miranda's bottle into her pocket while Mother Ezra shuffled over and waited for the rush of adrenaline but felt nothing. The old woman held out the tea with shaking hands. Despite her bent spine, she was younger than she first appeared, her cheeks free of wrinkles.

"What is it?" Willa asked, taking the cup.

The woman didn't answer, folding her hands back under her filthy shawl. Underneath, her dress was decorated with silver thread, an elaborate pattern that swirled and dipped around the seams. No doubt pilfered from a penthouse on the Upper East Side. It was a common sight these days—wedding dresses with hiking boots or eight thousand dollar silk-lined jackets pulled over ripped t-shirts.

Willa lifted the cup. The tea smelled like wet rags and cinnamon. She didn't put a lot of stock into the homeopathic remedies that were rampant on the streets, but what could be the harm in taking tea from an old lady? Even if it smelled like death.

She took a sip and winced at the acrid taste. The woman gestured for her to finish and for some reason she swallowed it down, shuddering.

"You see things others do not," Mother Ezra said quietly, tilting her head as if to get a better look.

Willa put the teacup down with a click. "I don't know what you're talking about."

The old woman held Willa's gaze, her aura a pewter mist. There was strength in those black eyes, and, for the first time, Willa wondered if there was more magic in the world than her own. If the streets were filled with people keeping secrets just like—

"Is everything okay here?"

Asher put a hand on her shoulder, giving Mother Ezra a curious look. Willa wondered what he saw—probably just a hungry old woman selling stolen medicine and tricking customers with her grass tea.

She forced herself to smile. "Just stocking up on painkillers. Let's go."

Asher nodded and melted back into the crowd. The taste of the tea had turned sour in the back of her throat. She turned to go.

Mother Ezra's bony fingers shot out, wrapping around her wrist. "You are the key in the lock, child," the old woman hissed, her hands still shaking. "You are the blue sky behind the storm."

· · · · ● · ● · · · ·

Willa caught up with Asher in front of his mother's office. It was sectioned off from the rest of the Night Market, a set of three temporary walls pressed against the shattered windows and a scuffed door closed tight. The cold wind whistled across the sharp edges of the glass—the sound lonely and haunted.

She shivered. The sweat from the stairs had cooled to a sticky film on her skin. Her stomach churned, the old woman's words nestled like shrapnel inside her.

Asher eyed her and then pulled his hoodie over his head, leaving his hair in disarray. "You look like shit. Here."

He held out his hoodie. Willa waved it away. "I'm fine."

"Darkness, why can't you just take some friendly help once in a while?"

Willa clenched her jaw. She was getting tired of people telling her who she should be. "Just leave it okay?"

"Don't be an idiot. I can see you're cold."

He shoved the hoodie into her hands, stepping into her to hold her elbow so she'd take it. She looked up and her breath caught. It was dark in this corner of the Market and he was too close, the moonlight painting his eyes silver.

He looked down at her, brow furrowing, but it wasn't in desire. It was—

Willa realized what was happening a second too late, flinching when he plucked the orange medicine bottle from her pocket and held it up, pills rattling.

His gaze snapped to hers. "What the actual fuck?"

She blinked, cheeks burned. *Who did this asshole think he was?*

Willa swallowed, poking him in the chest. "Let me make something clear, Asher Flint. Just because we're friends doesn't mean you get to tell me what to do."

Asher's eyes turned to flint. His fingers closed around the finger stabbing his chest, shadows flickering through his bright blue aura.

Willa's heart hollowed. She knew he had a right to his anger. Impulsive or not, he'd sacrificed everything for her that night with Frank and all she had done was take in return.

He leaned close, his aura as inky black as the hair falling across his forehead. She braced for him to call her a bitch (she was) or to tell her to go to hell (he should), but his grip was light on her elbow, holding her in place instead of bruising. His lips parted, but fury seemed to steal his words. Their breath mingled. Her heart thundered but it wasn't from fear.

Asher would never hurt her.

The knowledge was like ice water. Everyone hurt everyone. Dread curled in the pit of her stomach. Somehow he had burrowed under her skin, and she fucking *needed* him.

Asher must have seen something on her face because his rage evaporated and he released her. "It's your funeral," he muttered, shoving his hands deep into his pockets.

The box of bullets she'd stolen felt heavier than they had before. She imagined she could hear them clink together.

She put on the damn sweatshirt. It was still warm from the heat of his body.

Asher looked out over the dark city, his aura mottled, the frown still in place. Willa twisted her fingers inside the hoodie pocket. *What the fuck was wrong with her?*

She should apologize. That's what a decent person would do.

Asher rubbed a hand across the scruff of his jaw. He looked weary and cold in his thin t-shirt. The tiniest flakes of snow swirled through the broken window and settled in his hair.

"We're not friends, Asher," she said quietly, her voice catching on the lie.

His eyes darkening—silver to gunmetal. "What are we then?"

"Nothing," she whispered. "We're nothing."

His gaze drifted to her lips.

The office door slammed open next to them. Asher jumped. A large woman stood in the doorway, her orangish-red hair puffed around her head like cotton candy.

"How long were you planning on hovering, son?" she boomed around an unlit cigar, her stomach straining against a bright tie-dyed shirt.

"Linda," Asher said ruefully, the black in his aura dissipating like smoke.

The woman broke into a grin, enveloping him in a hug. Asher was tall, but Linda tucked him under her chin easily, crushing him to her chest.

Willa smiled despite the quiver in her stomach. Nothing had happened. Not really. Everything was fine.

Linda pulled back, patting Asher's cheek. Her aura was a bright tangerine that tangled with her wild hair. She turned to Willa. "So. Who is this little thief that you've brought into my Market, Ash?"

Willa stiffened, the pleasant mom-approved greeting dying on her lips.

"This is my...Willa," Asher finished lamely.

"Well," Linda crossed her arms. "Your Willa stole from me."

Asher shrugged, "No one's perfect."

Linda barked a laugh. "Indeed."

"Willa's okay. We met a couple of months ago," Asher said, following his mom into her office.

Willa shot him a look. They had *not* met a couple of months ago.

"It's nice to meet you, ma'am," Willa offered.

Linda waved a dismissive hand, settling behind an old teacher's desk. "Oh, don't shit a shitter girl. We both know I'm no ma'am and you're not glad to meet me."

Willa glanced nervously at Asher, but he just shrugged again.

The office was enormous, with a view of Central Park and the jagged teeth of the city beyond. Before the Pulse, it would have been an office fit for a CEO or real-estate mogul, but now the gray carpet smelled like mold, and the golden sconces were shattered.

It was filled with a dizzying variety of expensive clutter. A set of skis leaned next to a red espresso machine; a hospital bed was wedged between a marble statue of the Madonna and an old Sabrett's hot dog cart. Two fat marmalade cats dozed inside an unplugged refrigerator.

Willa couldn't tell if Linda was a genius or a madwoman. Judging by the stack of hundred dollar bills the woman was using to weigh down the mess of papers on her desk, she was leaning toward genius.

Asher sat in one of the three old movie theater seats situated across from the enormous desk, propping his feet on a pack of toilet paper. "How are things at the Market?"

Linda poured three fingers of vodka into a crystal glass. It was the real thing—the chilled bottle of Grey Goose still had the label. She knocked back her drink and wiped her lips with the back of her hand. She did not offer them any. "It's a shit show."

"More rumors about another uprising?" Asher asked.

"Their boy child leader visited me again the other day. Wants me to donate supplies." She laughed bitterly. "Fucking idiot is going to get himself killed."

Asher chewed on the inside of his cheek.

There had been rumblings about some sort of rebellion for years. She hadn't thought much about it. In the first few months after the Pulse, Central Park had been the makeshift headquarters for the Red Cross and the local police trying to a patchwork version of martial law. At first, it had been a relief to have someone in control, but unchecked power was a dangerous thing. Eventually, the men with guns became the enemy.

Since then, rebellions have risen and been quickly squashed. Willa had lost count of the number of people who'd been dragged past the Compound's barbed wire fence and never seen again.

Asher's fingers tapped on his knee. "Maybe we *should* help them."

Linda pointed at him with her glass. "Don't be naive, son. You think you can change this damn world? Well, you can't." Her eyes sliced toward Willa. "Don't forget who cleaned your wounds last time you tried."

Willa stared at Asher. She felt sick.

Linda filled two more glasses and nudged them across the table. Willa took hers immediately. She didn't know what she was doing here. She didn't really *do* mothers. It was the unconditional love she couldn't wrap her head around. She took a sip, trying to burn away the lump in her throat.

"It's been eight years. And there is still so much suffering," Asher pointed out, rolling his own glass between his palms.

Linda leaned forward, her face grim under the tuft of her hair. "And why do you think that is son? Why do you think that the nights are still filled with Darkness? Humanity *invented* electricity! We should have had things back up and running years ago. There's something else at work here."

Willa frowned, resting her glass on her knee. "What do you mean?"

"Don't you feel it, little thief?" Linda gestured in the direction of the Market outside her door. "Can't you taste it in the air? Something is *wrong*."

Willa thought about the hush that lingered in every crowded room and the thin, muddy auras. She thought about the thing that had whispered to her in the subway tunnel and the nightmares she couldn't seem to shake.

Linda poked her cigar in Asher's direction. "Whatever evil entered the world when that goddamn Pulse hit—it's here. It's all around us. The only thing to do is keep your head down and stay alive."

Chapter 10

"WHEN I STOPPED BY the garage to see if you wanted to hang out, this isn't exactly what I had in mind," Caspian said from somewhere above her head.

Willa could only see the soles of Caspian's boots from where she was lying underneath the abandoned Ford. She reached further into the engine, cursing when the bolt slipped from her grasp for the second time.

"Why don't you stop whining and make yourself useful?" she countered. "I need that 3/8th socket from my bag."

She grinned as he sighed and clattered around in her bag before ducking his head underneath the car to glare at her unconvincingly. Willa laughed and held out her hand. He arched an eyebrow, waggling the wrench.

"Uh, it would be cool if you handed me that now," she said.

Caspian pretended to consider. "I'm not so sure."

She shifted, the cold pavement biting into her back. Her arms ached from trying to disengage the exhaust manifold over her head for the past twenty minutes.

"It's not the best time for flirting you know."

"Oh, I think it's the perfect time. I can ask for anything I want."

"And what do you want?"

Caspian stretched out next to the car on his back, folding his arms behind his head and crossing his ankles. His shirt rode up, and she could see the bare curve of his hip. The wrench rested on his chest.

"I can think of a couple of things," he said, the low timber of his voice skittering across her skin.

She was still tingling from his enthusiastic greeting earlier, but they hadn't gone farther than stolen kisses yet. Willa's cheeks flushed, remembering the way his hands had roamed up her body as he pressed against her. Lord, he was all hard muscle and reckless passion.

"That could be arranged," she said, unable to keep the huskiness out of her voice.

He winked and slid the wrench across the pavement toward her. She caught it and went to work on the rusty bolt, trying to focus on the work instead of the heat in her stomach.

"You know you're incredibly sexy when you do that, right?" Caspian asked.

She rolled her eyes, fully aware that her hair was muddy and her face streaked with grease. "You must be desperate to get me in bed."

Caspian turned so he was lying on his side, head propped on his hand. "I'm on the cold ground just so I can talk to you. Clearly, I'm super desperate."

Willa chuckled and then shouted in success when the stubborn bolt finally dropped into her palm. She went to work on the last one.

"Since this is your idea of a date, maybe we should talk," Caspian mused.

She frowned at the gasket above her head. "About what?"

Willa knew this was coming. Had been dodging it for weeks.

The truth was, she didn't want a boyfriend. She didn't need someone to take care of her. She was fine on her own. All she wanted was someone who would drive too fast and kiss her too hard. Someone who would help her forget.

Willa blinked as rust fell in her eyes.

"Where were you?" Caspian asked.

She knew what he was asking. If there were still dating websites, this would be the first question on any profile page. The *only* question really.

Where were you when the world ended? When the past ended and the future began? Where were you when you stopped being who you were and started becoming who you are?

Willa shook her head as the gasket fell into her hands. "Subway platform," she said, making a big show of examining the part. It looked good. In need of some serious cleaning, but she was almost certain it would work on Asher's impossible Jeep.

She scooted out from under the car. Caspian helped her to her feet. Before she could protest, he plucked the gasket from her fingers, set it gently on the hood, and folded her into his arms.

Shit Fuck Damn. She should have just had sex with him.

His hand idly stroked her hair before she felt obligated to ask. "Where were *you?*"

There was a long pause before he said, "The eighty-sixth floor in Midtown. My mother was signing custody papers. She was releasing my little brother and me to live with my father."

"That must have sucked."

Caspian shrugged. "She was a junkie. The court had ordered her into rehab. My brother was already with my father in Ohio."

She dreaded the answer to the next question but knew she had to ask. "What happened?"

"There was a fire—in one of the floors below us. It took me two days to get to the ground. I was thirteen. My mother died."

Willa knew there was more to the story. Every person who had survived had one, and Caspian was no different. It didn't take a lot of imagination to picture the long endless stairwell. The heat of the fire.

"And your brother?"

She felt his throat bob and knew the answer. Millions of people had died those first few days, but even more had been lost, severed from their loved ones by unspeakable distance. There were no news reports filled with the names of the dead. No phone calls or plane rides home. Just a horrible silence—and miles and miles of Darkness.

Willa didn't know what to say. There *was* nothing to say. So she rose on her tiptoes and kissed him, giving him the only comfort she had to give.

· · · · ●· ● ● · · ·

Willa ignored the jostle of morning commuters and scowled at her father's text. He'd finally found the math test she'd left on the kitchen counter for him to sign. Apparently, she was grounded. Which was totally unfair—6th grade was hard and Ms. Gilbert was a bitch! Besides, it wasn't like it was the first D she'd ever gotten.

Her thumbs hovered over the keys for a second, but the right words (the ones that wouldn't make things worse) wouldn't come, so she just shoved her phone back into her jeans pocket.

Fuck him. There was no way she was going straight home after school. She had a date with the cute barista at Starbucks. Well, not a date exactly, but she was pretty sure the older boy was flirting with her every time he made her oat milk latte.

Willa slipped her Bose headphones over her ears, and let the crowd sweep her into the subway. She tapped her fingers impatiently against her backpack strap as she waited behind a bunch of German tourists all the way down the escalator.

Who the hell stands on an escalator?

At the bottom, she swerved around them with her Metro card in hand and was through the turnstile just in time to see the M train disappear down the tunnel.

Shit.

Willa sank onto her usual bench under the graffiti-covered tampon ad and checked the time. If the 6:51 was on time—which was highly unlikely—she might have time to slip into Mr. Welk's photography class before he noticed she was late. Again.

She leaned back without actually touching the filthy wall behind her and tried to will the train to appear. The air was oppressively hot, dredging up a thick soup of odors, but it didn't really bother her. There was something comforting about the smell of urine and body odor. It smelled like home.

Willa lifted the camera from her hip and took three quick shots of the homeless man crumbled nearby. The bum was sleeping on a pile of newspapers as if it were a fluffy king-sized bed. He was probably a drunk. She had no sympathy for the homeless, but she had a photo essay due on poverty, and Mr. Welk would eat that shit up.

A familiar vibration rumbled under her feet. Willa stood, weaving her way past briefcases and through clouds of expensive perfume until she found a place on the faded yellow line by the tracks. Sweat slicked the small of her back so she swung off her heavy backpack and wedged it between her feet.

A man in a pinstriped suit bumped her shoulder, and Willa jutted out her elbow to hold her place on the platform. The suit ignored her, barking commands at the invisible person inside his Bluetooth.

The train's breaks screeched in the distance. The station clock read 6:50

Willa tapped her foot to the music in her ears. Headlights appeared down the dark tunnel. The approaching train pushed cool air ahead of it, the breeze lifting strands of sweaty hair from her forehead. The man in the suit checked his watch as Willa reached for her bag.

The subway platform plunged into darkness.

There were two long beats of ringing silence before the crowd gasped. She blinked and pulled off her headphones. The man next to her was a shadow and people shifted restlessly, but no one panicked. They were New Yorkers. Brownouts were not uncommon during the heat of lingering summer, so Willa waited for the emergency lights to flicker on—waited for the world to whirl back into action. Her heart thudded twice. Nothing.

Nervous murmurs started to give way to a dangerous rumble, and nameless bodies pressed closer. Willa reached for her phone, surprised when the screen didn't light up. Uneasiness started to creep into her veins. What kind of brownout affected cell service?

BOOM!

The crash on the street above them was so loud the tunnel shook, tile and plaster from the curved ceiling raining on their heads. Someone screamed, and like a switch, the platform exploded into chaos.

The crowd surged against Willa's back, pushing her forward so violently her book bag slipped off the edge of the platform and tumbled onto the rails. Willa braced her feet to keep from following it.

Above the frantic yelling, the roar of the approaching train began to fill the station. She cursed and struggled to stay upright, getting an elbow to the side of her head for her trouble. The train was close, the noise filling the cavity of her chest. Willa pressed back against the wall of flesh behind her, watching the toes of her favorite red Converse slide across the cracked yellow line.

Her eyes had adjusted to the gloom, but Willa realized with a sinking stomach that she couldn't see the train's headlights even though it must be close. The crowd was a relentless tide as they fought their way to the stairs. An elbow caught her in the corner of the eye. Bright floating stars exploded in her vision.

The train burst through the dark tunnel with a roar.

The man in the suit next to her shrieked—a comical, womanly sound. He stumbled, grabbing her arm as his dress shoes slipped. His fingers found the sleeve of her flannel shirt, tangling in the fabric. They lurched forward.

It was Willa's turn to scream—her terror lost beneath the voice of the thundering train. She flailed in desperation. The stranger's fingers were dragging her down, and then Willa felt the rush of the train past her left cheek, sucking the air out of her lungs as it sailed past. Her hair whipped wildly, stinging her eyes. The man's grip became a heavyweight.

She swayed back, off balance as the train ripped past, swift and deadly, a dark snake caught in the current of a black river. The wind screamed. The sound should have been married with the shriek of breaks, but without electricity, the train was untethered.

Willa somehow caught a glimpse of a young girl through the train's dirty window, her eyes wide with terror, one tiny hand gripping a dingy blanket, and the other curled inside her mother's fist. They locked eyes, each of them frozen in their own nightmare, until the tail of the train disappeared and the little girl was swallowed by blackness.

Willa crumpled to her knees, listening to the sing of the rail as she pressed her palms against the pavement and tried to remember how to breathe.

The crowd was gone— escaping onto the street in the few seconds it took the train to pass. The man in the suit still clung to her shirt. She reached for him, but her fingers came back slick with blood.

The man was gone. Only his hand remained.

Willa clawed at the amputated limb, gagging at the bristly hair on the dead man's skin. The stiff fingers clung to her sleeve, twisted in the fabric. She shrieked in frustration, sobbing when she finally managed to tear it free.

She scrambled away, emptying the contents of her breakfast onto the platform. She wiped the bile from her lips, crawled a few feet away, and laid her cheek against the pavement. Her headphones were still around her neck. Spilled coffee soaked into her hair. As far as she could see, the ground was littered with abandoned purses, briefcases, and lost shoes. More than one dead body lay amongst the mess, trampled by the crowd.

She thought of the bum and his newspaper bed. Wondered if he'd escaped.

A stuffed animal lay near her hand. She touched its tattered foot. A dog, she guessed, although with one missing button eye, and was so ragged it was hard to tell what it had been in its—

A muffled boom brought her back to her knees.

The train crash blasted out of the dark tunnel like a bomb, metal shrapnel skittered across the pavement, sweeping away trash and debris into a brief whirlwind. The heat that followed made her turn her head.

She needed to get out of here. Needed to figure out what had happened above. Willa turned blindly toward the stairs.

"He can't save you," a voice said from behind her.

She turned slowly. Asher stood on the platform, the stuffed dog dangling from his fingers. Two drumsticks stuck out from his back pocket. He looked solid and real and terrifyingly familiar.

Willa's mind seized. He shouldn't be here.

The disaster in the subway station was Before. Asher was Now.

Terror burrowed into her gut and the world went dim around the edges. A strange mist slid down the subway stairs and drifted around her feet.

"Your dad. He can't save you," Asher repeated, moving closer. The soft blue of his aura was tinged with silver. He sounded sorry. Willa shook her head. This was a dream. Her mind knew it, but she put up her hand anyway, desperate to stop his approach.

"Why?" she pleaded.

His gaze was unwavering. "Because no one can save the savior."

She laughed, recognizing the hysteria in her voice. "I'm nobody."

"You are the key that turns the lock."

His skin started to glow, a silver fire burning under his flesh. Willa's heels hit the wall behind her, but she didn't remember moving. Asher's eyes blazed.

"This isn't real," she gasped.

He was so close. Willa suddenly knew with sickening certainty that his touch would burn her—that the heat of that smoldering skin would sear straight to her core. She cringed when he raised his hand.

"Stop," she begged.

He smiled softly and it was horrible.

Beneath the burning, he was just Asher—kind and good. Willa started to tremble. She couldn't be anyone's key. He lifted his burning fingers to her face. "Things are not as they seem," he whispered. "You are the blue sky behind the storm."

The back of his fingers grazed her cheek, lighting the fuse hidden inside her chest. She gasped. Gold and silver exploded in her vision, and she started to fall, blood roared in her ears. Willa tried to answer him, but she had no voice, so she just burned and fell into the sun with Asher's words echoing around her.

Chapter 11

WILLA WOKE WITH A jolt. The sudden movement launched her violently from the comfort of her couch, and she winced as her elbow connected with the coffee table. She landed in an undignified heap on the floor, tangled in her mother's old quilt.

It had been a dream. Just an everyday run-of-the-mill nightmare. That was a lie, but Willa stared at the ceiling and repeated it until her heartbeat slowed.

It had been years since that horrible day—since normal had ended and the long hell had begun, but it haunted her just the same. Willa kicked away the quilt and sat up. Coals still flickered in the fireplace, casting a soft orange glow around her apartment.

There were people sprawled everywhere. Asher was asleep on the armchair with Tink tucked in his lap, her boots dangling off the side, his chin resting on her neon purple hair. The sight of them together made Willa's chest throb.

Grayson was propped next to the fireplace, his long legs stretched out in front of him as he snored. A half-empty mason jar of moonshine glimmered in his limp hand.

Eden was sleeping in a dining room chair, burnished head buried in his folded arms. Even at rest, the boy looked tense, his whole body strung tight.

Caspian's friend had appeared last night after she'd invited Asher's band to crash at her house. Eden was a complete mystery. He rarely spoke and when he did he was terse to the point of being rude. She'd caught him watching her from a distance more than once. Caspian didn't appear to even like Eden that much, but for some reason they seemed to be a package deal. Tragedy made strange bedfellows.

Caspian was stretched out in her favorite armchair, broad shoulders hunched inside his leather jacket. His blonde hair gleamed in the flickering light. In her dream, Asher had been the one with lightning underneath his skin. Willa rubbed her throbbing elbow. Clearly, her mind was trying to make sense of the strange anomaly.

Willa rose to her feet and picked her way around the fallen partygoers. Through the loft windows, a hint of pink outlined the clouds on the horizon. It would be hours before anyone woke up. She probably had time to slip into her dark room and finish developing her latest roll of film.

Willa paused in front of her wall of photographs. She supposed, to the regular eye, it was just an artful array of faces—a study of tragedy and survival. But to her, it was an explosion of color.

She'd grouped the auras, starting with deep blues at the bottom and ending with shades of white at the ceiling. The wall was her way of trying to make sense of the colors.

Willa studied the picture of Asher she'd pinned up yesterday, in it he was playing the drums, the wild movement frozen in a fragment of time. The camera flash glinted off the sweat at his temples, his dark hair plastered to his forehead as he lifted the drumsticks. She could almost hear the complicated rhythm of his music

She touched a fingertip to the curling edge of the photo where his aura was deep blue. Was blue goodness or sorrow? Honesty or happiness?

The edge of his aura was tinged in red. She hesitated and then unpinned the picture and moved it closer to the cluster of red auras.

Most of these photographs were filled with violence, the auras the shade of old blood: a soldier beating a woman on the street, a man yelling in the water dispenser line, a child blinking away the flies caught in the hollows of his eyes. But in another, two lovers kissed their auras a bright red.

Near the ceiling, a picture of a mother breastfeeding her newborn in a dirty alley, her shoulder angled to protect her child from the rain. The woman's aura should have been black—filled with fear and despair, but it was a beautiful flame of white so clear and true that Willa couldn't look at it directly.

Red for anger? Passion? White for love? Willa shook her head, taking in the whole expanse of the wall. It should be simple but it wasn't.

It would be easier if there was just a neon sign labeling each person sad or happy, but it didn't really work that way. Humans were complex. The wall was a kaleidoscope of colors, but she felt even less enlightened than she did before she started capturing them on film.

Willa glanced back at the sleeping living room before slipping inside the large closet she'd converted into a dark room. She lit the lantern and crossed to a tiny table filled with stolen milk jugs of chemicals and photo paper.

She worked quietly for an hour, grateful for the stolen moment, mixing the chemicals and gently laying the photo paper in plastic tubs. After the right time had passed, she lifted each sheet with a pair of tongs and secured them to the clothesline that hung just above her head.

After a while, twenty photographs dripped from the line, and she slipped off her gloves, watching as they slowly developed, the images appearing like ghosts.

The first shot was of an old couple huddled over a burning barrel of trash, their auras threaded with so much black it looked like lace. The second was a teenager laughing in her girlfriend's arms, head thrown back, turquoise aura bright. The next was the closeup she'd taken of Caspian on the steps the night of their first date.

Willa stepped closer, eyes widening. When she'd crouched in the dark street to take the shot, there had been nothing unusual about him, but as the picture developed, golden fire sizzled across his cheekbones and arched across his lips.

He was a fallen angel. A burning bush.

Fear flooded her chest. The truth lurked just out of her vision, as if she turned her head fast enough she would see the meaning behind all of it—the auras and Caspian and the endless Darkness. It was all tied together.

· · · • • · • • · · ·

Caspian watched Willa stare up at her wall of photographs through half-slit eyes. Her hair was in a tangled bun and her feet were bare. She looked young in the moonlight—like a child standing in the glow of a Christmas tree.

She wasn't beautiful. Not like most girls he dated. But she was stubborn and smart and when he kissed her she was a wildfire. He liked her. And not just for the physical stuff. He liked the smell of her, subtle and sweet, a unique combination of vanilla and photography chemicals.

It had been years since he'd allowed himself to feel anything for anyone. He was a soldier, after all—a cog in a wheel. And cogs didn't fall in love.

Caspian watched Willa disappear into the makeshift darkroom. It didn't matter how he felt, of course. She'd hate him soon.

Eden was fed up with waiting, and Caspian couldn't blame him. But still, he hesitated. There was something off about her that he couldn't quite put his finger on. It was the way she stiffened when she looked at the world; the way her eyes traced his profile when she thought he wasn't looking.

It was almost as if she knew. Knew about him. Knew about everything.

Maybe it was just an excuse. Eden thought so. But Caspian had learned to trust his instincts. So he waited.

He met Eden's eyes across the room, nodding once before unfolding himself from the armchair. The redhead followed, adjusting the leather jacket that hid the secret he carried between his shoulder blades.

Caspian scanned the room. The rest of the partygoers were still sleeping. Asher was tangled with the cute pink-haired girl on the oversized chair. The singer kid snored by the fireplace.

Willa would have to leave these people behind. The sooner he initiated the Harvesting, the easier it would be for her. He picked his way silently across the room with a fluid grace that he usually kept hidden.

Eden glowered at him, sweeping one hand in a sarcastic bow. "Now, oh wise one?" he asked, keeping his voice low.

"With all these people here?"

Eden's eyes flashed. "Why in Darkness not? It didn't stop you when you came for me. "

"That was different," Caspian snapped. He wished Eden would get over his own Harvesting. It was three years ago. Not that he blamed him for being angry, but enemies don't make the best teammates.

"Maybe if you weren't screwing her..."

Caspian wasn't sure how the knife got into his hand. How it had gone from the sheath at his hip to press against Eden's throat. It was like that sometimes, his movements so swift it took a moment for his brain to catch up.

Eden just sneered, hands still tucked inside his pockets.

Caspian cursed and pulled back. He didn't have to check the room to see if anyone had seen—the steady beat of a half dozen hearts only he could hear hadn't wavered. He headed for the door, not bothering to see if Eden would follow.

"I explained why I'm waiting a couple more days—you don't have to be such a dick about it," Caspian said as they stepped into the hallway. Eden leaned against the opposite wall and shrugged obstinately.

Caspian frowned. "There is something different about her, Eden. I can't put my finger on it. But it makes me nervous."

"Yeah. I feel it too. But we can't wait much longer."

"I know." Caspian glanced toward the closed door, trying not to think about wrapping the part of himself that was falling in love with her in steel. "Give me just a couple more days, and then we'll do what needs to be done."

Caspian rubbed the dull pain that sat behind his eyes. He hadn't signed up for any of this. When the Pulse hit, he had thought the worst thing that could happen *had* happened. He'd been naïve.

"What are you going to do?" Eden asked.

"You know," he responded, the words bitter.

"Caspian..."

"It's fine. It's my job." Caspian said sharply, zipping up his jacket. Inside the apartment, he heard voices. It was time to go.

"She's going to hate you," Eden said softly.

Caspian met his partner's eyes, hating the pity he saw there. "It has to be done."

It was false confidence, built around arrogance he had honed into a sharp weapon years ago. The truth was, he was tipping on a precipice as if the dirty hallway carpet was the edge of some cliff his whole life had always been hurtling towards.

He could say no. Could walk away from this life. Could go back to being helpless and afraid. Until they hunted him down.

Eden pushed off the wall and took his hands out of his pockets—normal-looking hands.

Caspian braced himself. The Traveler touched his shoulder and the hallway vanished in a burst of blinding white. The air turned bitterly cold, stealing his breath, as if he had just been shoved into a howling blizzard.

They vanished—Hunter and Traveler both—leaving the dark hallway as empty as if they had never stood there at all.

Chapter 12

WILLA KNEW GOING ON a double date with Asher and Tink had the potential to be a disaster, but Caspian had insisted, which was more than a little suspicious, since she was fairly certain he barely tolerated her friends.

She stared up at the rising half-moon and decided she didn't care. Caspian's thigh was warm the back of her neck and grass tickled her bare arms. He ran his fingers idly through her hair and she couldn't help a satisfied little hum.

Tink sat in the circle of Asher's arms nearby, leaning against the large oak, her fur-lined boot tapping against Willa's calf. Willa closed her eyes while the others talked quietly about safe subjects, like which market had the best sweet bread, their comfort books, and the new song the band was trying out.

Willa loved this little park tucked between two apartment buildings. The fiercely private, exclusive community kept it clean and heavily guarded. Entry was not free. She'd sacrificed the stolen bullets from the Market as payment, pretending not to feel lighter when they clinked into the silver bucket on top of reading glasses and half-empty bottles of Tylenol.

The fee was worth it. In the summer, wildflowers bloomed between corn stalks and fattening watermelons, the air filled with the buzz of bees and the happy shouts of children playing. But it was quiet now and cold; the nearby jungle gym was decorated with battery-powered Christmas lights, each strand twinkling happily. Above their heads, hundreds of white paper snowflakes fluttered in the branches of the oak tree as if fairies had blessed this place. It was as close to magic as anyone could muster these days.

Willa smiled when Caspian traced her lips with his fingertip. The wet grass soaked into the back of the sheer blouse she'd borrowed from Tink, but she didn't care about that either. If all went as planned, she wouldn't be wearing it very long anyway.

She drifted, listening to Tink singing "White Christmas" in her high clear tone, and tried not to love the moment too much. Happiness was a double-edged sword. It always took something in the end.

Caspian's fingers twined with her own. There was a scar across his knuckles, thin and almost hidden. She traced it with her thumb.

In another lifetime, something had cut him to the bone.

Willa sat up at the thought, chiding herself for her foolish drifting. There was only one lifetime. And it was this one—hard and brutal. It did no good pretending it was otherwise.

She avoided Caspian's eye, brushing grass from her hair. He glanced at her curiously but then just held up a silver thermos. "Coffee?"

Her shoulders relaxed. She shook her head so he passed it to Asher, who took a swallow and promptly started to choke and sputter. Willa snorted. Caspian's version of coffee was 80% rot-gut liquor.

"Jesus, what the hell," Asher wheezed.

Caspian chuckled, "Sorry about that."

Asher wiped his lips with the back of his hand and took another swig. Willa suppressed the urge to roll her eyes.

"So—Caspian," Asher said too casually, passing the thermos to Tink. "What's your story?"

Willa tensed, but Caspian just leaned back on his elbows. "What do you mean?"

Asher's fingers tapped on Tink's thigh. "I mean...you never talk about yourself."

Caspian shrugged, fiddling with a piece of grass. "Not much to tell. Lights went out. Dead family. Blah, blah, blah."

Willa frowned. "Asher, he doesn't have to—"

"What do you do? Where do you live?" Asher interrupted.

Caspian looked up at Asher then, going eerily still as if the air itself was afraid to touch him, the grass frozen in his hand.

Asher stiffened but didn't look away. Willa wished she was imagining the threat that hung between the two boys, but even Tink's eyes widened.

Until a sharp clatter cut through the tense silence—guns exchanging hands at the gate. Guard duty change. It was a small distraction but enough to make Caspian drop his gaze, sweeping a hand through his blonde hair as if to shake off the stillness.

Asher let out a breath, thick ribbons of black marbling his aura.

"I don't live anywhere," Caspian said mildly as if nothing out of the ordinary had happened. He plucked another piece of grass, smiling up at her.

A chill ran through her. She didn't believe that smile. Not one bit.

Asher's eyes darted to her and then away again, "Where do you sleep?"

Caspian looked amused. "I've got a couple of bolt holes around the city." He pressed the grass between his thumbs and blew. It made a whistling sound. "I like to keep my options open. It helps in my line of work."

"Which is?" Tink interjected, shooting a sympathetic glance in Willa's direction.

"I solve problems for people."

Willa frowned. "That sounds dangerous."

"I'm still alive."

She stared at her boyfriend. They'd been together for weeks, and she'd never asked what he did during the day. Maybe she hadn't wanted to know.

"What kind of problems?" Asher asked.

"The kind that's none of your business," Caspian replied easily, dropping the grass and turning away from them to rummage in his bag.

The conversation was clearly over. Asher raised an eyebrow in her direction, but Willa just shook her head. It made sense. Caspian had a smoothness to his movements that seemed unnatural at times. She'd seen him handle his weapon and it was always with deadly precision. That he was some sort of man-for-hire answered a lot of questions. She just wasn't sure she liked the answers.

"My job does have a few benefits," Caspian said, turning back to them. Four silver Hershey kisses sat on his open palm.

Tink lunged forward. "Mother of Darkness, is that chocolate?"

Caspian laughed and handed a piece to each of them.

"Where the hell did you get these?" Tink asked as she reverently peeled back the foil and popped it into her mouth. She groaned and collapsed back on the ground dramatically.

"Who did you have to kill is more like it," Asher muttered, inspecting his piece as if it might be poison.

Willa shot him a look, but she didn't blame him. Two years after the Pulse, chocolate was a luxury. After four years, it was scarce. Now it was unheard of.

"Like I said," Caspian said, as if that answered the question.

Willa held her chocolate flat on her palm, afraid it would melt. It was like holding a chunk of gold. She tucked it into the front pocket of her bag for later. When she needed a piece of joy.

"How do you find clients?" Asher asked, taking a bite of the chocolate with just his front teeth, leaving a half in his hand.

Caspian rolled the silver wrapping between his fingers. "It finds me mostly. There's no shortage of bad people doing bad things in the world these days." He flicked the silver ball into the dark, frowning. "Why do you think that is?"

"Why do we think what is?" Asher said, his teeth stained with chocolate.

"Why do you think there is more evil in the world now?"

Willa looked up in surprise. It was not a Caspian sort of question. He was staring up at the stars again, golden fire shimmering down the line of his neck.

Asher just shrugged, but Willa thought about Linda's words—about the hush and the waiting. "Desperation makes people do bad things I guess," she said quietly.

Caspian's eyes were distant as if he were making calculations in his head. "I don't think that's it."

He looked heavy suddenly as if he might be more than just a hot guy with a motorcycle, a quick smile, and a dangerous job. She touched his knee. He traced a finger across the back of her hand for a moment before pushing to his feet. "Better get you home before you turn into a pumpkin or glass slipper."

Willa let him haul her to her feet, stumbling a bit. His chest was solid muscle against her palm, and she suddenly remembered what the plan was for the night.

She made herself smile up into his handsome face, trying to forget his tense stillness and the questions she knew she should ask. Caspian tucked her hand into the crook of his arm as they said goodnight.

Willa knew she wasn't imagining Asher's eyes on her as they left.

Outside the gate, the streets were empty. She leaned against Caspian as they walked, the pale moon lighting their way. "Do you really think that?" she asked

He glanced down at her, his messy hair caught in his lashes. He looked normal again. Just a boy walking his girlfriend home. "Think what?"

"That there is something wrong with people? That some sort of...I don't know, mystical darkness is at work?"

"Don't you?"

A man passed them on the sidewalk, his filthy trench coat hanging from gaunt shoulders. There were track marks between his dirty fingers, and his aura was nearly translucent, a sickly gray.

"I don't know," she answered honestly. "Maybe we were just awful before, and the Darkness brought out our true nature."

"It's more than that. Haven't you ever seen anything that made you question if there is something more?" He paused, glancing back at the retreating man. "Something most people can't see?"

She should tell him about the auras. He was her boyfriend. But the words stuck in the back of her throat.

A militia jeep turned onto the street, the headlights blinding as it rounded the corner. She froze, but Caspian was already pulling her into an empty doorway, crowding her into the shadows. The doorknob dug into the small of her back but his lips settled into the curve of her neck—just two kids making out.

From over his shoulder, Willa watched the hulking jeep slide by, engine rumbling. A soldier stood on the runner, the DHS on his bulletproof vest luminous as he scanned the street, weapon in hand. His aura was a dull, faded brown.

"Easy," Caspian breathed.

The beam of the spotlight swept just above their heads, trailed down the sidewalk, and caught on the junkie who was just shuffling out of view. The jeep sped up and disappeared around the corner. She sagged.

"Idiots," Caspian murmured, kissing the underside of her jaw. He smelled good, like soap and cologne, like men smelled Before.

"If I didn't know better, I'd think you planned all this," she whispered, turning her head. He smiled against her mouth. Willa threaded her fingers through the golden silk of his hair and kissed him. He tasted like chocolate.

Dimly, she knew that what they were doing was dangerous and stupid. Their backs were exposed—vulnerable to anyone. Or any*thing*.

His hands slipped inside her shirt. She gasped, wanting to be the kind of girl who didn't love the way danger heightened the press of his body, bringing it into bright vibrant focus. Caspian traced her bottom lip with his tongue. Darkness, they had to stop or she was going to let him do unthinkable things to her right here on the sidewalk.

Willa pulled away, staring up at the stars as he feasted on her neck. The street behind him was empty now and quiet. The night pressed all around them, twisting into something sinister.

"We should go," she whispered.

He lifted his head, "What's wrong?"

Willa swallowed, staring out into the darkness. She'd almost forgotten the pale flash of that thing in the subway and the terror that had scraped across the inside of her skull. But now the feeling was back, thick and hot on her tongue.

"We should just go."

Caspian nodded and tugged her down the sidewalk, his fingers twined with hers. He walked like someone who wasn't afraid, and by the time they stopped in front of a stately old hotel, her pulse had settled.

The murky glass doors were held open with a stack of bricks, pale light spilling onto the street. Inside the lobby, someone had attempted to clean the black and white tile but the dried sweep of dirty mop water streaks swirled on the floor. The hotel sign above the doors was impossible to read, half of the letters missing and one golden S hanging upside down by a nail.

Caspian turned to her and pulled her close, his eyes were filled with something dark and secret and just for her. "Come up with me?"

Willa swallowed, desire stirring back to life like forgotten coals, but somewhere below the heat, just underneath her rib cage, was a twinge of doubt. The echo of that eerie stillness and Asher's warning eyes and all the things she didn't know about him made her hesitate.

He was dangerous, but she wanted him. Wanted *it*.

Fuck it.

Willa took his hand and led him inside.

It had been an opulent hotel once, with a soaring ceiling and gold finishes. Now mold crept up the wallpaper, despair dripping from the tarnished chandelier.

Willa tried not to be awkward as Caspian negotiated a room price with the greasy-haired girl at the front desk, sliding a dime bag of salt across the marble counter. The girl scooped it up eagerly and handed over the key, leering with a mouth full of rotting teeth. Willa grimaced.

"Fourth floor," Caspian said. She admired the fit of his jeans as they headed up the stairs.

At the landing, he held the heavy fire door open for her, his shirt riding up just enough to give her a tantalizing glimpse above his waistband. She slid by him far closer than necessary, grazing a fingernail across the exposed skin.

His eyes glittered. "Stop stalling, Celadon."

She laughed as he dragged her down the hallway, pausing only after he put the key in the lock. Willa knew this was the moment—his hesitation, the question he wasn't asking.

This was stupid, but she'd never believed in denying herself pleasure. Caspian was gorgeous and wild: why shouldn't she sleep with him?

He gave her a lazy smile. Willa pushed past him.

Caspian kicked the door shut and pressed her against the wall. Willa swallowed a groan, tipping her head to nip at the sensitive spot below his jaw, savoring the salt of his skin before he dragged her face up toward his. He said her name against her lips, his voice thick and rough. For a moment she was lost in the heat of his kiss, but then he was tugging at the hem of her shirt, pulling it off with one smooth movement. She shivered as his hands found her bare waist and he bent to kiss his way down her neck. And then lower.

Desire unfurled inside of her like warm honey.

He muttered something dark under his breath and then spun them, lowering her to the ground with startling grace before hauling off his shirt. Willa ran her hands through the crisp hair on his chest as he held himself above her. Darkness, he was gorgeous.

He was panting, and Willa grinned, delight spinning out inside of her as her fingers danced down the hard plane of his stomach to find the zipper of his jeans. The muscles in his arms trembled. "Harlot," he breathed.

Willa laughed and then he rose above her and she was lost.

· · • • • • • • · ·

The night air was cool as Caspian slipped onto the hotel balcony, but he hadn't bothered to find his shirt in the dark. Willa was still sleeping, curled on the threadbare carpet underneath her jacket.

There was no furniture in the dingy room, and he wouldn't have trusted a mattress in this shit hole anyway. She looked beautiful and sad huddled there on the floor of his makeshift home—just another lost girl.

He wished he could give her better. She deserved better.

There was no such thing as luxury in the world anymore, but a bed would have been nice, at least. They could have slept until noon, curled around each other and waking only for more sex and a trip out to a vendor's cart for a slice of warm, sweet bread.

Willa didn't seem to mind the modest accommodations and maybe that was the saddest part of all.

He'd done the best he could as they'd laid together afterward, sweat cooling, her leg heavy over his. They had talked about normal things. About what they missed and the small ways they held the despair at bay; reminiscing about ocean sunrises and movie theaters and the taste of chocolate chip cookies. It had been good.

Caspian swallowed his bitterness as the glass door on the next balcony slid open and Eden stepped out. He expected a sarcastic remark—something biting and vicious that cut to the bone—but the Traveler seemed unusually subdued. He glanced at Caspian's bare chest before propping his elbows against the railing, wrapping his fingers around a steaming mug of tea. "What did you find out?"

Caspian knew the side of the mug read, I love NY, the same way he knew that the room behind Eden had two comfortable beds and an armory of weapons laid out on the tiny kitchenette's counter.

He ran a hand across his face, looking up at the silent stars. "She acted weird when I mentioned that there might be things she couldn't see. I think she knows something."

Eden considered, taking a sip from his mug. "Could mean anything." He waved a hand to encompass the whole city. "Everyone is walking around with fucking PTSD these days." His lips twisted, glancing at the door behind Caspian as if he could see through it to the girl curled on the floor. "You couldn't get more out of her, lover boy?"

"I can't exactly ask her directly," Caspian snapped. "Don't be an asshole."

He was surprised when Eden fell silent, avoiding his eyes. Caspian supposed neither of them was proud of what they were doing here. Suddenly his muscles ached, as if he'd just come back from a hard day of training.

He hated this. Hated what he would have to do to her. But everything beautiful had to be broken before it could be strong.

"Have you ever heard of someone knowing about us before their Harvesting?" Caspian asked.

Eden frowned. "No. But you've been around longer than I have."

"I thought you might have heard something from Beckett."

That was a lie. The truth was that he wasn't the sort of person that people trusted back at the Triad. No one invited him to sit next to them around the evening fire or wanted to chat at the breakfast table. He only knew what the Council told him, which was never enough.

But everyone fell in love with Eden eventually, despite his sarcasm and black silences, as if drawn to his darkness by their own despair. No matter what the Council had done to him, Eden managed to be good, his integrity a shard of glass they couldn't remove.

Now though, Eden was glaring at him from the other balcony. "Beckett and I aren't a thing."

Caspian lifted an eyebrow, which was about as close as he came to banter.

"Fuck you very much," Eden retorted mildly. "I don't know shit and even if I—"

Inside, Willa's heart rate changed.

Caspian stiffened, holding up a hand. Eden shut up, his eyes shooting daggers, but he turned and slipped back into their room, just as Willa stepped out onto the balcony.

Caspian turned, arranging his face into a soft smile. The kind a boy gave a girl he loved.

She was wearing his shirt. A soft black t-shirt that barely grazed the tops of her thighs. It looked a lot better on her. Willa smiled sleepily, stretching and shaking out her dark hair in a way that immediately made him forget Eden existed.

"It's cold out here," she said softly, rubbing her arms. The shirt rode up higher and it was clear she wasn't wearing anything underneath.

Caspian brushed the hair from her face and pulled her closer. She let him, winding her hands behind his neck, meeting his lips with her own.

It was a lazy kiss and soft. She was warm and solid in his arms, all their passion burned away into something softer. His stomach twisted. He pulled away gently, pressing his lips to the top of her head.

He knew everything about this girl. The Council had briefed him before he came. He knew her history and inevitable future. Had seen the length and breadth of her suffering laid out on crisp sheets of paper.

Caspian knew she was using him too. For sex. For forgetting.

But for tonight they could both pretend, so he just smiled and kissed her for the last time.

Chapter 13

A SHER DIDN'T LOOK UP from the engine when Willa pulled up on Caspian's motorcycle. He tightened the already secure radiator bolt and tried not to listen to the murmur of their conversation.

At the sound of her footsteps, he slammed the hood shut a little too hard and turned. "Don't take off your jacket."

Willa paused halfway through putting down her bag. "Um, why?"

Asher tossed his greasy rag into the nearby wash bucket. She was wearing Caspian's too-big shirt from the night before, but she'd tucked it into her jeans and altered it somehow so it was annoyingly feminine. Her hair was down for once and swept the small of her back.

She looked soft and lovely.

He crossed his arms. "We're going on a scouting mission. For parts. I got a tip about a private parking garage that is fairly intact."

Willa nodded, gathering her hair into a ponytail. The movement made the collar gape, showing off the delicate line of her collarbone.

Asher brushed past her, placing the wrench in the white outline of itself in his toolbox. He touched the other tools, moving each of them a fraction until they were straight. "I was going to go this morning, but you're late."

Willa flushed.

Asher snapped off the lantern. He was being an asshole. Willa *was* late, but that wasn't the reason he was angry. Not by a long shot.

He stalked outside, trying not to think about how he'd left Tink sleeping naked and warm in his bed. Willa trailed behind him silently. He had no right to be annoyed. But *Caspian*, for Darkness's sake? Goddamn perfect-hair, motorcycle-riding, creepy Caspian?

Asher hauled down the garage door, wincing as it screeched and hit the pavement with a loud clang. Willa squinted in the morning light. "Sorry boss."

"When you didn't show up, I was worried," he snapped. He watched wariness wash over the brightness in her eyes, tension bleeding back into her face.

Asher swore under his breath. He really *was* an asshole.

"I'm not used to having anyone...um, waiting for me," she said.

He let out a breath. "I know."

"I won't do it again?"

She said it like a question. Asher couldn't help but laugh as he started down the street. Willa fell into step beside him. To fill the awkward silence, he pulled out the crumpled directions his informant had scribbled on a piece of notebook paper. The parking lot was about ten minutes away. He cleared his throat. "So...Caspian."

Willa scrunched up her nose. "Listen, I know you don't like him. You don't have to say anything."

"It's not that I don't like him..."

She snorted. "Liar."

He threw up his hands. "Fine. You caught me. I think he's a self-involved pretty boy with a dangerous job and questionable morals. Are you happy?"

"Yes," she said primly, tucking a loose hair behind her ear. "You have officially outed yourself as a horrible friend."

Asher rolled his eyes as they gave a wide berth to a group of teenagers passed out on the sidewalk. Needles littered the ground between empty bottles of booze. The parking garage was on the outskirts of a bad part of town, buried under what used to be an affluent apartment complex. His hand drifted to the knife at his hip, checking what he already knew was there.

"I'm not naïve, you know," Willa said.

He gave her the side-eye. "What does that mean exactly?"

"I *mean*...I don't have any delusions about Caspian."

Asher pressed his lips together. He wasn't gonna touch that one.

"He's not bad," Willa continued, glancing over her shoulder at the junkies they had left behind. "He's just fucked up. Like the rest of us."

Asher stopped. Willa smiled, and he tried not to notice the curve of her lips.

"Fine." He waved a hand. "If golden boy makes you happy, I'll deal with it."

It was her turn to laugh. "Well, that *is* a relief."

The knot loosened in Asher's chest. He didn't know what was between them. Didn't want to examine the silent current that slid beneath their interactions too closely. But he liked this. Being with her. Making her laugh.

He turned away from the thought and pointed at the narrow corridor between a burned-out pawn shop and an abandoned deli. "It's just down here."

She nodded, crouching down to adjust a loose boot lace as Asher ducked into the alley. His clever retort turned to ash on his tongue.

It was freezing in the alley, as if he'd just stumbled inside an industrial-sized refrigerator, the hair in his nostrils crystallizing. His breath plumed in front of him as he fumbled for the knife at his hip.

It wasn't just the cold. There was also the weight of the silence, like the percussion left behind after a gunshot, this place seemed to swallow sound. Fear slithered down his spine. It was never quiet in the city. Even after the Pulse, there was always the shuffle of feet, the burble of pigeons, or the distant murmur of voices. The alley *looked* normal—piles of trash, a mason jar filled with urine, a dead rat—but all his other senses told him otherwise.

Asher recognized the texture of the silence. In another lifetime, a foster father had taken him deer hunting in Connecticut. Quality time, the forgotten man had said. But Asher remembered the stillness as they lay hidden amongst the pines and snow—the silence of a predator hunting.

All this registered in a few beats of his heart. Long enough to slip his fingers around the hilt of his knife, but not enough for a warning.

Willa rounded the corner, her voice shockingly loud. "Sorry, I—"

Asher threw his hand up, but it was too late. She collided against his back, sending forward a half step.

She stiffened and he sensed her reach for her own weapon. "What the hell?"

He shook his head, not daring to drag his eyes away from the empty alley. He heard her thumbed off her safety. He tightened his grip on his knife. The silence deepened and then—

The air in front of them shimmered like heat over hot pavement, warping the brick wall behind it. The anomaly was vaguely circular and stretched to just above his head.

"What the fuck is that?" Willa whispered.

Asher didn't respond, words frozen in his throat, praying for this to be a bad dream or a trick of the light, but the temperature continued to plummet.

The outline of two ghostly figures flickered in the center of the fractured air.

Willa cursed, her fingers twisted in the back of his flannel, urging him backward.

The silhouettes guttered and then—Darkness help them—solidified into two flesh-and-blood men. They didn't step through the shimmering portal; suddenly they were just *there*, throbbing into focus between blinks.

Every instinct told him to run, but somehow he knew that there would be no escaping. They wore long vests that brushed the top of scuffed boots, the hems frayed like a flag kept out during a storm. The deep blue fabric looked heavy, exposing muscular arms to the cold, deep hoods hanging low over their faces. Silver thread climbed the edges of the garment in an intricate swirling filigree that made them appear other-worldly as if they had just stepped out of a castle onto a lonely moonlit moor.

"Willa..." he managed, trailing off when he saw the glint of their weapons. Fear nestled in his stomach like a tangle of vipers.

One of them held knives, the sharp blades curving around his knuckles. Asher had only seen knives like that in video games. Krimbits—inelegant weapons, designed for slashing and killing in close combat. Asher's fingers tightened on his narrow switchblade.

The taller one held a bow, the fletching of the arrows in his quiver glinting over his shoulder. They were unlike anything Asher had ever seen, shiny and silver as if they were made of impossibly thin metal.

It was those foreign arrows that finally unlocked his muscles.

He knew how to fight. He'd spent more nights than he'd like to admit, bloody and bruised on the floor of his cell. But this was different. Whoever these people were—*whatever* they were—they reeked of death.

Asher lunged. He aimed for the knife man's throat, figuring he had a better chance against blades than arrows. The hooded man moved fast—faster than should have been humanly possible, dancing smoothly to the left, the edge of the knife slipping inches past his face.

Asher stumbled and the hooded man caught him easily, pulling him into an embrace. He smelled like cheap cologne. Like sandalwood and spice, the smell so out of place that Asher hesitated, just long enough for the man to sheath a curved blade between his ribs.

He saw white. Blinding pain erupted in his chest, tearing at his breath. He heard Willa's gun go off but the sound was muffled like his head had slipped underwater.

Time flickered. Somehow he was on the ground. He tried to force air into his lungs but they were broken so he just stared up at the narrow wedge of sky, cold concrete bleeding into his spine. There are no stars tonight, he thought. There should be stars.

Willa was yelling his name. He waited for the peaceful calm to descend. For the soft tunnel of light to ease his pain, and whatever god there might be to carry him away. But there was only pain—only his own staggering pain.

Willa's hand was like ice on his cheek. He focused on the bright green of her eyes, unable to make sense of her words until she pulled the knife from his chest and the ocean of pain became a tsunami. His body curled around the agony, but she pressed on his wound, trying to stop the hot gush of blood.

Her dark hair fell over her face. He wished she would pull it back so he could see her eyes one last time.

And then.

A gentle heat spread from her fingers. The warmth curled around his lungs, the claws of agony retracting. Asher sighed. His muscles relaxed.

He barely noticed the strange viridescent glow that filled the dark alley as his eyes drifted shut. Willa was calling his name again, her fingers soft on his cheek, but he was so tired.

· · · · ●·● ● · · ·

Willa had seen something Asher couldn't when the hooded men stepped from the broken circle of air. Their auras were threaded with gold, the flax threads woven through their normal colors like lace. She was trying to unravel that terrible mystery when Asher lunged forward.

The man with the silver fletched arrows spun toward her and there was no more thinking. Her fingers spasmed, the gun kicking hard in her hand. The shot went wild, bits of brick raining into her hair and tinkling

Willa saw Asher fall, a curved blade protruding from his chest. She screamed, but the archer was stalking forward, backing her against the wall. He loomed over her, the long bow still empty in his grip. She got a glimpse of pale skin before he grabbed the hot muzzle of her gun, twisted it from her grip, and tossed it to the side. It skidded to a stop in a puddle.

Somehow her blade was in her hand. She thrashed out blindly. The archer circled closer, moving easily as if a girl with a knife was no concern. Willa's heart thudded. She had to run. It was her only hope of surviving this insane nightmare—*their* only hope.

Willa hurled herself toward Asher, trying to skirt the archer's long reach but he caught her around the waist, disarming her again in one swift movement. Asher was on the ground, his breath a whistle, blood pooling around his body.

She shrieked and clawed frantically at the archer's forearm. He grunted, red blood welling up in three long deep marks across his skin. He threw her to the ground as easily as he'd discarded the gun. Gravel tore through her jeans, biting into her knees. Willa cringed and threw her hands up to ward off the killing blow she knew was coming.

But the archer had stopped, his hooded face turned toward Asher, bow still loose in his left hand. Blood slid down his pale skin and dripped from the tips of his fingers, unnoticed.

Willa scrambled backward. He ignored her, watching his partner lower Asher gently to the ground. It seemed strange. Why not just let him fall?

She didn't have time to analyze the thought. Her fingers glanced off her discarded gun. She fumbled with it, rising on her knees, sobbing. The two strangers turned to her silently, but neither bothered to lift their weapons. She didn't blame them. The muzzle shook so badly, she'd be lucky to hit the wall behind them.

The one who stabbed Asher wore a watch. It was analog, the face glowing dimly in the dark alley. It was the sort of watch your grandma would have given you for Christmas Before, cheap but functional. The sight of it unnerved her, because he held one of those strange curved daggers in the same hand, his palm still slick with Asher's blood.

He took one step toward her, and she pulled the trigger. The shot glanced off the wall a dozen feet above their heads, chips of brick and mortar rained down on his hood. His aura pulsing—burnt orange and gold.

There was something she needed to understand here. Something she needed to *see*. But her mind was sluggish, foggy with adrenaline.

Behind the hooded men, Asher struggled for breath on the ground, one limp hand outstretched toward her. The wound in his chest made a sucking sound.

She staggered forward, not sure how she planned to get around these two fuckers, and not caring, just knowing that she needed to get to Asher—needed to touch his face. Needed to save him.

Willa expected them to grab her as she scurried past them. She expected a curved blade to slip into her flesh or those eerie silver arrows to pierce her heart, but instead, the archer gripped his companion's shoulder.

She froze as some sort of silent communication passed between the two men. A shudder ran through the archer's body, and he hunched his shoulders. His aura pulsed black, a wave of pain that obliterated the lavender shade, leaving only gilded gold edges. There was a sound like tearing paper, horrible and wet.

Silver wings sliced through his flesh, razor-sharp feathers unfurling like magic, the tips arching high above his head.

Willa cried out, falling back. Everything she knew about the world shifted and rearranged itself into something new and terrifying. Because those wings—*Darkness help them.*

They were metal—those horrible wings—and they glinted like the fletching of his arrows, each feather as fine as a razor blade. The archer flexed his shoulders and the wings unfurled further, the tips scrapping each side of the alley. They sang when he unfolded them like a blade being sharpened, metal on metal. They were beautiful and terrible and she couldn't breathe.

He looked down at her then, his aura violet again, wings singing. Sorrow curled within his aura and she hated that most of all because only *people* felt regret and sorrow. These were monsters.

Willa pressed a hand to her mouth as they took off, the whistle of steel cutting the air. The gun was forgotten in her hand. The frayed hem of their long vests rippled as they disappeared.

She stared at the empty sky until Asher's tortured breath snapped her back to reality. She fell to her knees at his side, her mind filled with white noise as she frantically ripped at his shirt. Her hands slipped in the oil slick of his blood.

The knife wound was paper thin but pulsed with gore at every breath. She pressed the remains of his shirt against it.

"Ash!" she rasped, surprised her voice worked at all. The gray storm of his eyes fluttered.

She pressed harder. He grunted, his body bowing around the pressure. In the old days, she would have called 911. Before, she would have screamed for help, would have run into the street for a passing doctor or nurse or goddamn chiropractor. But now she just knelt in the abandoned alley and tried to hold her friend's blood inside his body with the palm of her hand.

Willa didn't know much about knife wounds, but she knew enough to know that his lung had collapsed. Distantly she knew that even if there *was* a doctor, Asher was dying. Hot tears dripped off the tip of her nose and mingled with his blood.

Please. Please. Please.

But no help was coming. Willa pressed her forehead against his shoulder, Asher's pulse slowing under her palm. The beautiful blue flicker of his aura was fading, turning thin and transparent as a pane of colored glass.

She blinked at that aura. Something only she could see. And reached inside herself.

There was no explanation for why she did it, or how—only desperation. It was a prayer of sorts. A plea to whatever god had cursed her. A hope that there might be something *more* to her strange, useless magic.

She closed her eyes, listening to Asher's struggling heart.

For a moment, there was nothing. And then something flickered inside of her.

A light—forest green and familiar—glimmered behind her eyelids. She reached for it with her mind's eye.

The color pulsed and grew.

Beneath her hands, Asher shuddered. Willa held the soft green light in her mind, letting it fill her senses. It was warm, like sinking into the summer ocean.

Asher's fingers circled her wrist. The color curled inside her. A soft hum filled the air, and she realized dimly that it was her. Somewhere, crouched in the middle of an alley, she was humming tonelessly, the sound mingling with the strengthening beat of Asher's pulse.

She opened her eyes, barely catching a glimpse of the edges of that green glow as it whispered away until she was just a girl kneeling in a pool of her friend's blood.

Asher was terribly still, but his chest rose and fell steadily. Willa sagged, ignoring the blood that mingled with her eyelashes and started waiting.

The Umbra

Part Two

Chapter 14

I T WAS THE RAT that woke her.

Willa grimaced at the cheerful sunlight filtering into the alley as she peeled her bloody face off Asher's chest. Her head was pounding so loudly she was sure people passing on the street would hear it. Darkness, how long had they been unconscious?

She lifted Asher's wrist, momentarily startled by how fragile it seemed, and smeared gore from his watch. 7:13 am. Somehow it was morning.

She needed to get him out of there. He needed a doctor and then...

Willa's thoughts stumbled. Everything about the attack the night before was jumbled, like she was trying to do a puzzle in a drunken haze. There were things she needed to think about. Things she needed to DO. Her eyes drooped. If she could just sleep for a few more—

The angry skitter of claws on the pavement forced her eyes open again. The light in the alley had shifted, the sunlight hitting higher on the wall. Willa squinted as the rat crept closer. She tried to swallow, but the movement made her lips crack. She'd kill for a sip of water.

She hunched over Asher's still body, touching the rough stubble of his jaw. He was so pale she could see the fragile veins etched under his eyelids, but his breathing was steady and strong.

Willa lifted the bloody shreds of what was left of his shirt. His wound was an angry red slash, puckered but healing, the edges purple and mottled where the hilt of the knife had collided with his ribs. It would leave a glorious scar.

Did she do this?

Her hands trembled as she shook him. His breath caught, but he didn't open his eyes. Willa looked around, half convinced she would see a man with wings swoop out of the sky. Or maybe a dragon? That was just as plausible.

But it was just a normal alley. A rusty can of corn lay nearby, framed in a golden rectangle of morning light. Pigeons fluttered overhead. Willa ran a hand across her face. Maybe it had been her imagination? Maybe someone had slipped her drugs? Or she had finally bowed under the stress of this life and suffered a mental break?

Those were ridiculous, outlandish theories, but no more outlandish than a man with metal wings who stepped through a magic portal. Or the ability to heal a dying friend.

She needed to get out of here. Get out of this moment, so she could sort things out. She shook Asher harder. He groaned, eyelids fluttering. Willa glanced up at the wall. It was covered in faded graffiti, but she could still make out the chipped brick where her shot had gone wild last night.

Not a dream.

The rat was close now, licking the congealing pool around Asher's body. She kicked at it with her boot. The rodent chittered angrily and disappeared into a storm drain.

Asher had slipped back into unconsciousness. She patted him lightly on the cheek. He moaned.

"Come on, Don't be a pansy, Flint. Open your goddamn eyes."

His eyes opened, the smoke of his irises cracked with red. He lifted a hand to his forehead, streaking the dried blood and mud caked on his face. He looked as shitty as she felt.

He should be dead right now. Her stomach flipped.

She attempted a feeble smile. "There you are."

Asher blinked. Willa watched reality sink its claws into him, a storm of emotions flickering across his eyes. She put a hand on his shoulder, but he batted her away, lurching violently into a sitting position.

"Easy," Willa soothed. Asher ignored her, ripping frantically at his chest. His nails were half-moons of his blood. The remnants of his shirt slipped off his shoulders, the rail of his spine unbelievably fragile as he examined the ragged scar underneath his ribs. He shivered violently, but she doubted it had anything to do with the cold.

Will touched the bare skin of his shoulder. He stilled. For a moment, there was nothing but the harsh rasp of their breath in the quiet morning air.

"Asher?" Her voice wavered when his eyes met hers, bright and wild. He looked unhinged, his hair sticking up as if blood was some sort of morbid hair product.

"Am I dead?" he rasped, spreading his palm over the angry scar. "What is this? Willa, what the hell *is* this?"

Willa swallowed. "You're not dead."

He scrambled to his feet, backing away. "What the hell happened, Willa?"

She stood slowly, muscles trembling. Her head felt unnaturally heavy on the delicate stem of her neck. Asher's knife was suddenly in his hands. Willa took a deep breath. Exhaustion was a relentless weight on her shoulders, but she needed to get them somewhere safe so Asher could rest and she could figure out...well, figure out *something*.

"No one else is here, Asher. We're okay. We're both okay," she said. His frantic gaze settled on her, and she smiled—the kind of smile you give a rabid animal or a screaming child. His knife lowered a fraction.

She inched closer. "We need to get out of here. Rest. Put your knife away, okay? Can you do that for me?"

After a moment he nodded, sagging back against the wall. He was shaking so violently, that she wasn't sure how he was still upright. She slipped under his arm, staggering when his body settled against hers. They took a tentative step. Dried blood flaked from his skin, floating around them like a nightmare version of snow.

"We're okay?" he asked, his breath ruffling her hair.

Willa's fingers tightened on his waist as they slowly made their way toward the light. "Yes," she lied. "We're okay."

• • • • • • • • • •

"He punctured my lung," Asher announced.

Willa peeled open her eyes, staring at the ceiling of the abandoned Goodwill. Her head felt like the inside of a drum.

"I felt it happen," he continued. "Hell, I *heard* it happen. It was like trying to breathe fire. 0 out of 10 do not recommend."

Willa groaned, rolling into a sitting position. It had taken them an hour to stagger a few blocks. She'd been almost delirious by the time she'd dragged him inside the old thrift shop. Asher had been muttering under his breath by then, and she'd been afraid he'd snapped—that whatever she had done to heal his body had destroyed his mind.

"I'm pretty sure I died," Asher continued conversationally. He was sitting against the wall across from her, legs tangled in the nest of discarded clothes she had fashioned before passing out beside him. "I'm pretty sure those two bastards magically appeared out of nowhere and shanked me with a fucking medieval dagger."

Willa tried to lick her cracked lips, but her tongue was a swollen piece of meat. Gore still clung to Asher's bare chest, but there was color in his cheeks. A wave of relief made her light-headed.

"You want to tell me what the hell happened?" Asher asked, nudging her leg with his boot. "Aside from the stabbing part, it was mostly a blur."

Something in her chest tightened. Willa picked up a t-shirt from the nest. It was more holes than fabric, eaten away by moths and time, but she folded it anyway, trying to organize her thoughts into something that would pass for believable. When she opened her mouth, only a strangled sob escaped.

"Hey," he said gently, scooting closer. "Hey, don't do that."

Willa shook her head, squeezing her eyes closed. Her throat burned. She barely registered when he pulled her into his lap, but she pressed her face into the curve of his neck, letting the fear fill her chest till she was shaking and clinging to him.

He murmured soothing words and eventually her sobs dwindled to watery hiccups. She sat up a little, wiping her nose on an old baby onesie. Asher patted her back awkwardly.

Oh, God.

Shame blazed across her cheeks, and Willa was suddenly aware of the way her cheek was pressed against his warm chest. She tried to shuffle off of his lap with some dignity still in place, but he held her firm.

Something fluttered behind her ribcage.

"You okay?" Asher asked, his fingers brushing the hair from her damp cheeks. The movement made her shiver. She nodded.

"You blubbered all over me," he noted, wiping at his damp shoulder.

Willa sniffled. "I'd kill for a hot bath right now. Like, literally stab someone with a medieval dagger."

Asher laughed, and Willa felt the knot of terror loosen. She crawled out of his lap, and this time he let her. She wrapped her arms around her knees. Asher's eyes were soft. "I guess we need to figure this thing out, huh?"

"I honestly don't know where to start," she admitted.

"Let's start with how I'm not dead?"

"I, um, healed you?"

He ran a finger across the puckered scar on his chest. "You healed me?"

"Yeah?"

Asher examined the healing wound. It was still raw, but the skin around it had become a mottled yellow color. It looked weeks old instead of hours. "You want to elaborate?"

She closed her eyes for a moment. When she opened them he was still sitting there, his eyes steady. No matter what she said next, it would sound crazy. "You were dying, Ash. I was trying to save you when suddenly I just..." She trailed off, unsure of how to explain the unexplainable.

Asher looked like he had been in a car accident. The blue in his eyes was unusually bright peering out from the gore streaked across his face. She wondered what it must have felt like to die. "Have you ever done something like that before?" he asked finally.

"Not exactly."

He arched one dirty eyebrow.

Willa sighed and ran her hand through her matted hair. The last time she had told someone about the colors—Sara Beth Carter in 3rd grade—she'd spent the rest of the school year in the guidance counselor's office. And eating lunch by herself.

But Asher had seen what she had seen last night and had the jagged scar to prove it.

Willa cleared her throat. "I see auras. Around people. They're like fingerprints, I guess. Everyone's is unique but they also change depending on how someone's feeling."

Asher was quiet, so she worked at a tangle at the nape of her neck.

"How long?" he asked.

"When I was a little girl, I thought everyone could see them." She laughed but the sound had no humor. "I learned my lesson the hard way. People are afraid of things they don't understand. So I stopped talking about it."

Asher tapped a finger on his knee. "Can you read them? The auras? Can you tell what a person is thinking? Feeling?"

Willa winced as she worked to untangle her hair. "Not really. People are not that simple."

Asher rubbed the healing wound on his chest. Willa waited for the inevitable.

"So you can see, uh, my aura right now?" he asked.

She glanced at him, smoothing her fingers through her hair. Asher's aura was shot through with black so thick that it threatened to drown out the soft blue. Willa hated those dark tendrils almost as much as the wariness in his eyes.

"Maybe you should just get out of here," she said, braiding her hair to hide the tremble in her fingers. Her heart was a hot stone in her chest. "I mean, this isn't your problem. I wouldn't blame you."

There was a beat of silence as she tied off the end of her braid with a discarded shoelace, but then Asher said, "Don't be an idiot. There is no way I'm going to leave you in the middle of this mess."

"If you were smart, you'd run." She paused. "I would." It was true. The bitter thought burrowed into her heart.

"And miss all this excitement?"

Asher climbed slowly to his feet. He held out a hand. And after a second she took it.

Willa watched as he dug through the pile of clothes and pulled out a moth-eaten flannel shirt. He sniffed it and winced. She felt herself smile.

She didn't want to need him. Had, in fact, spent the past few months waiting for him to betray her. Not in a bad way. But in the way everyone did these days.

Asher hooked a smile in her direction. "Let's get out of here. If I have to be covered in blood for any longer, I think I'll lose my damn mind."

"God, yes."

He was still buttoning the borrowed shirt when they stepped out onto the street. More time had gone past than she had thought—it was late afternoon. She squinted up at the gray sky. "Of course, it's raining."

Asher grunted in agreement as they set off, hugging the edges of the buildings to stay dry. They were moving slower than normal, but it was obvious the impromptu nap had done them some good.

They'd gone a few blocks in silence when Asher stopped underneath a torn awning. Rain was coming down in heavy sheets, shrouding them in a curtain of water on all sides. His dark hair hung in limp spikes, dripping into his eyes. She had to resist the urge to brush it to the side.

"So here's what we know so far," Asher said, counting off on his fingers. "One, you see magical auras. Two, you think that is somehow connected to healing me. And C, two mysterious assholes stepped through a magical portal and attacked us for no apparent reason?"

Willa nodded. Her teeth started to chatter. Asher took her hands, rubbing them vigorously between his own. The tips of her fingers tingled at the warmth. "So is that it? Is that the end of the crazy?"

She looked up at him through the wet spikes of her eyelashes. "Well."

He lifted her numb hands to his mouth and blew on them. His lips brushed her fingertips.

"So after you lost consciousness?" she said, not looking at his mouth.

Asher's brow furrowed. "Yeah?"

Willa took a deep breath. "The one who attacked me sprouted metal wings and flew away."

His hands stopped moving.

"Seriously," she said.

"Well, sure," Asher responded casually. Willa couldn't help but laugh as he dragged her back out into the rain.

Chapter 15

WILLA BURROWED DEEPER INTO the couch across from Asher and stared at the roaring fire, cheeks tingling from the heat. It was foolish to waste so much firewood this early in the winter, but after the night they'd had she couldn't help herself. She took a sip of tea. The shot of bourbon Asher had added burned, warming her from the inside.

He'd been quiet since they'd stumbled, cold and wet, into the apartment. She had saved Mr. McMurtry from Donut's exuberant company, grudgingly taking the dog out to pee while regretting her decision to be a pet owner. By the time she'd trudged back up the stairs, leftover stew bubbled over the fire, and Asher had left a steaming bowl of water on the bathroom counter. Willa momentarily considered marrying him.

Shivering on the frigid bathroom tile, she had stripped down to her soaked underwear and dragged the washcloth across her skin, wincing as she cleaned out the shallow cut on her cheek. Willa didn't remember getting cut. It must have been the asshole with the knives.

Trying not to look too closely at the nightmare of her life, she pulled on her softest sweatshirt. It was littered with holes, a faded, long-forgotten cartoon Sponge danced across the front. It wasn't her best look, but Asher had seen her worst.

"You're spoiling him," Willa said now, eyeing the enormous dog who had wedged himself next to Asher's armchair. Donut gave her a baleful glance. Asher just chuckled and continued to rub the dog's head.

He had pulled the pink comforter from the bed she never slept in and was wrapped in it like a mummy. It should have looked ridiculous but the rough shadow of his beard and the darkness around his eyes was strangely appealing.

When he'd come out of the bathroom drying his hair, damp boxers hanging from his hips, Willa had fumbled the piece of firewood she was holding. The puckered red slash under his ribs was not the only scar on his lean body. Just above the curve of his hip bone was a faded silver line and when he had turned to change into one of her dad's old concert t-shirts, Willa had noticed the rough burn marks across his back.

She sometimes forgot Asher had his own secrets.

Willa settled deeper into the couch. Asher took a drink. He hadn't bothered with the tea part. She watched the way the alcohol clung to his lips.

"He's a good dog," Asher said, still scratching Donut behind the ear. "I can see why you keep him."

"I'm glad you do because I sure as hell don't," she teased, only half kidding. After the night they had been through, it hadn't been very fun standing on the street in the cold rain while Donut sniffed every piece of trash.

"Well. He loves you. No strings attached." The reflection of the fire flickered in Asher's eyes. "But I don't think that's why you keep him."

Willa curled her hands around the warm mug. "Why do you think?"

"He's a relic." Asher smiled when the dog started snoring softly, chin resting on his knee. "He reminds you of a time when walking the dog was just an annoying chore you had to finish before you snuck out with your boyfriend. He's a fossil of the past."

Willa glanced up at the mantel. There was only one picture up there, dusty in its silver frame. A sepia-toned shot of her as a baby in her mother's arms. Both of them were squinting into the summer sun, bathing suits dripping onto the Coney Island boardwalk, shoulders tanned and freckled. Willa's chubby baby face was covered in ice cream, sticky fingers tangled in her mother's wet hair. They were laughing.

"That's really gone forever isn't it?" Willa said quietly.

Asher followed the line of her gaze. "I think so."

She nodded, watching the coals spark and dance in the hearth. The same way the light had gleamed underneath Caspian's skin.

"Are you sure you didn't see their faces?" Asher asked, changing the subject. "Or something that would help us identify them?"

Willa shook her head. So much had happened. It had been a blur.

Asher frowned, sitting forward. "There must be something."

She closed her eyes, forcing herself to remember despite the fear that rattled against her ribs. The sudden bitter cold. The horrible scream of those metal wings. The golden glow woven through their auras like shattered glass.

A glow she had only seen once before.

Willa lurched forward, hot tea splashing across her fingers.

No.

The blood drained from her face. She must have made a sound because Asher was suddenly next to her on the couch. She pressed a trembling hand to her racing heart as if she could hold the truth there.

"What? What is it? What did you remember?"

Willa tried to push the knowing out of her mind, but suddenly it was there—in the familiar golden aura, the grace of his movements, and a flash of those glacial eyes.

Something splintered inside of her. They had...

She was gripping Asher's hand so hard she must have been crushing his bones, but he held on. "Whatever it is, we'll figure it out, okay? Just tell me what you remember."

"Caspian," Willa rasped, pushing his name past her raw throat. She'd thought she was done crying, but as the heavy stone of truth settled in her gut, tears spilled over her cheeks.

Asher sagged back against the couch, and Willa wearily closed her eyes.

· · ● ● ● ● ● ● · · ·

Caspian leaned against the window jamb and watched Willa's apartment building through the afternoon drizzle. The cold seeped through the thin glass, and he pulled his vest tighter. He couldn't stop remembering Willa bent over Asher's limp body. It was burned on his retinas, like an image left too long on an old television screen.

She'd been hurt.

He hadn't meant to hurt her—well, not physically at least—but somehow she had gotten that cut on her cheek in the scuffle. It was shallow and superficial but it was the thing that kept nagging him.

He'd brushed his lips against that cheek the night before.

None of that mattered. He was a soldier, and a soldier did his duty even when it was ugly. So Caspian waited silently, watching the rain forming puddles on the street below.

Willa should have been home by now. The conflict in the alley had been hours ago.

"Maybe he died," Eden offered unhelpfully. "I mean, you got him pretty good. Punctured his damned lung. Maybe she didn't get to him in time."

Caspian turned to glare at the Traveler. The lanky redhead was lounging on the only piece of furniture in the abandoned apartment. The couch was so filthy Caspian would have caught fire rather than let the musty fabric touch his skin. It was hard to tell if the piece of ancient furniture had an elaborate pattern or if it was just caked with mildew, but Eden was stretched across it casually, the frayed edge of his vest trailing onto the dusty floor.

"She got to him in time," Caspian said flatly.

Eden took a thin blade from inside his vest and started cleaning the dirt from under his nails. "Maybe she wasn't ready."

Caspian turned sideways, watching the empty street. "She was ready."

Eden scoffed. "No one is ready. One day you're just a normal guy trying to survive the apocalypse with your cute boyfriend and family, and the next—surprise!—you have freakin' wings!" He glanced over his knife. "You and I both know she will never be okay again."

Caspian could see the reflection of Eden's dead boyfriend in his partner's hard gaze. He knew that the Traveler was remembering too. Knew Eden's dreams were haunted by the horrific sound of his lover's screams being cut off by the hard, unforgiving pavement.

No one should hold a memory like that.

Caspian tried not to remember who Eden had been before his Harvesting. Tried not to remember the night he'd found himself crouching outside a steamed-over window on a cold metal fire escape, peering inside Eden's tiny kitchen. It had been packed, a long table crammed into the small space and spilling into the living room. The air had smelled like roasting meat and carried the sound of laughter out to where Caspian shivered in the snow.

Every single one of them had been a redhead except the boy next to Eden with the mop of black hair and an easy smile. A toddler sat in the boy's lap, playing with his crooked glass. Eden's arm had been slung casually over the back of his chair, twisting one dark curl absently as he chatted with an old woman.

They'd been happy. Even in a world buried in darkness, somehow Eden had found his way into the light. It would have been easier if he had been miserable. If he had been holed up under a bridge using damp cardboard for a bed. But he hadn't. And when it was time for the Harvest, Eden had lost everything.

Caspian watched now as the Traveler slipped the blade back inside his jacket and stood. There was nothing he could say to soothe pain like that. No amount of words could fix losing your family, your lover, and your life in one night. So he didn't bother. It was easier on both of them if he was an asshole.

Caspian turned back to Willa's window. He knew what they whispered behind his back at the Triad, that he was cold and heartless. They were half right. The sting of a sword was the only time he ever really felt alive—his breath born the moment a blade parted his skin.

Until Willa.

Caspian touched the glass, watching condensation drip from his fingers. She would accept his betrayal eventually. Everyone did. Even Eden, who had left his boyfriend's body crumpled on a city sidewalk.

The Harvesting was brutal for a reason. It was the only way to trigger their powers. Willa would work with them because it was her destiny, but she would never forgive him.

In the street below, a kid rode by on his bike, tires hitting every puddle. Eden leaned his forehead against the window, the rain casting strange shadows across his face. "Maybe she won't come with us."

"She doesn't belong here anymore. She belongs to us."

He felt Eden look at him, bitterness carved into his emerald eyes. But even Eden understood. By destroying Willa's life, they were saving countless others. Including, perhaps, their own.

Chapter 16

"**T**HIS IS A STUPID idea," Willa said as they reached the twentieth-floor landing.

"We have to start somewhere," Asher insisted, shouldering open the door to the Night Market.

Willa wrinkled her nose at his back. He was probably sick of listening to her complain, but she was tired and sad, and it was easier than examining the shitstorm of her life.

The market was nearly empty. She could see the red glow of the rising sun through the broken windows on every side of the building. The wind whipped through the empty stalls, carrying in a whisper of snow. Willa pulled her coat tighter.

It had been a long night. They had stayed up for hours, picking apart their memories for some sort of clue. But it turned out Willa knew next to nothing about her boyfriend, and all she could think of was the crazy old woman at the market.

You are the key in the door. Whatever the hell that meant.

"Come on," Asher said. Willa followed, moving aside as a hunched figure slid past them pushing an empty grocery cart. It was strange here without the bustle of the crowd as if ghosts had seeped back into the empty spaces the living had left behind.

Willa quickened her step, nearly running into Asher when he stopped in front of Mother Ezra's tent. It was abandoned—the curtain flapping. The old wooden sign was face-down on the empty table.

"We could wait," Asher said.

"No," Willa picked up a forgotten orange prescription bottle. One pill rattled inside. She stuck it in her pocket. "This is a waste of time. She's probably just a senile old lady trying to make a quick buck."

Asher wandered over to the bank of windows. She followed, watching the heavy snow blanket the city. He rubbed his jaw wearily. He was desperately in need of a shave. And twelve hours of sleep. "Any ideas where to look next?" he asked.

Every time they'd been together, Caspian had picked her up at her apartment or the garage. She had no idea where he slept. At the time, she had rationalized that he was probably embarrassed—holed up under a bridge maybe. Now she knew the truth.

Willa shook her head, fighting the shame that burned across her cheeks. "I have no idea."

They were silent for a long minute, listening to the wind howl through the broken glass. She could feel Asher's eyes on her. "I'm sure Caspian has a good explanation for what happened, Willa."

Willa snorted. Asher had hated Caspian on sight. He was only trying to make her feel better. It was sweet but unnecessary. She didn't have particularly high boyfriend standards, but not trying to kill her was definitely on the list. There weren't many things—

A loud crack cut through the room. Willa jerked away from the window as a fissure spiderwebbed across the surface, frost racing across the glass. The air beside them wavered as the temperature plummeted, stiffening her fingers.

So much faster this time.

Asher drew his knife, but Willa resisted reaching for her weapon. They needed answers, not revenge. Her skin pricked as the two dark figures stepped through the shimmering portal. Their weapons were sheathed, hoods pulled up to hide their faces, but she stepped back anyway, feet crunched on broken glass.

The one with curved knives strapped across his chest had a narrow scar across his knuckle. A pale white line that she had traced with her thumb.

The stranger reached for his hood with the hand she recognized.

Maybe she was wrong, Willa thought wildly. Maybe this craziness had nothing to do with Caspian. *Oh Darkness, please let this have nothing to do with Caspian.* But when the thick fabric pooled around his shoulders, Willa found herself staring into her boyfriend's blue eyes.

She pressed her lips together to keep them from trembling. He met her gaze without expression, his face like stone. Caspian had the same golden hair and handsome face, but there was a fierceness that she had never seen before. A part of himself he had kept hidden.

Willa reached behind her blindly and found Asher's hand.

It was one thing to suspect that the boy you were sleeping with was a murderer. One thing to wonder if the boy who had pressed his lips to the inside of your thigh was a demon. It was another to know for sure.

When the second figure dropped his hood, it was just a formality. Willa was not surprised to see Eden's burnished hair. She should have been angry, but all she felt was the hole inside her yawning open. Numbly, she watched Asher shift in front of her as if he could protect her, but the pain was forged inside her own heart.

"Willa," Caspian said, stepping forward, his aura flowing around his shoulders, burnt orange threaded with gold. She wanted to run, but the open window was so close that the cold wind buffeted her back as if the air was trying to help keep her standing.

Caspian spread his hands as he approached to show that he was unarmed.

Willa felt something shift inside of her.

It was the naked expanse of those vulnerable palms that did it. She welcomed the hot rage that rushed through her, obliterating the soft underbelly of her sorrow. Suddenly she wanted to scream and lash out until Caspian felt the agony she felt.

Willa lurched forward, ignoring Asher's startled warning, and hit Caspian square in the jaw. It was like punching stone. Caspian swayed but didn't step back, his expression impenetrable.

"Why?" she hissed, raising her hand again. He caught her wrist, and Willa wished his grip was tighter—wished his fingers would dig and bruise. She couldn't stomach gentleness. Not from him.

"It's a long story, Willa," he said, his voice calm and measured as if she was a crazy jilted ex-girlfriend. It made her want to kill him.

Willa jerked free, stepping back into Asher's chest so she didn't rip out his beautiful fucking eyes. "Don't say my name."

Caspian held up his hands. "Fine. What do you need to hear first?"

Willa paused, pressing her palm against her belly to stop the shaking. It was a cruel question because what she needed to know had nothing to do with wings or magical portals.

"Why did you let me..." She waved a hand between them weakly. Nausea rolled through her. Something other than mild indifference flickered across the granite of his face. "Why did we...what was even the point..."

She stopped. It didn't matter. Her heart wanted answers that couldn't be given.

Asher's arms went around her, warm and solid. Suddenly she was tired. So tired. All she wanted, was to get through this horrible moment so she could move on to the forgetting. "Just tell me what is going on, you backstabbing asshole, so we can get to the part where I never see your face again."

Eden chuckled. "Well, this is super fun. I told you this was going to be a shit show, Caspian."

"Shut up," Caspian snapped without turning around.

Eden shrugged and leaned against a concrete pillar. Because she couldn't bear to watch Caspian formulate his next lie, Willa turned to study the lanky redhead. The boy with wings.

She barely knew him. It seemed like he was always standing off to the side—around, but never part of anything. His friendship with Caspian had been a complete mystery. But now...

Now he made sense.

And somehow, suddenly, it seemed like it would be easier to hear whatever was coming next from someone who hadn't kissed her. From someone whose lies didn't hurt so much. Willa pulled away from Asher, brushing past Caspian.

Eden watched her approach in stony silence. Between the vest and the black combat boots, he looked more like a sullen teenager than some sort of supernatural angel. She stopped a few feet away. "You flew."

It was a ridiculous statement, but no one laughed.

Eden arched an eyebrow. "Yes."

Willa tapped a finger against her jeans. "How?"

"Well, princess, that is a long story indeed." He pulled a knife from out of a side pocket and started to clean his fingernails.

Willa crossed her arms. She was done playing games. "What the hell *are* you?"

"Are you sure you want to know?"

She couldn't help but notice that Eden's nails were impeccably clean and manicured despite the rest of his appearance as if the disheveled loner were just a mask he wore. She nodded at his question.

"I'm a Traveler," he said, watching her carefully. "I can move myself and my Trinity wherever I choose. I have wings. There's a lot more to it. But that's the Cliff Notes version."

Willa didn't like how that sounded.

"Your backstabbing boyfriend is a Hunter. He has heightened senses that make him a real pain in the ass with a blade." Eden slid the knife back into his pocket and straightened. "But that's not what you want to know. Is it?"

Eden's freckles were so dense they practically swallowed his pale skin. There were wrinkles at the corners of his eyes. The kind of lines you got from squinting at the sun too long. Or laughing.

He watched her study him, his face impassive, but she thought she saw something in his green eyes that looked suspiciously like pity. Or maybe it was sympathy.

"No," she said slowly. "That's not what I want to know."

Eden nodded and abruptly shoved past her. He smelled like snow and wind—as if he had just blown in with the winter weather. He walked up to the broken floor-to-ceiling window and gripped the sill with one hand, the toe of his boot hanging casually over the edge. The shattered glass dug into his palm, but Eden didn't seem to notice the line of red trickling down his wrist or the drop below.

"Willa," Caspian said to the back of her head, this time with an edge in his voice. She glanced back at him. The tattered edges of his vest pulled around his shins in the wind. "We don't have time for this. Come with me and—"

"She's not going anywhere with you," Asher sneered. Willa glanced at him in surprise, noticing the knife in his hand. She'd practically forgotten he was there.

Caspian laughed. "If I wanted to take her, there is nothing you could do to stop me."

"You fucking bastard," Asher growled.

"Stop it," Willa said quietly.

Asher froze, chest heaved, eyes sliding toward her. He had every right to be furious. Caspian had nearly *killed* him. But she'd been haunted by the auras since the Pulse. Wondering what they meant. Wondering if there was *more*. Caspian and Eden might have answers.

"I need to know, okay?"

It wasn't fair. He had a right to answers, but she knew he'd let her go. Willa turned back to the broken window before she could change her mind. Eden was leaning out over the edge, holding on with his fingertips. The wind fanned the flame of his hair, his violet aura licking around his face.

"Are you ready to be someone new, Willa Celadon?"

She didn't answer. *Couldn't* answer. So she just took his hand. Eden grinned, the black sky bleeding snow and stars behind him, and pulled her into the frozen night.

· · · · ● · ● · · ·

They fell.

She wanted to scream, but the sound was stolen by the wind. Eden held her against his chest, but it did nothing to protect her from the sharp needles of snow that pricked her skin. The sidewalk rushed up through the blur of her frozen tears, coming closer with every thundering heartbeat. The air shrieked.

This was not flying. This was suicide.

She was going to die. This was some sort of horrible game. There was no such thing as Hunters and Travelers and superpowers. She was just a stupid girl who followed some stupid boy out a damned window.

Every detail snapped into clarity. The broken yellow line on the approaching street half hidden by snow, and the blur of candlelight in a window as they tumbled. Willa panicked, throwing an elbow against Eden's chest, but he ignored her.

"Hold on!" he shouted.

It was stupid advice. The only thing she could *do* was hold on. Metal screamed against metal over the roar of the wind. And they stopped falling. The abrupt change of direction was so violent Willa was sure her neck would snap as Eden's shoulders flexed, his strange wings catching the frozen current as they shot back into the air.

And just like that, they were flying.

Willa swallowed the shriek caught in her throat, stomach rolling, as Eden banked around the building, the movement smooth and controlled.

She swore, brushing the frost from her cheeks with a shaking hand.

Eden was polite enough to pretend he didn't hear, his gaze on the horizon. The dark city stretched under them, silent and beautiful, the snow muffling everything but the strange singing of his wings. They climbed in long swooping arches that made her stomach dip.

Her pulse slowed to match the lazy rhythm of his beating wings. They were beautiful, his wings, each silver feather sharp as a razor. Script swirled along the edges of each one, an inscription carved in a language she didn't recognize.

Eden looked down at her, emerald eyes glittering. "You want to go to the top?"

"You're an asshole," she replied easily.

Eden smiled. The tip of one wing touched the outside of the Market building, concrete dust tumbling into the night as they shot into the moonlight.

Chapter 17

WILLA PEERED OVER THE edge of the skyscraper, her fingers tight on the rough stone ledge. They were at least a hundred stories above the city, the curve of the building hiding the sidewalk from view. She should have been terrified, but all she felt was numb—as if the fall had burned through all the fear left inside her.

Eden perched silently next to her, his chin resting on one knee as he gazed at the dark silhouette of the skyline. He was a living gargoyle, his unbelievable wings arching over his shoulders; the edges of his frayed vest trailing behind him.

"You tried to kill me," she said, snow soaking into her jeans. She had a million questions but they crowded against the back of her throat, so she settled on a fact. Facts were easier.

Eden flexed his wings, the unearthly ring of them like a death knell. "Trauma triggers power."

Willa could still feel Asher's blood slipping through her fingers, hot and slick. For the first time since it happened, she wondered about the extent of her strange new gift. Could she fuse broken bone? Knit together a severed limb? Heal the delicate flesh within the brain?

"I'm sorry," Eden said, his words nearly swallowed by the wind howling up the side of the building. "I know that doesn't make it better. But I am. Sorry. "

Willa turned and stared at his profile. A long silver chain hung around his neck, shaken loose by the flight. A thin guitar pick dangled from the end. Eden rubbed it with his thumb absently. These days, everyone had a keepsake: a tattoo or a ring or ratty t-shirt. A living gravestone for someone they had lost.

"How long have you been like this?" she asked.

Eden tucked the chain back inside his vest. "It's been two years since Caspian Harvested me."

"What was it like?" she asked, certain he wouldn't tell her, but he twisted toward her.

"Let's just say that my boyfriend wasn't as lucky as Asher."

Willa pressed her hand into the snowy ledge at her hip. She wanted desperately to believe Eden and Caspian were heartless monsters, so she finally had a place to rest all the hatred and helplessness inside of her, but she only saw regret in Eden's eyes.

"Just tell me," she said, welcoming the sharp numbness that started creeping up her wrist.

"What do you want to know first?"

Nothing. Take me back to my life. Wake me up. I don't want any of this.

"Everything."

Eden waved a hand. "All this bullshit: Caspian, the attack in the alley, Asher almost dying—even this fun little recruitment speech—is part of your Harvesting. You're a warrior now, sweetheart, and we've come to take you to the Umbra to, you know, increase your badassery."

Willa's mind stuttered over the word warrior but settled on another. "The Umbra?"

Eden shrugged one shoulder. "If you want a history lesson, you'll have to talk to Caspian. I'm a horrible student. The short version is that the Umbra is a magical hiccup in the time-space continuum."

Willa screwed up her face. "Um?"

"A friend of mine described it like this: imagine Time is a river and the Umbra is an upside down glass in that river. The water trapped inside the glass is still part of the river—part of Time—but it ceases to flow. The Umbra is stagnant—forgotten. It is also our home. And now it will be yours."

She thought about her apartment with Donut curled too close to the fire, filling the room with the smell of his singed fur. She thought of late nights with

Asher in the shop; the sharp bang of tools punctuating the smooth current of their conversation.

The numbness in her hand had turned to pain, but she kept her palm pressing into the snow. "Why me?"

Eden unfurled himself, balancing on the precipice of the skyscraper as if it were just a sidewalk instead of a narrow ledge in the sky. Wispy flakes of snow swirling around him. "You know why."

She did. But so far there had been no mention of the aura that ghosted around the edges of Eden's shoulders. Willa pushed herself to her feet gingerly. Her hand ached. "This is ridiculous. I'm nobody."

Eden nodded thoughtfully and pulled a long, thin sword from behind his back. Willa hadn't noticed it before, tucked next to his quiver of sharp silver arrows. She wondered how many other weapons he had hidden on his body. Wondered what it would be like to be more weapon than man.

He slashed the sword between the flakes of snow lazily. "We don't get this way overnight princess. Each of us has some sort of...anomaly—flying, heightened senses, knitting flesh—but we are *trained* to become warriors."

Eden sparred on the edge with an invisible partner. "You'll go to the training mat on your first day feeling like an imposter, but you will leave with the nagging sense that you were made for this—like a key turning in a lock."

Willa stiffened.

The pain in her hand had turned into hot needle pricks. She flexed her fingers, swaying as the wind gusted up the side of the building. "Let me get this straight. You want to take me to some sad dying world and train me to become part of your weird supernatural cult?"

This time Eden laughed out loud. "Just wait until you hear about the monsters."

Willa crossed her arms. Eden did something complicated with his wrist, twirling the thin blade through the air. "You are part of our Trinity. A group of warriors that isn't quite complete without all three parts: a Healer, a Traveler, and a Hunter. You're the last piece of our puzzle."

She waved a hand at the empty city below. "The Pulse killed millions. We've been starving and dying in the Dark for eight years. I think I would have remembered if a supernatural warrior had come out of the clouds to save us. Where the hell have you been?"

He turned to her, his feet sending snow tumbling off of the precipice. "The Triad is not concerned with the problem of men. They fight the monsters—Skotos—that feed in the darkness."

Willa thought of the pale nightmare that had slipped inside her skull in the subway. Remembered the sick feeling of invasion and the incandescent fear that followed. "Monsters."

Eden tilted his head, the tip of his sword resting on his boot. "You don't seem surprised."

"I've heard the rumors." She shivered despite Asher's hoodie. "And there was one time..."

Eden cursed. "They are supposed to be confined to the Umbra, but no prison is completely effective. Sometimes thin places appear in the magic where the Skotos can slip through. The Trinity had been patrolling these weaknesses for centuries but since the Pulse..." He shook his head. "Things have changed."

Willa could tell there was more to the story. Things Eden wasn't saying. But there was only so much she could take.

She stared down into the whispering abyss. There was only one question left that mattered. "What if I say no?"

Eden's aura darkened. "Caspian will kill Asher."

Willa froze. "He wouldn't."

Eden wouldn't look at her. Something hot and slippery uncurled in her gut. When he finally spoke, his words were solemn and final. "Caspian would cut Asher's throat and force you to watch while he bled out if it meant completing the Trinity. And I would let him."

Willa breathed in. Eden wasn't a friend, but she knew him well enough to know that he liked to dance. That he smoked when he was drunk. She had caught him sneaking treats to Donut more than once.

"Why would you do that?"

Eden looked out at the city, lips twisting. "There are people I care about trapped in the Umbra. If the Skotos win they will die."

The wind whipped up the side of the building, tangling her hair. When she was a girl, she'd read the Hobbit underneath her dead mother's quilt and dreamed of being whisked into another life with a knock on a perfectly round door. Anything to save herself from the sight of her mother's coffee cup gathering dust inside the kitchen cabinet.

She lifted her icy palm, pressing it to her hot cheek.

Now that the moment was here, she didn't want it. Now that the storm of power curled behind her ribs and her Gandalf was waiting for an answer with his magnificent wings all she wanted was her small, sad life back

But Asher—the boy who'd sacrificed himself without asking for anything in return. Asher, who held the chips of a debt she could never repay.

Willa lowered her cold, empty hand. There was no choice to be made. Her whole life was in the past.

· · · ● · ● · · · ·

Asher's knuckles throbbed from where they had connected with Caspian's face. He flexed them inside the pocket of his hoodie—tender but not broken, and glared at the asshole in question. Caspian sat against a concrete pillar, oblivious to the bruise blooming along his jaw, eyes closed, his fingers resting loosely on the curved blade in his lap.

Asher was not fooled. The first punch had been as much a surprise to him as it had been to Caspian. He wouldn't get a second shot. So he started pacing instead, broken glass crackling under his boots. Eden and Willa had been gone too long. Mother of Darkness, what had she been thinking?

Caspian cracked one eye. "Bloody hell, would you cut that out."

"Your pet bird dragged Willa out the freakin' window. For all we know, they could both be dead right now."

"They aren't dead. Birds can fly, you idiot. Eden won't hurt her."

Asher slid down the office wall and seethed in Caspian's general direction. The Hunter, or whatever the hell he was, didn't look so good. His eyes were hollow, and he seemed to have misplaced his normal swagger, as if betraying Willa might have mattered more than he'd like to admit.

Well, fuck him.

Asher knew plenty of guys like Caspian. The Golden Boy only cared about the people he destroyed if the consequences spoiled his plans. There was not enough room in his ego for guilt. Or love.

"You tried to kill me," Asher said, trying for accusatory and ending up somewhere around petulant.

Caspian rolled his head in Asher's direction, his hand still resting on the knife like some sort of damn taunt. The rising sun turned his hair into spun gold, the V of his vest dipping just low enough to show off his movie star chest. "I've got bad news for you friend."

Asher felt every muscle in his body pull taught. "Don't fucking call me that."

Caspian's lips curved into the shape of a smile. "I know you think you are important—the best friend—her protector. But almost dying was your only purpose here. You should go. Save yourself."

Around them, the light of day had twisted the Market floor into something small and sad—just a few scattered booths on a dirty concrete floor. Asher gritted his teeth and contemplated Caspian's murder. "I'm not leaving without Willa."

The Hunter shrugged, his head lolling away again. He closed his eyes again. "She doesn't need you, best friend—if she ever did at all."

Asher pushed himself to his feet, restlessness trying to gnaw its way out of his chest. Willa better get back here soon because he couldn't stand to be in the presence of this self-righteous, egotistical, dick weasel for one more—

Eden and Willa blinked into existence, scraps of trash and snow swirling around them. Willa's cheeks were rosy, the cold wind whipping her dark hair as she stepped out of the broken air. She shot him a crooked half-smile. He sucked in a breath. She was beautiful, the way a wild thing is beautiful when caught in a moment of stillness.

And then she turned, shrugged off Eden's hand, glaring up at the redhead. "Was that really necessary?"

The Traveler gave her a lazy smirk. "You're gonna have to get used to it sometime, sweetheart. Might as well be now."

Caspian rose smoothly to his feet, doing nothing now to hide the unnatural grace in his movements. "You can dispense with the dramatics, Eden."

"You're just mad that I got to her first, lover boy."

Caspian's gaze shifted to Willa. Asher expected to see hurt on her face, but her spine stiffened.

"I can explain everything," Caspian said softly.

Asher's hand curled into a fist, the bruise on his knuckles pulling tight. He would give his drum kit to wipe that smarmy smile off Caspian's damn face, but Willa beat him to it.

"Oh, I seriously doubt that," Willa responded, eyes glinting.

"Everything that happened was necessary," he said.

"Including fucking me?"

Caspian flinched, but Willa continued ruthlessly, "Because Eden filled me in. He told me about the Harvesting and the Umbra and a bunch of other nightmare shit, but he didn't mention sleeping with me."

"It wasn't all about Harvesting, Willa. I wanted—"

"Don't you dare."

Caspian stumbled to a stop, the briefest emotion skirting his face before he straightened. "You are coming with us. This is not a negotiation. You have a right to be mad, but—"

"No," Willa said, quieter this time. She looked over at Asher through the fringe of her tangled hair—underneath the fierce glare and unreasonable courage was a broken girl.

"Do you want to get out of here?" he asked.

Willa's chest heaved. "Please."

It was all the answer he needed. Asher walked between the two warriors—with their lethal weapons and unnatural power—and took Willa's hand. It felt small inside his own.

"You can't leave," Caspian said, but the venom had leached from his words. It sounded more like a question.

"If you care about me at all, you'll give me time," Willa said

"That's not—"

"Let her go, Caspian." Eden interrupted, the steel of his wings ringing behind him. "We need her willing. It will be easier that way."

Agony flickered briefly across Caspian's face, but when he spoke, his voice was cold. "Twelve hours, Willa Celadon—and then you are ours."

Willa nodded as they turned to go, and Asher could see the gallows in her eyes.

Chapter 18

WILLA HAD NEVER BEEN to Asher's house, but whatever she'd expected, it wasn't this. He shouldered open the door to the elegant brownstone, pausing to knock snow from his boots. She followed him into the foyer only to find herself gaping upward, frozen on the doormat.

Dozens of brightly colored paintings stretched from the baseboard to the edge of the vaulted ceiling—each piece of art more stunning than the next. It should have felt cluttered, the frame of a stark black and white photograph of snow-peaked mountains touching the gilded edge of a whimsical abstract, but instead the space breathed life.

She moved closer to a shadowy still life featuring a broken skull and a bright riot of peonies. It was spartan and vivid all at the same time, each brush stroke beautiful and precise. It had been ages since she'd seen so much color outside of the auras. After the pulse, darkness, and despair had leached the pigment from the world.

Behind her, Asher stripped off his coat and kicked his boots into a pile as if having dozens of priceless pieces of art in his foyer was completely normal. How much time had he spent looting art museums after the Pulse? Like most people, she had spent the better part of the first year scavenging for food and water just to stay alive. Beauty had been the last thing on her mind.

Willa touched the corner of a dreamy watercolor half hidden by a leaning coat rack. The name Monet was scribbled in pale white script in the right corner. "How do you have this?" she breathed.

Asher added his scarf to a hook. "Stole it."

Willa followed him into the kitchen. "I *know* you stole it."

He stepped behind the counter and started pulling things from a red igloo cooler. "Well. Then you asked the wrong question."

Willa shook her head. It was stupid and impractical—dangerous even to have so much art. The world didn't value what it used to, but someone would want such beauty. Someone would kill for it.

She watched Asher unwrap crumpled newspaper from around a piece of dried meat. She was hardly in a position to judge him on his stupid decisions. Hell, she'd been putting Asher in danger since the moment they'd met.

He pulled a tin out from underneath the counter, peeling back the plastic lid and filling the room with the smell of coffee. Tink's guitar was propped in one corner and a bottle of silver nail polish sat forgotten on the kitchen table. In the corner, a pink bra was mixed in with a pile of Asher's laundry.

"Does Tink live with you?" Willa asked suddenly, startled that she didn't already know the answer.

Asher paused in the middle of scooping coffee into a French press. "Yeah."

"I didn't realize the two of you were so..." she waved a hand, "serious."

Asher started scooping again. "We aren't."

Willa raised an eyebrow. He cleared his throat. "When I first moved in, there were six of us: Grayson, Tink, a bunch of other musicians." He turned and pulled two coffee mugs from a cupboard. "Eventually they all drifted off and only Tink was left."

She picked up the nail polish, tapping it against her palm. "I guess I didn't take you for the casual sex kind of guy."

Asher's gray eyes glinted with something she couldn't name. "That's kind of personal don't you think? Seems like you have more important things to worry about than my love life."

"Sorry," she mumbled, looking away. Exhaustion pressed on her shoulders. She should have gone home and gotten some sleep, but being alone somehow felt even more impossible than being with Asher.

"Do you mind starting the fire?" he asked without glancing up from his coffee.

"Sure," Willa said, glad for something to do as she headed into the living room.

It couldn't have been more different than the foyer. The walls were bare except for a single abstract painting hanging above the mahogany fireplace. It seemed to glow from the inside, the paint layered so thick it looked too heavy to be hanging. The painting made her feel warm—large strokes of yellow and orange reminiscent of summer sunsets, as if it was giving off its own magical heat.

Willa passed the soft leather couch to crouch in front of the hearth, reaching for the neat stack of old paper nearby. She crumbled a few pieces, adding them to the cold ashes, followed by a few sticks of kindling. She lit a match, watching the fire take, finding comfort in the familiar ritual.

Willa wondered if there were fireplaces where she was going. Or coffee. Or photographs. She imagined a military school filled with stone-faced Caspians nursing their battle wounds and drinking whisky straight from the bottle. She hugged her knees, digging her socked toes into the rag rug.

In her mind, she could see all the broken pieces of her life: a dead mother, a negligent father, the taste of the cold as Eden pulled her into the sky, Caspian's lips against her skin, the exact shade of Asher's eyes.

Willa stared into the flames until the heat dried her tears. listening to Asher move around the kitchen. Eight hours—just eight hours until she became someone else.

She fiddled with the neat stack of paper by the hearth to distract herself. A map sat on top, crumpled and then smoothed out as if someone had remembered at the last minute not to be wasteful. She picked it up. It was hand-drawn in pencil, the sketch remarkably detailed. In loopy script along the top of the page was the heading: Central Park. Willa frowned.

In the beginning, the compound in Central Park had been a temporary shelter set up by FIMA. Now it was a pseudo-government, swarming with militia and vigilantes. It was where the rules were made. And the rule breakers disappeared.

Willa held up the map, as Asher entered the room with two steaming mugs. "What's this?"

He plucked the paper from her hand with two fingers and settled on the couch beside her, his leg brushing her shoulder as he stretched them out. He turned the paper right side up, chewing on a piece of jerky. "I don't know." His brow furrowed. "It's Tink's handwriting."

Willa helped herself to a piece of dried meat. It was delicious, spiced with something she couldn't quite pinpoint. Cinnamon maybe.

"Has Tink ever spent time in the Compound?" Willa asked with her mouth full.

Asher squinted at the map, tracing the outline with one finger. Doubt flickered across his face and rippled across his aura. He shook his head. "No. But I have."

Willa's stomach twisted. Of course, he had. It's where Frank had taken him after the cop car turned the corner and disappeared from her sight and mind.

"It's probably nothing," he said, folding the paper neatly into four and tucking it into his pocket.

He seemed to shake himself before glancing down at her. "You have a lot of questions about my life considering you just discovered you're part of a supernatural cult. Maybe we should talk about that instead."

Willa took a bite of bread from the plate he'd set on the coffee table. It was soft and tasted faintly of honey. "Where did you learn how to cook?" she asked, skirting the question.

"Same place you did. The school of trial and error.

Willa took another bite. "My bread does not taste like this."

He chuckled. Willa wiggled her foot until she could see her toenail through the hole in her sock. She leaned her head back against the couch and studied the painting. In the firelight, the colors seemed to move. Asher absently fiddled with the ends of her hair. The subtle motion sent electricity skittering down her spine. "So what's the plan?" he asked quietly.

"What do you mean?"

"Where will you go?"

Willa frowned. "Go?"

Asher waved a hand. "You can't go with those guys. They're dangerous. Not to mention dicks. I assumed you asked for time so you could run—get a head start."

The fire had died down to golden embers dancing along the edges of the wood. It reminded Willa of Caspian. Her chest tightened. He had known the whole time and had slept with her anyway. She hated him, but it didn't change anything.

Willa didn't think Caspian would really harm Asher, but she couldn't take a chance. She pushed to her feet, sweeping a hand through her wind-tangled hair. "I'm going with them."

Asher blinked up at her. "What are you talking about?"

Willa leaned over and threw another log into the fire, watching the burning pyramid collapse. "You heard me."

"Are you crazy?" His gaze never left her face as he unfolded himself from the couch.

Her hands were trembling so she shoved them into her pockets. "I need answers. About who I am. *What* I am. Maybe Caspian and Eden can explain the auras. I have to—"

"Like hell," he hissed, grabbing her arm. "You don't need those bastards to tell you anything. *I* know who you are." His fingers dug into her bicep. "Willa, this is insane."

She wrenched her arm away. "I don't need your permission."

He threw up his hands. "They tried to kill us. How much proof do you need that this is a bad idea?"

"This isn't about them! You aren't listening."

"Why don't you explain it to me," he snapped.

Willa swallowed. There was a clock on the mantel behind Asher's head. It ticked quietly in the center of her chest. "I've always been different. Asher. *Felt* different. As if I wasn't a part of this world. And now I have the chance to find out why."

He shook his head. "Jesus, Willa, everybody feels different. It's part of being human."

"That's the thing, Ash. I'm *not* human."

He stared down at her, too close, eyes flashing. "Once they have you, they'll never let go."

Willa lifted her chin. "Eden said—"

"Oh, well if the damn psycho with wings said it's okay, then let me pack you a suitcase," Asher ground out.

Willa shoved him in the chest. "Stop it. You're being a douche. It's not a good look."

Asher caught her hand, pressing it to his heart. She tried to yank it away but he leaned in even closer. She stubbornly stared at the collar of his shirt. "Let me help you," he pleaded. "We'll run. We'll find a place to go."

He would do it. She knew he would. He would leave his whole life to save hers.

"Willa?"

There was blood underneath his fingernails. His own blood. Asher had died less than twenty-four hours ago. He had almost bled out in a dirty alley for no damn reason other than he was a pawn in some horrible game.

Willa met his eyes with the flint of her own, infusing as much venom into her words as she could stomach. "There is no *we*, Asher. Do you think I don't know what is happening here? What do you want?" She laughed bitterly, ignoring the thud of his heart under her palm.

"I'm not the enemy."

She hated herself, but she held his gaze. "I'm going."

His lips thinned. "Fine. You've been making stupid decisions since the minute I fucking met you. Why would it be any different now?"

Willa felt a wave of regret so sharp it stole her breath. A small part of her hadn't expected him to give up.

She started to step back, but Asher still had her wrist. He pulled her into him roughly, their hips colliding. He brought his head down to hers and she caught the smell of rain and grease. Her stomach clenched. "I just want to make one thing crystal clear," he said, low and quiet, his bottom lip brushing her earlobe. "If I wanted to be more than your friend, Willa...I would be."

Asher lifted his head and her breath tangled with the smoke of his eyes. She didn't sway forward. She was almost sure of it.

Willa pulled her hand away and fled like a coward, pausing only to grab her coat from the hook, buttoning it with unsteady fingers on the welcome mat. The beautiful art in the foyer seemed garish now and wrong.

"You don't have to go," Asher said from behind her.

Willa looked up at the giant Calder mobile bolted to the high ceiling. Each brightly colored panel caught the candlelight as it spun lazily. Before the world fell apart, it would have been worth a fortune. But now...

"Why do you keep them?" she asked, pulling on her wool beanie as if nothing at all had happened between them. As if this were just a conversation between friends.

Asher was silent for so long that she finally turned, her throat tightening at the sight of him leaning against the banister. He touched the corner of a nearby painting with his thumb—a muted portrait of a girl sitting alone in a field of wheat. "I keep them because some things are worth saving."

Willa opened the front door before his storm-cloud eyes could change her mind, letting the snow swirl into the room.

"Will you come back?" Asher asked, his voice half stolen by the wind. She stared down at the rectangle of light etched onto the snow in front of her. He touched her shoulder. She wanted to turn back into the circle of his arms. Wanted to follow him upstairs and write the ending of her own story.

"I don't know," she said instead, holding her breath until his hand dropped away and she could step out into the cold street alone.

· · · · ●· ● · · ·

Willa slept curled on the floor of her apartment in front of the cold fireplace until Donut pushed under the blanket, nudging the small of her back with his wet nose.

After a restless hour listening to the dog's soft snore, she gave up. She needed a bath. A good night's sleep in a cozy bed. Maybe sex with someone who didn't know her name.

Willa climbed to her feet, smiling when Donut let out a grumbly huff and shifted his big body into the warm spot she'd left behind. She padded toward the bathroom, stripping off each layer of filthy clothing as she went, leaving a haphazard trail down the hallway. Two hours. That's how much time she had until Caspian and Eden came for her. Laundry hardly mattered.

Willa lit the candle on the vanity, shivering as she dipped the washcloth in the bucket of cold water she'd left inside the sink and dragged it over her skin. She tried to run her fingers through her hair but it was hopelessly tangled from the impromptu flight with Eden.

She cursed and yanked off her underwear, kicking them behind her before grabbing the sink bucket and folding herself into the tub. The porcelain was hard against her spine as she dumped the water over her head, gasping at the brutal cold. She tried not to remember all the hot showers she hadn't bothered to savor before the Pulse, but it was hard on days like today. Goosebumps peppered her skin. She scrubbed at her hair, soap stinging her eyes.

She wasn't sure when she started crying, but the shudders from the icy water turned into deep hopeless sobs. Willa rested her cheek on her knee, hot tears dripping sideways down her face. How many times did life have to show her that there was no one she could trust? That it was hard and unyielding and miserable?

Willa watched the soap bubbles circle the rusty drain dully. When the tub was empty, she rose bonelessly, drying off with the stiff towel until her skin was red and chafed. She dipped her fingers into the silver pot of oil sitting on the back of the toilet, smoothing it into her hair until it hung heavy and loose down her back.

The bathroom was filled with the smell of coconut and the unwanted memory of her mother. She died long before the Pulse, but she tended to show up at moments like this, awakened by the smell of coconut oil the taste of saltwater taffy, or the quiet sound of a woman singing.

Willa stared at her naked reflection. Her eyes were bloodshot and rimmed in red, but her dark hair glistened and curled at the tips—her mother's hair.

She should cut it.

That's what girls in the movies did when they were about to become someone else. They stood in dirty gas station bathrooms and hacked at it with giant sheers or a jagged knife until it hung in sharp ragged lines around their chin.

She was clean now, but the fragile skin under her eyes was almost translucent in the candlelight. She looked small and lost and not remotely magical.

Willa pulled her mother's hair into a loose bun and forced the corners of her mouth up. It felt unnatural, like putting on a mask, but the girl in the mirror smiled just the same.

Chapter 19

I T WAS NOT QUITE morning when Asher slipped out of bed. He pulled a wrinkled t-shirt over his head, stumbling over Tink's boots in the dark. Behind him, his girlfriend was stretched across their mattress like a starfish, the comforter bunched at the small of her bare back, socks still on.

Tink had come home hours after Willa had left. Asher didn't know where she'd been or with whom, but he had reached for her, pulling her body underneath him. She hadn't questioned the rough desperation in his touch. Tink had always been like that—twisting his darkness into her light with the arch of her back and the laughter she pressed into his skin.

He wished he could love her; wished there was a way to fold love into a place where it didn't belong.

Now he was questioning everything, the crumpled map and Tink's scribbled handwriting detailing things she couldn't have known unless she had gleaned them from a dozen private conversations.

He picked his way carefully down the stairs in the dark and into the kitchen. There were more important things than his girlfriend's secrets. Things like magic and monsters and mystical warriors who appeared out of shimmering portals. And coffee.

He yawned, scooping fragrant grounds into the—

Something shuffled in the darkness.

Asher froze, staring into the living room. There was just the outline of the couch and the dirty plates still balanced on the coffee table. The oil lamp they kept burning low on the mantel flickered. Nothing else moved.

Still.

The hair on his neck pricked. Asher quietly slid open the utensil drawer at his hip, feeling for the handle of the chef knife. It was dull, the tip chipped off, but it would slice through a murderer if necessary.

It was probably just Grayson. The singer sometimes crashed on the couch after a late-night gig. Or maybe it was a stray drunk Tink had picked up on her way home last night. It wouldn't be the first time Asher had almost stabbed a perfectly friendly stranger in his own living room.

He picked up a flashlight with his other hand, praying Tink hadn't let the batteries die again as he inched around the kitchen counter.

A dark lump was huddled on the rug in front of the cold fireplace. It lifted his head. Asher adjusted his grip on the long chef knife and thumbed on the flashlight.

Donut blinked up at him.

"Mother of Darkness, Willa." Asher lowered the light as his heart somersaulted. Donut let out a lazy harumph in response and rolled onto his back, tongue lolling.

Asher crouched, rubbing the dog's belly while he twisted in ecstasy. A pang ran through him. She was really gone. He detached the note pinned to Donut's collar and leaned back against the couch.

Asher,

I know you hate me, but there is no one else. Please take care of my dog.

He is stupid, but I love him.

Love,

Willa

Asher rested his hand on Donut's head. He was used to being left behind, but every time it happened, he told himself that he would never fall for it again. That this world wasn't made for softness.

He'd been doing fine until Willa.

Maybe she had the right idea. Maybe dogs were the only safe place to store your love.

The first pale tendrils of morning were just starting to filter through the curtains. Donut snored softly in his lap, paws kicking. Asher didn't blame him. Running seemed like a pretty decent idea right now.

Asher rubbed a hand across his face, contemplating the distance to the kitchen. He would kill for a coffee. Not the kind that required building a fire and boiling water. The kind that appeared in his hand, steaming and warm and made by a bored, hipster barista in a beanie. The coffee of Before.

He pushed to his feet, shifting the dog's head to the rug. Donut didn't even—

"That is a horrible watchdog," a voice said from the shadows.

Asher straightened fast.

Caspian was leaning against the wall, arms crossed, as if he belonged there. The supernatural asshole was in his living room.

Asher made a lame attempt to find the forgotten steak knife with his foot, but Caspian raised an eyebrow at the furtive movement. Asher stopped searching. He might as well fight a grizzly bear with a frying pan. Instead, he turned his back, bending to throw kindling into the warm coals hidden underneath the ash. He might not be as quick or as strong as Caspian, but he knew quite a bit about bullies. He could stay small and quiet until the moment it mattered.

"Donut doesn't appreciate being referred to as 'that,'" Asher said over his shoulder, forcing himself not to tense when Caspian moved into the room behind him. "What are you doing in my damn house?"

He turned to find Caspian half sitting on the arm of the couch, twirling the kitchen knife between his fingers. The frayed hem of his vest trailed across the cushions, the silver thread catching in the candlelight light. "I came to warn you. Well, to threaten you actually."

Asher moved behind the kitchen counter. "Fun."

Caspian embedded the tip of the chef's blade into a sheet of music Asher had left on the coffee table. The handle vibrated. "I need you to let her go."

Asher took a pot from the dirty sink. "I'm confused. You already won. Willa went with you. Why bother coming here?"

Caspian drifted around the living room, picking up things and putting them back down as if Asher's home was some sort of curious archeology dig. He gritted his teeth while the Hunter flipped through his well-worn paperback of The Stand.

"Willa is stubborn. The training will be hard." Caspian glanced up. "If she tries to run—and she probably will eventually—she'll undoubtedly come here."

"Why do you think that?"

He knew the answer, but he wanted to hear Caspian say it.

The Hunter's lips tightened. He tossed the book onto the couch. "The two of you have a thing that I don't get."

Asher laughed, knowing he'd regret it and not caring. "Yes, I can see how friendship could be a baffling concept."

Caspian went still. It wasn't normal human stillness, but that eerie otherworldly kind that sucked the air from Asher's lungs. He swallowed, reminded again who he was dealing with. There was a wolf in his living room and you did not throw stones at a wolf.

Caspian prowled closer, leaning across the counter to take the full pot from Asher's hands. "Be careful how you speak to me, human."

He took the pot into the living room, crouching in front of the fireplace to tuck it next to the hot embers. Asher pressed his damp palms against the countertop. "How would she possibly run away?"

The Hunter tapped a finger against his knee, staring into the flames as the water warmed. "Eden," he said without turning as if that answered everything. And maybe it did.

It didn't surprise Asher that Caspian was worried about Eden's loyalty. He'd known a lot of kids like Caspian in foster care. He'd shared sparse rooms with dozens of boys with hate in their eyes and a wall around their hearts.

Caspian lifted the boiling pot out of the flames. The handle must be hot, but the Hunter didn't flinch when he handed it over. Underneath the counter, Donut leaned like a drunk against Asher's leg.

He should probably lie: *Yes, Exalted Great One—I will erase Willa from my consciousness.* But he couldn't make himself form the words, unwilling to betray her even after she was gone.

"If she comes to me," Asher said, keeping his voice light as he poured the coffee. "I would help her run to fucking Antarctica to get away from you."

"I'm not sure if you're stupid or brave."

Asher added a healthy swig of liquor to Caspian's mug before sliding it across the counter. "Oh, definitely stupid."

Caspian took a drink, humming in satisfaction. It was a normal sound. A human sound. But Asher knew there was more. He braced himself, burying his fingers in Donut's soft fur.

Caspian's eyes were splintered bone, but Asher forced himself not to look away. The Hunter smiled, just a small uptick at the corner of his mouth as if he saw Asher's bravery and found it charming.

"I need her alive, but I *can* hurt her, best friend," Caspian said quietly, his voice like silk and daggers. "And if you don't stay out of this—I will."

· · · · ·· · · · ·

Caspian wasn't sure what to expect when they appeared in Willa's apartment. A girl whose eyes were filled with hate. Or maybe just an empty room. He dreaded the idea of hunting her down like an animal—of using the memory of her smell to drag her into the Umbra. But he found none of those things.

Willa leaned calmly against the kitchen counter as they materialized, arms crossed. She'd changed into a pair of simple black jeans and a matching shirt that hugged her frame in an annoyingly distracting way. A stuffed army duffle bag sat at her feet, an expensive-looking camera slung at her hip.

She raised an eyebrow. "Let's get this over with."

He glanced toward Eden. The bastard shrugged. Caspian cleared his throat. "Willa, I want you to know—"

She straightened, anger snapping across her face. "Let's get a couple of things straight before you whisk me off to some sort of fucking fairyland."

"Oh, I do believe I'm going to enjoy this," Eden muttered.

Caspian glared at him and the Traveler held up his hands in mock surrender.

"Listen carefully you lying bastard," Willa said through clenched teeth. "You mean nothing to me—less than nothing."

There was no hesitation in her hatred. Exhaustion pressed against the back of his eyes. He shouldn't have slept with her. It was selfish and stupid and he would be paying for it for a long time.

He'd wanted one good memory to add to the meager pile that kept him warm at night. Something pure and good to remind him that the world wasn't smoldering ash. That there was something worth fighting for.

"I'm sorry," he said, knowing it wouldn't be enough.

"You were lying the whole time you were touching me," she hissed, color high on her cheeks. She wiped her hands on the front of her jeans as if trying to erase the touch of his skin. "I'll come with you. But we are not friends."

He nodded sharply, relief choking out despair as she shrugged the duffle bag onto her shoulder.

Willa looked at Eden. "Will I ever be able to come home?"

The Traveler nodded. "I'll take you whenever you need."

Caspian tensed. "Eden—"

Eden slid a glance his way—a secret look that spoke volumes. Caspian relaxed. He sometimes forgot which side Eden was on, but the Traveler had as much to lose as Caspian. Maybe more.

Eden took her bag, his expression friendly and open—his own sort of weapon. "Whenever you want. I promise, Willa."

It was her name that did it—a bullet of sincerity. She glanced around the apartment one last time. When she turned back there was fire in her red-rimmed eyes. "I'm ready."

Caspian could hear her breathing. It was strong and deep. The fingers wrapped around the strap of her bag were steady. Eden must have seen it too. "Let's go home," he said.

Willa grimaced but took the Traveler's outstretched hand. Caspian's heart stuttered. This was it—the moment his life had been hurtling towards since his own Harvesting. Once the three of them Traveled to the Umbra together, their Trinity would be complete—a bond that could only be broken by death. He should be happy, but the darkness inside him was a black tumor of anger and regret.

The girl with the broken heart held out her hand to him, and Caspian took it.

Chapter 20

WILLA THOUGHT TRAVELING WOULD be like being struck by lightning—a wave of power that would leave her gasping on her living room floor. But she was wrong. Caspian and Eden's power was like sinking into a warm sea.

A soft roar filled her ears. She could still feel the callouses on their hands and the strap of the duffle cutting into her shoulder, but it seemed far away.

Behind her eyelids, Caspian's burnt orange aura tangled with Eden's violet. It was familiar and yet buried beneath were vivid colors she had never seen before: deep amber, onyx, and cobalt like the shine of an oil slick, as if her whole life she'd been floating on the surface of the vast ocean, only to discover the fathomless depths below.

She could feel Caspian and Eden as if they were inside her chest. Could dip her palms into their loneliness and let their anguish slip through her fingers.

Her newfound power wanted to heal and soothe; wanted to knit together happiness the same way she stitched torn flesh, but all she could do was let the glorious tide of their auras crash over her.

It had been forever or a minute when Caspian laughed breathlessly beside her and let go of her hand. Her eyes snapped open. They were in her living room, Eden's palm still slick against hers. The lines of her bones sizzled.

Caspian collapsed onto the couch, eyes wild. "Well, fuck me."

Willa rubbed her sternum. It felt full as if the shards of Caspian and Eden's aura had slipped into the splintered holes inside her heart and fixed something she hadn't known was broken.

Eden untangled his finger from her, angling his shoulder so she couldn't see his face. The bright lavender of his aura had deepened to a dark wine.

Willa hesitated and touched his wrist with her fingertips. "Are you okay?"

Eden stiffened. "Yes."

Willa didn't believe him. There was a part of her that could see him now—all his emotions exposed like the glistening entrails of a gutted fish. And Eden knew it.

But Caspian seemed oblivious, sprawled on the couch and grinning up at the ceiling. There was something that blinded him—a dark place even their new bond couldn't touch.

Willa ran a shaking hand across her forehead, still struggling to hold in the effervescent power, and saw the apartment for the first time.

She frowned. When they'd linked hands, morning light had been streaming through the windows, dust drifting through the sparkling sunshine, but now the air was a strange mustard yellow, filled with the eerie crouching stillness that sometimes proceeded a storm.

Willa stared at the empty fireplace mantel. The silver frame with the picture of her mother was gone. Fear slithered in her gut. Her mother's quilt was no longer tangled on the floor, and Donut's frayed leash was missing. The furniture was all there—the lumpy couch and her dad's favorite armchair—but all the details were missing; the refrigerator magnet from Coney Island, the dirty dishes in the sink, and the teetering stack of books by the coffee table.

Her wall of pictures was gone. Every shot. Every face. Leaving behind only cold brick.

"What is this?" she whispered.

"Do you smell that?" Eden asked, still pale beneath his freckles.

It wasn't what she expected him to say, but she *did* smell something—had smelled it, in fact, since the minute Caspian had let go of her hand. The scent tickled the back of her mind, sweet but unpleasant, like a peach that had been left out in the bowl too long—like something good that was dying.

"What *is* that?"

Caspian rose from the couch, eyes bright. His aura was a bronze current gilded with gold. One hand rested easily on the hilt of the knife strapped across his chest. He gestured at the window. "Go see for yourself."

Eden must have felt her hesitation, because he crossed the room first, looking down at the street. She followed. On the wrought iron balcony outside her apartment, the tomato plants were withered stalks, fruit rotting on the shriveled vines.

And the sun was a black hole.

She'd seen a total eclipse once in fourth grade. The class had made viewing boxes from milk cartons and stood on the gravel playground as the shadow moved across the sun. The birds had gone silent when the false dusk had descended and so had her classmates.

Eden squinted up at the black sun. "Welcome to the Umbra, Willa."

She pressed her feverish forehead against the cool glass. Last night she'd crouched in the snow in the shadow of Asher's brownstone until Donut's neck was damp from her tears. Now there was only ugly gray slush in the street below as if this terrible new world couldn't abide beauty. The ugliness pressed all around her—the sweet rotting smell and the sick light—like standing in a morgue.

"You get used to it," Eden said quietly. "It's not so bad in the Triad—that's where we live. You can't smell it so much and...well, it's not so bad."

Down on the street, a nightmare lurched from the shadows.

They'd told her about the Skotos—warned her about the monsters trapped in the Umbra. Imprisoned in this horrible left-behind place, but she wasn't prepared for the sight of it.

Human-like and impossibly tall despite its hunched back, the creature leaned heavily against the alley wall, the loose folds of its ragged flesh catching on the rough brick, leaving behind wet streaks of blood. White bones broke through its thin weeping skin at all the sharp places, elbows and cheeks, and the jagged ladder of its spine. The Skotos shambled forward, long limbs twisted and distorted, claws tapping the sidewalk like a blind man's cane. Its head moved rhythmically from side to side, and Willa knew not being able to clearly see its face from this distance was a mercy.

She pressed closer to the glass. "Mother of Darkness."

Eden crouched next to her. "You remember when I told you that the Umbra was a glass tipped upside down in the river of time?"

She nodded numbly.

His emerald eyes tracked the Skotos' ghostly movement. "Well, the glass is cracked. We don't know why—only that it had to do with the Pulse. And if it breaks…"

Her lips felt numb. "How many?"

Eden rubbed the back of his neck. "Thousands."

The number was too big to understand. Her heart thudded. What the hell had she agreed to?

The street was empty again. The Skotos had disappeared around the corner.

"Where is everyone else?" she whispered.

Caspian leaned against the glass, scanning the street. "There's just the Triad here in New York. There might have been humans once—we don't know. There are other Triads: Mexico City, Vancouver, and another where San Francisco used to be."

Willa thought about Asher's show in the subway all those weeks ago. Remembered the bodies pressed against her as she had danced. Now she was trapped in a world where the number of people on that subway dance floor was nearly the same as on the whole damn continent. She pushed to her feet, tucking her trembling hands in her pockets. "So. What now?"

"Do you want the good news or the bad news?" Caspian said.

Willa eyed the place where the Skotos had disappeared. "How could there possibly be more bad news?"

Eden rubbed his temple. "Oh, there's more."

Caspian pulled a pair of knives from the leather sheaths that crisscrossed his chest. Willa tried to forget what they looked like slick with Asher's blood. "The *good* news," he said. "Is that Eden and I can protect you."

She did not like the sound of that. "Protect me?"

Eden flicked his bowstring with a thumb. "The bad news is that this day is just getting started."

Willa felt lightheaded. "Just tell me."

The two warriors exchanged a glance. Eden cleared his throat. "Every new Trinity has to go through a test. To, you know, see if we're...if we're—"

Caspian interrupted. "We have to make our way back to the Triad on foot."

Willa squinted. "And where exactly is that?"

Eden waved vaguely at the window. Willa sat down hard, not caring if there was a couch to catch her or not.

Thousands. There were thousands of those monsters in Manhattan. The sterile apartment suddenly seemed downright comfy. "I'm just doing the math here but..."

Eden pulled an arrow from behind his back, testing the sharpness with the pad of his thumb. "No, yeah, it is completely terrible."

Willa stared dumbly at her overstuffed duffle. She'd been generous, filling it with clothes and boots and her favorite books. A few keepsakes. Her camera equipment. The things you packed when you left one life to start another. Now it just felt foolish.

She glanced down at her gun. It seemed like a human weapon, insufficient for killing corpses, but she was fresh out of katanas.

Eden's face was grim. She liked the sarcasm better. "Any chance you can do a little magic to get us out of here?"

He nocked his arrow and shook his head. "That would be cheating. An automatic fail."

Willa stared at the dead sun, her power pulsing, thin and weak inside her chest. "This is suicide."

"Probably."

· · · ● · ● · ● · · ·

They went down to the street through the front door. There was no point in keeping to the shadows. Like rats and roaches, the Skotos preferred the darkness.

The boys had briefed her while she repacked her meager belongings into a backpack, a stream of facts—each worse than the other:

- The Skotos could control minds—seizing your will so you died smiling in a pool of your own blood.

- Their teeth were filled with so much rot and bacteria that one nick led to a slow, painful death.

- Everything else led to a *quick*, painful death. Which was fun.

Willa squinted up at the blackhole sun, the edges of the ring as bright as the center was dark. The smell of rotting flesh was thick and greasy. She swallowed a gag, covering her nose with the collar of her shirt, eyes watering.

"Keep your hand on your weapon," Caspian growled.

Willa let her shirt drop, trying to breathe through her mouth.

Eden nudged her, holding out a small vile. "Try this."

She dabbed the peppermint oil underneath her nose. It didn't entirely mask the stench of dead flesh but it made it bearable.

"You know they can smell that stuff," Caspian grumbled. "You're going to bring them right to us."

"If she pukes, they're definitely going to smell it," Eden retorted.

Caspian muttered something under his breath but let the matter drop. His feet were bare, silent on the concrete stairs. She hadn't asked why they'd slipped off their boots on the way out, too exhausted from knowing things to absorb more.

Across the street, a rusted yellow cab sagged onto the pavement, its metal guts spilling onto the ground. The same as on her block back in the real world and yet different. She'd taken a dozen pictures of it in various states of disrepair since the Pulse. It was strange to see it here, frozen in time.

"We need to move," Eden said, his bow drawn. The string cut into his cheek as he scanned the street.

Caspian murmured his agreement. The boys flanked her, circling slowly as they walked down the center of the street, weapons aimed at every dark corner. Overhead the empty buildings loomed, broken teeth cutting into the gray sky.

They passed the corner where old man Frick traded homemade maple candy for cigarettes, and the store filled with junkies strung out on dirty mattresses. But in the Umbra, none of those things existed. Just eerie silence.

"What are the chances we get to this Triad place without seeing one of these things?" she whispered.

Eden chuckled darkly, "Oh, I'd say about negative 100%."

Willa pressed her lips around the rest of her questions.

Ten steps later, Caspian stopped, his gaze trained on the dark crevice between buildings. Willa held her breath.

Something hissed. It was not a human sound.

"Fuck," Eden breathed.

A rotting corpse slipped out of the shadows.

The Skotos was even more terrifying up close. Shreds of skin hung from the sharp bones of its jaw, black teeth visible through the gaping holes in its face. Long strands of scraggly gray hair dangled in sickly patches from its skull and through the shattered cage of its ribs, mottled pink lungs expanded and contracted. Nothing that looked like that should be breathing.

Caspian shouted something, but she was already running, the boys on either side. Their feet echoed in the cavern of buildings.

The Skotos made a wet guttural sound that vibrated in the back of her teeth. She didn't dare look over her shoulder, but she could feel its hot carrion breath on the back of her neck as they fled.

Eden cut his long strides short, one hand pressed between her shoulder blades, propelling her forward faster. She focused on not stumbling, surrounded by the horrible click-scrape of the monster's claws on the pavement.

Already a dozen steps ahead of them, Caspian took a sharp left, angling toward a stone church that stood on the corner. A tall construction fence surrounded it as if someone had once tried to protect the holy place from the horrors of the world. He hit the fence at full speed, launching over it in two swift movements. The Skotos shrieked, the sound wet and sharp.

Without breaking stride, Eden grabbed Willa under the armpits and spread his wings. They lifted off the ground, her boots barely clearing the barbs topping the fence.

Willa grunted when he dropped her unceremoniously on the other side, tumbling awkwardly into the dead grass. Eden and Caspian were already up, breath ragged, weapons drawn.

The Skotos had stopped, chest heaving.

She staggered to her feet. The churchyard was empty except for a few crooked gravestones and a statue of Mary, her vacant eyes raised to the heavens. Thick vines nearly swallowed the church's stone facade. A forgotten place of worship. A god that had abandoned them all.

Caspian pushed her behind him, falling into a fighting stance, as the Skotos wrapped its claw around the chain link. Willa blinked. No. Not claws—the boney ends of fingers poking from the ragged flesh of long fingers.

"You've got to be fucking kidding me," she breathed.

"Lie down." The creature's voice was raspy, its milky eyes pinning her in place. The gash of its mouth never moved. It spoke inside her mind.

Willa shuddered. It was the worst type of invasion. Personal and close and impossible to fight, like an uncle touching your thigh underneath the dining room table.

"Sleep," the monster crooned.

Next to her, Eden's wings drooped, the silver tips carving groves in the dirt. His bow rolled out of his boneless fingers.

"I *am* tired," he murmured, folding slowly to the ground.

"What are you doing," Willa hissed, grasping at his collar. Eden batted at her weakly, mumbling something incoherent.

On the other side of her, Caspian fell to his knees, placing his sword neatly next to Eden's bow, as if he were just putting it away after the end of a long battle. Terror turned the world technicolor, amplifying the scarlet blood on the Skotos' lips and the bright yellow of Caspian's hair as he bent his head.

Willa tried to breathe. Somehow she was alone. Despite the two warriors at her side, she was alone again.

The Skotos hissed again, rattling the chain links. The long rags of its skin caught and tore on the sharp metal as it started to climb.

Caspian laid his cheek against the ground.

Willa discovered the gun in her hand, cocking it with trembling hands. The monster sneered, perched on the top of the fence like a vulture. She pulled the trigger.

The bullet sailed over the Skotos' head. It leered and licked its teeth with the gray meat of its tongue. Willa snagged back a half step, but the church loomed behind her. There was nowhere to run.

She tugged blindly at Eden's hair. "Get up. Darkness, please get up."

The Skotos laughed—a horrible sound that reminded her of grinding bones. The gun bucked in her hand, but Willa didn't remember giving her finger permission to pull the trigger.

The creature swayed when the bullet shattered its cheek, shards of bone and flesh pattering on the concrete, but it held onto the fence.

Willa held her breath as it turned its blind eyes back to her, face dripping gore. "I see you, Healer," the monster breathed inside her mind. "You will die screaming like the others before you."

Beside her, Caspian's pale lashes fluttered closed. Willa shoved her gun back into her waistband. The violence of men was not going to defeat this nightmare, so she did the only thing she could think to do.

She knelt in the grass in front of Eden.

His eyes were dull but he still knelt in the damp grass, as if somewhere inside of himself he still fought the creature that had his mind. Willa touched his shoulder and reached for the supernova of power waiting inside of her. It was there, bright and steady and good. She muttered a prayer to the blind statue of Mary that she wouldn't kill them all, and released it.

She gasped, every nerve in her body pulling tight as the power settled around them, a lacy bubble of pale green light. Her aura, visible for the first time, the color dappled like a forest floor.

Eden grabbed her wrist.

"What the hell?" he rasped, but she was already dragging him to his feet. Or maybe he was dragging her. Pain lanced down her spine. Her aura shimmered around them, but it hurt to keep it there.

Caspian struggled to his knees. "What happened?"

"No time," she choked as the Skotos leaped into the churchyard.

Caspian cursed and leaped to his feet. The Skotos was so close she could see the broken blood vessels in its white eyes. Its mind slithered against her consciousness, raking across the thin skin of her aura. She staggered, but Caspian was already there, holding her up.

Eden aimed and shot, his hand a blur. The arrow pierced the Skotos' pale eye, viscous fluid bursting over its tattered cheek. The creature shrieked, the mental claws digging deeper. Her power buckled, but Caspian was already pulling her away and back.

Somehow they ended up on the church steps, her aura wavering around them. Eden nocking another arrow. "I'll hold it off!"

Caspian nodded, pulling Willa behind the silver curtain of the Traveler's wings.

The weathered church door was swallowed in thick vines. Caspian twisted the rusty doorknob, but it only opened a fraction before catching against the vegetation. Willa's head throbbed like a rotten tooth. She leaned against the door frame as he tried to work it free.

"Faster," Eden hollered. Caspian said something unpleasant about Eden's virtue but tugged harder.

The Skotos mentally prodded her shield. It hurt. Like someone working a finger into an open wound. "Faster," she whispered, tasting blood.

Caspian put a foot against the wall, muscles straining as he yanked. The vines gave way. The door scraped open. He shouted in relief, twisting sideways to squeeze into the tight space, pulling her with him. She collapsed into the church's cool interior, turning in time to see a claw swipe through the air as Eden tumbled on top of her, his wings barely clearing the door jam.

The boys were up immediately, shoving the door closed behind them.

The Skotos screamed, wet and inhuman. Willa gripped her head, the sound of a seismic pulse that splintered her power. She shouted a warning, but the boys were already heaving a wooden pew against the door. It shuddered once and then stopped.

The church descended into silence. Eden's chest heaved, an arrow poised against his cheek like a flashing star. Caspian pulled Willa to her feet, blood dripping unnoticed down his bicep.

The chapel was untouched by time and tragedy. Mustard light streamed through the stained glass rosette, painting the wood floor a muted rainbow. The ceiling soared above them, faded frescos still gilded with gold. It seemed strange to find a place like this in this dead world, like stumbling upon while crossing the river Styx.

They hurried down the center aisle, stepping over hymnals and bones. There was nothing on the elevated pulpit except a moth-eaten Bible and two melted candles. On one side of the dias was a door that went down to the basement, and on the other, a set of stairs leading up to the choir loft.

Eden waved a hand at the steps.

"Horrible idea," Caspian said, showing his empty palms.

With a sinking stomach, Willa realized his sword was back where he had placed it in the grass. Only the knives strapped across his chest remained and they suddenly seemed small—good for stabbing unarmed best friends in dark alleys, but not so good for terrifying ten-foot skeleton monsters.

Eden shrugged. "If things get sticky, we can just jump out a window. I'll get us to the ground."

"Can you carry us both?" she asked.

He winked, oblivious to the blood spattered across his face. "It would be more like falling, but we probably wouldn't die."

"Comforting."

Eden chuckled.

Caspian scowled as they started up the steps. "Ladies, can we keep the witty banter to a minimum? We're—"

The Skotos hurled itself against the church door just below them, rattling the building and sending a golden framed picture of Mary swinging drunkenly on the wall. They fell quiet.

Her heart sank when they reached the empty choir loft. It stretched the full length of the chapel. There was no escape up here. Just dusty boxes and a broken nativity display. Caspian kicked at a rat that scurried across his feet.

The church vibrated again, followed by an unnerving crack, and the sound of wood scraping. Willa could feel the slick midnight of the Skate's mind as it slipped into the church below them.

"It's in here with us," she breathed.

They pressed deeper into the darkness.

"Now seems like a good time to tell the new girl how we kill that thing," she whispered.

Caspian shrugged. "It breaths just like us. It dies like us too."

Her lips thinned. "I shot it in the face."

"Well, maybe not quite like us," Caspian responded, rummaging quietly through the nearest box.

The church was quiet, but she could sense it searching for them below. Somehow the silence was more unnerving than the noise of the hunt.

She started flipping through the boxes, pushing aside scratchy garland and old bibles. There had to be something here they could use to save themselves. "What about the other like me? Couldn't they help?" she asked.

The boys exchanged a glance. Willa's hands stilled on a cigar box of broken crayons.

"Uh, that thing you did..." Eden hedged. "Shielding us from the Skotos? That's not...we've never seen that before."

Willa's stomach clenched. She didn't want to be different here too.

"Aha!" Eden whispered triumphantly, pulling two pipes from behind a tipped choir chair, cobwebs caught in his burnished hair. They were rusty and thick, each the length of her arm. She had never been so happy to see an inanimate object before.

He tossed one in Caspian's direction, who caught it easily. They took a position on either side of the staircase, only half hidden by shadows. Willa would have taken the time to be offended if she wasn't about to be eaten by something that looked like a child's drawing of a nightmare. She picked her way back over to them through the boxes. "What can I do?"

"Can you do that shield thing again?" Caspian asked.

Willa could feel her power curled inside her, like a warm, sleeping cat. It felt a bit tender and bruised. "I think... I think I can hold it off for a second. But I can't promise anything."

"We'll take what we can get." He looked at Eden who nodded grimly. "A second is all we need."

The Skotos appeared at the bottom of the stairs, the bony tips of their fingers wrapping around the banister. It leered at them, the silver fletching of Asher's arrow still poking from its ruined eye, the rotten stench of its breath drifting up to them. Caspian raised his pipe.

She expected it to move slowly since it was injured, but it launched itself upward, eating upstairs in two long strides, claws skittering on each step.

Willa threw out her power recklessly, but somehow the soft green aura fell around them in a graceful arch. The Skotos collided with it a full speed sending a shockwave of pain through her body. She sunk to her knees in the dust.

"Hurry," she gasped as the shield wavered, but Caspian was already moving, swinging the pipe like a batter reaching for a home run. It connected with the Skotos' head with a wet thwack, scraping flesh from its white skull.

The creature teetered on the top step but didn't fall.

Its single sightless eye turned to her, the viscous white threaded red. Willa pressed a hand to her head, pain spiking through her mind as vividly as if the Skotos had pierced her flesh with its claws. There was a sickening ripping sound and her vision went white. She tried to call out as the shield failed, but Eden had already plunged his pipe into the Skotos' chest, ripping already torn flesh. Caspian snarled, kicking it in the stomach. Dimly, Willa heard a snap and then the monster tumbled over the banister, hitting the pews below with a deafening crash.

Willa wiped at her nose, the back of her hand coming away red. Dust motes glinted in the yellow air. Eden and Caspian grinned at each other.

"If you two high-five, I'm going to kick your asses," Willa rasped.

Eden shrugged at Caspian. "Guess we'll do the manly chest bump later."

She staggered to her feet. Her head felt like it was filled with cotton. She swayed. Eden put a hand on her elbow. "You good?"

Willa nodded. She was definitely not good.

Caspian flipped the gore-covered pipe in his hand, sliding it into the empty sheath at his hip. "This is my new favorite weapon."

Eden snorted. "When you spread rumors around the Triad about your epic heroism, don't forget to mention who did the actual killing."

Willa rubbed her forehead. "I'd like to point out that you two would have been drooling zombies if it wasn't for me."

Caspian's eyes were bright, still feverish from battle. "Willa, that was amazing. What you can do with your power...it's a game changer. With a weapon like that..."

She stiffened. She did not like being called a weapon. "What do we—"

The choir floor exploded in a storm of splintering wood.

The Skotos balanced on the edge of the ragged hole, bringing the smell of death in its wake. Willa barely had time to register what was happening before she was running. They launched over boxes and toppled chairs, the Skotos crashing after them, Eden's pipe caught in the ribs of its chest. Ahead of them, there was nothing but the church wall and their terrified reflections in the stained glass window.

"Don't stop," Caspian shouted, hitting the window with his shoulder, and launching himself out into the air in a shower of colored glass. His arms and legs pinwheeled in the air. With a curse, Willa followed. It wasn't like a cartoon. There was no moment of suspension in the morning sky, no hesitation in her trajectory. They started dropping immediately—fast and hard.

Until Eden snatched them from the sky.

Willa's neck snapped back painfully, Caspian's shoulder knocking hard against her own. They dangled precariously from Eden's hand, his wings booming overhead, silver blades whistling. Twenty feet below, the dirt-packed ground twinkled with a mosaic of broken glass.

There was no time to be grateful. Eden screamed.

Willa heaved herself up, grabbing his wrist to steady her wild swing, and looked past the flare of his wings. One long finger bone was curled around Eden's thigh, the tip piercing the meat of his leg.

The Skotos was hanging from the church window, its body folded nearly in half. It leaned heavily on a large shard of broken glass, the edge sticking out grotesquely from its back. Black blood washed down the stone wall in a macabre waterfall.

Willa felt Eden's grip loosen. He choked on a curse. She had no idea how he was keeping them in the air.

"Here!" Caspian yelled, swinging wildly beside her. He slapped the second pipe into her palm. Without thinking, she swung. It hit the Skotos' arm, shattering bone. Hot blood sprayed down her cheeks, catching in her eyelashes.

She had just enough time to see its bony claw slip from Eden's torn thigh before they were tumbling and everything became a blur of silver wings and the black sun.

Chapter 21

T HE FLOOR WAS COLD. It was her first thought when she swam back into consciousness. They should be crumbled on the dying grass in an abandoned churchyard, but she could feel hard marble under her spine.

Willa turned her head, trying to focus through the pounding in her head. Eden's fingers were tangled with her own. There was glass in his hair, a dusting of colored chips that caught the candlelight. His pant leg was soaked in blood.

She concentrated on their connected hands and healed him, the warmth and power inside of her blossoming easily, like exercising a well-used muscle. Eden's eyes fluttered open.

A few feet away, Caspian was already on his feet, smoothing his hair and shaking glass from his shoulders. He did not ask to be healed, so Willa took a breath and soothed her own body, each ache and bruise fading until her headache became just a whisper.

"It's official," Eden groaned, pushing up on his forearms, shards tinkling onto the marble floor. "I'm in love with you."

"You're the one who saved us," she managed, sitting up. The world tumbled and swung before settling into place.

They were in the sky. Or as close as you could get without dying.

The Triad was on the top floor of a building that towered over the rest of the city, a giant among giants. The interior walls had been stripped, leaving a vast open floor. Through the large windows, Willa could see the broken, outstretched arm of Lady Liberty through the yellow haze, the iconic statue's familiar torch long since lost to the bottom of the Hudson. They were at least ninety stories above the city, the distant horizon curving, the black sun hovering like an ominous eye.

"Is this the Freedom Tower?" she asked, arranging the city in her mind.

Eden nodded, grimacing as he stretched his healed leg.

"Ironic," she murmured, gazing overhead.

He chuckled. "We thought so."

The half-dozen floors above them had been gutted, the ceiling tapered so far in the distance she could barely make it out. The circle of tall windows around the perimeter at twenty-foot increments was the only mark there had ever been floors there at all. It was dizzying, like looking up an elevator shaft lined with glass.

A skeleton of steel beams crisscrossed the space, each missing floor marked by a grand candelabra in the corner—the kind you were more likely to encounter in a Parisian Opera house than a Manhattan skyscraper. They groaned with candles, filling the cold space with a warm glow.

But none of that was as stunning as the Traveler's who glided between the exposed beams like supernatural bats, the sharp edge of their wings catching in the candlelight.

"Holy shit," Willa murmured.

The Triad was busy. Other Trinity strode across the gleaming marble floor in long vests, the cavernous space swallowing the whisper of a hundred bare feet. They reminded Willa of businessmen rushing through the soaring beauty of Grand Central station on their way to the L train—only they carried weapons instead of briefcases.

A boy with a broken crescent tattoo cupping his left eye passed close by, a stack of books tucked under one arm, a trio of throwing stars strapped across his chest. Willa saw the exact moment he noticed her, his footsteps faltering slightly. He didn't stare, but his aura flashed yellow as it trailed after him.

Heat flared across Willa's cheeks. She was sprawled across the floor, covered in blood and dirt, and gawking like a dopey tourist in Time Square. She tried to stand and failed, her stomach swooping lazily.

Caspian crouched in front of her, his face littered with small cuts. He touched her forehead, his fingertips coming away red. "Looks like a concussion."

She made a pathetic sound of dismay when he hauled her to her feet.

They were in a study area of sorts, with worn leather chairs and mahogany tables littered with open books and empty coffee cups. It all looked startlingly familiar, like a college library during exams. A few people were sprawled nearby, studiously ignoring them as if magically appearing out of nowhere covered in blood was completely normal.

She tried to focus on what Caspian was saying to Eden—something about the Council and a meeting—but ended up just concentrating on staying upright. She closed her eyes. Maybe this was normal for them—a near-death experience just a small hiccup in an otherwise boring Tuesday.

"Darkness you two," a voice interrupted. Willa blinked as someone bullied Caspian to the side and slipped something warm into her shaking hands.

She frowned down at the bright red mug. It appeared to be hot chocolate, topped with a mountain of whipped cream. The smell of nutmeg drifted up to her on delicate wisps of steam.

Willa looked up at her savior. He had an open face and the longest lashes she had ever seen, like a grown-up cherub. A faded crescent moon tattoo curved underneath his left eye. Willa tried to push past the lump in her throat to thank him but ended up just smiling weakly.

"Sit down, love" the boy soothed, steering her into the nearby armchair. "Don't let these inconsiderate Neanderthals push you around."

She sunk gratefully into the chair, clutching the warm mug like a life raft. The cherub knelt in front of her. "I know all this is a lot to take in, but things aren't as bad as they look right now. I promise."

Before she could respond, he touched the back of her hand and his reassuring words dissolved into a soft buzz. The cherub's aura was the deepest blue she had ever seen—the color of the cold ocean deep out at sea. Her muscles relaxed, eyes drifting—

"That's enough, Beckett," Caspian snapped.

The boy let go of her hand and the sea disappeared.

She made an embarrassing mew of disappointment, but her breath was deep and even; her heart a steady beat. When she opened her eyes again, the world had come back into sharp clarity.

"Your hot chocolate is getting cold," the cherub observed, settling back on his heels. "You like hot chocolate, right? I mean, who doesn't? Even Eden likes it...although he'd never admit it to me. The secret is nutmeg. It's in short supply these days, but he managed to get me a whole bottle during a supply raid last month." Beckett put a hand to the side of his mouth, "That's how I know he loves it despite all the scowling."

Willa took a sip. It was thick and sweet, the rich chocolate coating her raw throat. "It's delicious," she said softly. "Thank you."

The cherub nodded, his dark curls bouncing as he rose to his feet. Willa pushed herself back up even though her knees still felt like water.

"I'm a Healer too," Beckett said, helping her to her feet. He held up his hand ticking off imaginary points on his fingers. "Also: mentor, hot chocolate master chef, excellent guitarist, a bloody horrible card player, and—"

"And all-around pain in the ass." Eden interrupted.

Beckett winked at the Traveler and patted his backside. "How would you know? Have you been looking?"

Eden shifted uncomfortably, his gaze fixed firmly somewhere over Beckett's head. "Stop messing around." He wore his no-nonsense battle face, but the effect was ruined by the flush that crept up his neck.

Willa murmured a greeting and took another sip of hot chocolate. A boy wearing circle glasses in a chair nearby met her gaze over the top of his book and then looked down quickly. She straightened, adjusting her blood-soaked top, feeling like a neon sign.

Beckett nudged her, glaring at the kid. "Don't worry, no one is going to notice you."

She didn't bother acknowledging the lie. Willa could feel their eyes.

Caspian didn't seem to mind the extra attention, his gaze fixed on a Traveler striding toward them through the crowd. The girl couldn't have been more than twelve, her blond hair pulled into a severe ponytail, silver wings tucked tightly against the back of her vest. She stopped in front of him, and Willa was pretty sure the girl would have clicked her heels together if she hadn't been barefoot. "Sir. Counselor Lyra requests your immediate presence."

Willa glanced at Caspian, amused by the formality, but her smile quickly faded. She'd been preoccupied earlier, but now she realized that he looked different as if the Umbra had changed him. His golden hair was slicked away from his bloody face, the blue in his vest bringing out the ice of his eyes. He looked dangerous, like a beautiful knife that you only pull in the most pressing emergency.

"I'll debrief the Counselor," he ordered, clearly addressing Eden. "You get Willa orientated."

To her surprise, Eden nodded curtly as Caspian strode off with the young Traveler in tow. The crowd parted for him as soldiers for a general. For the first time, Willa considered that the boys might be leaders in this strange world and that she might be too, by proxy. The thought made her nauseous again.

On the other side of the cold Triad floor, two girls spun and parried inside a training ring. The clash of their swords reverberated like bells in the cavernous space. They were stripped down to tank tops and loose cotton pants, a small crowd watching as they fought. Even from a distance, Willa could see blood mingling with their sweat.

·· • • •· • • •· ··

Caspian pulled back the war room's heavy, velvet curtain. It took up one corner of the Triad, the only space hidden from the rest by the lush fabric dotted with silver whorls and embroidered stars. The only furniture was a long wooden table lined with straight-backed chairs. He'd heard that the scarred table was almost a thousand years old, hewn from an ancient spruce tree from North America's first-growth forest. His bare feet sunk into the scarlet rug as he approached.

The war room was like the rest of the Triad—sparse and opulent all at the same time, as if muted humility were their unofficial motto.

Counselor Lyra stood alone by the window, gazing out at the dark city, hands cupped behind her back. She'd hidden her wings. Without them, she looked small and mild but Caspian wasn't fooled.

Lyra commanded his actions and demanded his loyalty, but that didn't mean he was immune to her tactics. The Counselor's favorite weapon was subtle manipulation.

She turned, her smile dazzling. "Caspian."

Her voice was light and almost musical. Caspian wondered if she practiced it. He dipped his head, not because it was required, but because he knew it earned him points. "Counselor."

She was beautiful, with delicate features and cascading white blonde hair. Her eyes were the color of honey and when her wings were fully extended she looked like the angel Caspian knew she wished to be.

Lyra lifted one pale eyebrow. "I see you procured your Healer. Finally. "

"I didn't realize there was a deadline."

That wasn't entirely true. Everyone in the Triad—Fractured and Trinity alike—sensed the urgency in the air.

Lyra breezed past him, smelling like rosewater. "Yes, well, you've had your fun with that girl. I expect you both to report to training first thing in the morning."

He frowned. *That girl.*

Lyra's scarlet vest was cut low in the back, dipping almost to her waist. It showed off the enticing line of her spine and the Traveler scars on her shoulder blades.

"It's customary to give her a few weeks to acclimate before—"

"This is not a democracy, Hunter."

His mouth snapped shut.

They had slept together once. Soon after he'd turned eighteen. It had been physical—just a momentary release. An indiscretion. They'd never spoken of it, but he could see the remembering in her eyes.

Her back arched subtly as she leaned to touch the hilt of one of the many swords that crisscrossed the center of the weathered table. It was a macabre centerpiece—each a weapon of a fallen Counselor. A memorial to those who fought and sacrificed. "I added three swords to the table yesterday," Lyra said.

Without the smile she looked older; a general of armies instead of a politician. The pommel of her thin rapier peaked over her diminutive shoulder. Most Travelers preferred the bow for its long-range capability, but Caspian had seen Lyra use her sword with deadly accuracy, her white hair spattered with Skotos blood. There was a rumor that she'd once taken on three of them alone and lived to tell about it.

Caspian studied her profile. "London?"

Lyra nodded. He'd heard rumors of other Triads falling to the Skotos—Cairo, Sydney, Moscow—but to hear it confirmed…

"What happened?"

She ran her fingertip down one of the blades. Blood bloomed in a thin line, dripping into her palm. "It would be easier to show you."

Unease stirred in his gut, but he was a soldier, so when Lyra held her bloody hand across the fallen swords, Caspian took it.

It was different than Traveling with Eden—smoother. Still, he clenched his abdominal muscles as they plummeted through the nauseating vortex of time. He regulated his breathing, keeping his mouth closed so that the frigid air wouldn't sear his lungs. But Lyra was powerful and frost barely had time to crisp in his eyelashes before she was letting go.

His skin pricked at the sudden rush of warmth, although London could rarely be called warm. The faint foreboding and hazy yellow air of the Umbra had been replaced by the startling clarity of a place still in step with time. The real world.

He recognized the pub. It was a favorite amongst the London Triad, frequented particularly by Travelers and clueless locals. Not a clean, touristy place near the city center, but a dingy hovel in Camden that served good chips and cheap off-brand Guinness. He'd been here with Eden a few times, tagging along under the guise of wanting to sleep with a pretty Yorkshire girl.

The pub smelled familiar, like malt vinegar and cigarettes, but everything else was wrong. A growler of beer had spilled across the bar, solidifying into a sticky goo. Half the stools had been tipped over as if people had left in a hurry and the glass had been shattered in the heavy front door. The Tavern was set down from the street, the feet of the smokers on the sidewalk and scurrying wharf rats the only view.

Now, something large moved past the window, the familiar shadow crawling across the pine floor. Caspian's hand went to the hilt of his sword. He recognized the sound of claws on cobblestones. Lyra nodded at the window. "Take a look."

She hadn't drawn her weapon, so he kept his knives sheathed, relaxing his grip on his power as he crossed the room. The world burst into technicolor. His footsteps became lighter as if some of the gravity had been sucked away.

The truth was, he didn't need to see what was out the window anymore. He could hear what had become of London. Could hear the moist suck of Skotos' lungs and smell death. The street outside the pub was a war zone, dead bodies littered everywhere; black crows feasting on torn throats and sightless eyes. The sky above the old city was gray, and it was drizzling. The gutters were a river of red. In the distance, London burned.

Bile rose in Caspian's throat. He should be used to the copper smell of blood mixed with the stench of burning flesh, but he reeled in his power, muting the gruesome scent so he could breathe.

A Traveler lay crumbled in front of the pub, cheek pressed against the broken sidewalk. One of her wings had been ripped off, her shoulder mangled. Blood pooled in the small of her back.

"What happened?" Caspian asked, staring into the dead girl's eyes. He wondered if he'd known her. If he'd bought her a drink— pressing her against the sticky bar wall and forgetting her all in the same night.

Caspian turned away from the horror. Lyra had moved behind the bar and was pouring two fingers of something clear into a crystal tumbler. "They came through a rift. A big one."

He stepped over shattered plates and upturned tables. Caspian knew the Umbra had been unstable since the Pulse. Everyone knew. No prison was completely infallible and they'd been hunting down escaped Skotos for centuries, but things had been getting worse since the world ended.

"Lyra."

She looked at him over the rim of her glass, her blue eyes shrewd. He could see her mind spinning. He kept his gaze steady, ignoring the nausea that rolled through his stomach.

Lyra finished her drink and poured herself another. "The Umbra isn't just unstable, Hunter. It is failing. We have already lost cities—Cairo, Auckland, Singapore. The Skotos are practically pouring out of the Umbra."

"What will happen if it fails?"

She lifted her glass, blood drying on her palm. Her hands were shaking. "If the Umbra shatters, then both worlds will fall."

Fear crackled in the lining of Caspian's stomach. "How long?"

Lyra's eyes slid past him to the window and the carnage beyond. "A month if we're lucky. Maybe days."

Chapter 22

B ECKETT LED WILLA PAST the training circle, his arm threaded through hers and keeping up a steady stream of gossip that she only half heard. Eden had left soon after Caspian, and Willa couldn't be sure if he was running from his responsibility or Beckett's relentless flirting.

Only one girl remained on the mat, parrying with an invisible partner, dark hair escaping from her braid and blood dripping from one elbow. She stared at them until Beckett said something unflattering about her mother. The girl gave him the finger.

"Don't worry. You'll fit in soon enough," Beckett said, patting her hand.

"I don't fit in anywhere," she said, glancing back over her shoulder as the girl added her rapier to a wall of weapons.

"Well, you do now."

The back of her throat ached. It was all too much. She needed a moment to herself—preferably somewhere with a thick-down comforter and unlimited access to cookies—where she could cry with dignity. But Beckett was already catching the arm of a passing girl.

"This is Mae," he said, waving at the girl whose wings curled behind her as gracefully as the flick of her eyeliner. Her skin was the warm taupe only the melting pot of New York City could mix, her curls wrestled into a purple scarf that trailed down the back of her long vest.

"She's going to take you up to the Healer's quarters," Beckett continued.

Willa's eyes flickered to the crisscrossing beams above her head. "Up?"

Mae smiled, revealing dimples in each of her round cheeks. Willa barely had time to register what was happening before the girl unfurled her wings and hauled her unceremoniously into the air, but she managed to not flail her arms when Mae deposited her onto one of the steel beams.

"Is there some reason there isn't a freaking handrail up here?" Willa squeaked.

Mae hovered in front of her with lazy sweeps of her sharp wings. "It's more efficient than stairs." Her voice was soft and cultured—British, maybe. "You're Eden and Caspian's new Healer?"

Willa swallowed, watching the tiny ant people swarm below her. "Guilty."

Mae nodded, her dark eyes as kind as Beckett's. Willa wondered if maybe everyone was nice here except for her two douchebag partners.

"I'm glad they finally found you," Mae said. "Everyone knows they'll be part of the Council one day and they're bloody good fighters. You're practically royalty around here."

Willa swayed uneasily. "Dear God, I hope for your sake that isn't true."

Mae laughed, her cool lilac aura buffering around each sweep of her wings. "We could use all the help we can get. Stay here while I get Beckett."

Willa tried to play it cool as Mae dove back to the Triad floor. Her boots felt clunky and unstable on the narrow beam. She suddenly understood the appeal of bare feet.

From up here, she could see the whole Triad floor, sectioned off with grand rugs like an expensive New York loft. There was a classroom with chairs set in a semi-circle around an old chalkboard, a laundry with steaming tubs, and a long set of tables where people were eating. The smell of warm spices masked the faint stench of the Umbra. Her stomach rumbled. Willa couldn't remember the last time she ate.

There were only two areas sectioned off from the rest of the floor by thick curtains. Beckett had pointed them out; the war room and the bathhouse. Dust and blood still coated her skin. Willa hoped the bathhouse was as wonderful as it sounded.

The largest section held a series of hospital cots arranged on two overlapping rugs. She was surprised at the quiet beep of machines and the number of people who tended to the sick and injured. Every bed was full, which seemed odd for a world with magical Healers at its disposal.

Mae dropped Beckett next to her and then swept away with a little wave.

"Sorry about that," he said, smoothing his curls. "I should have come up first. I forget how scary it can be up here when you're new."

"I'm okay," she said, muscles aching from trying to balance.

He nodded at the lie and gestured for her to follow him down the girder. "We'll go slow."

She resisted the urge to put her hand on his shoulder as they moved, dozens of Travelers flying between her and the unforgiving floor. They'd catch her if she fell. She could at least pretend to be brave.

"How long have you been here in the...uh, Umbra?" she asked, trying to distract herself as they inched along. Beyond Beckett, the rafter disappeared inside a velvet curtain that stretched twenty feet in both directions, a circus tent in the sky.

"Ten years," he replied. "I was harvested before the Pulse."

Two Travelers swooped alarmingly close, laughing. Willa put her hand on Beckett's shoulder, grateful when he didn't comment on her death grip. "What about your family?"

He stopped in front of the curtain. "This *is* my family."

"But, I mean, what about your real family?"

Beckett's brow furrowed. He touched the crescent moon tattoo on his cheek. "I'm Fractured, Willa."

She didn't know what that meant, but there was something about the way he said it that made her stomach twist. His expression morphed from surprise to anger before settling on pity. "They didn't tell you—those spineless cowards."

Willa shook her head, wondering if her heart could take one more betrayal or if it would crumble like burnt paper.

"Once you are bonded with your Trinity, your lives are tethered—to each other and the Umbra. If Caspian or Eden die, you become Fractured like me. Willa..." His voice became achingly gentle. "The Fractured are trapped in this world forever."

Her burnt heart was thin and fragile but it didn't blow away. She hadn't expected the truth from Caspian or Eden. And they hadn't promised it.

He squeezed her elbow. "You know, it's okay to be mad at them. I would be."

She took a breath, lifting her chin. "Caspian and Eden happen to be a lot more dangerous than me. Maybe I'll just wait a couple years and then murder them in their sleep."

Beckett chuckled, leading her through the thick curtain. "Sounds fair."

Willa was relieved when they stepped onto a wide wooden platform. Hidden behind the massive curtain was an intricate series of ladders and landings that climbed thirty feet over their heads. It was like a treehouse; a complicated scaffolding filled with dozens of black net hammocks that swung out over nothing. The whole place was lit up like a college dorm room at Christmas, the reflection of a hundred strings of twinkle lights dancing in the windows.

She could hear the hum of the generator just underneath the quiet strum of a guitar and low voices. The air smelled like warm spices mingled with smoke from the crackle of fire. It was beautiful, in the way a home filled with messy, laughing children is beautiful.

Delighted, she turned to Beckett. He smiled. "Welcome to the Healer's quarters. It's not all bad."

"How is this possible?" she whispered.

Beckett shrugged. "We live in an empty world with Travelers who can go anywhere. It's not hard to get what we need."

Nearby, a short ladder led to the largest platform. Dozens of Trinity lounged around a massive fire, sparks dancing in the sky above like fireflies. The group was sprawled on a haphazard array of colorful pillows. Willa could hear laughter.

"Shall we go say hello?" Beckett asked. "Or I could show you to your hammock—you must be exhausted."

She *was* tired. Her bones ached from it. But that wasn't why she hesitated. All this supernatural nonsense and she was suddenly terribly nervous about meeting the people who were going to become her new family.

Willa thought of Asher then and the night in the garage when they had all reminisced about Matzo ball soup and cafes and life Before. She'd thought her time being on the outside was over.

At least pretend to be brave.

"I am a little hungry," she admitted quietly.

Beckett thumped her on the back. "Atta girl."

The voices around the fire died when she descended the ladder. Willa forced herself to meet everyone's curious stare as Beckett swept an arm out dramatically. "Gentleman...Ladies..." He pointed at a cute girl with a short purple mohawk. "Not-quite-ladies."

The girl in question grinned and flashed him the middle finger. The turbulence in Willa's stomach eased. Maybe this wouldn't be so bad.

He nudged her forward. "This is Willa. She's having kinda a bad day, so at least pretend to be nice."

She blushed as a chorus of hellos followed them to an empty set of pillows next to the mohawk girl who was wearing a crop top that featured a ninja cartoon cat. Willa relaxed another fraction, sinking gratefully onto an enormous cushion. It smelled like smoke and incense. She immediately wanted to curl up and sleep forever.

Beckett gestured to the purple mohawk girl. "This is Zara. She's your bunkmate."

Zara leaned closer, her silver eyebrow ring glinting. "You're lucky Beckett's the one showing you around. He's the boss around here—although he'd never brag."

A smattering of acne marred Zara's chin. She was young, thirteen at most, but the curved daggers at her hip were as sharp as Caspian's, and her bicep was wrapped in a ragged bandage that oozed blood.

"Boss?" Willa asked.

"Yup," Zara replied, handing Willa a steaming bowl of rice topped with some sort of chunky stew. "The Fractured kinda run this place. Active Trinities are too busy saving the world."

The lanky kid on the other side of Beckett snorted and shoveled a bite into his mouth. He was closer to Willa's age, glasses slipping down his nose. A dirty silk tie was knotted around his forehead like Rambo and a well-loved copy of *The Hobbit* lay open on the cushion next to him. Beckett introduced him as CJ.

She'd expected a bunch of quiet Buddha types or stoic warriors, but this felt safe and familiar. Willa took a bite of her stew. It was warm, with roasted peppers and a few hunks of meat that might be pork.

After a few bites, she recovered enough to ask. "So the Fractured are in charge?"

Zara laughed, waving her fork. "More like managers. You know, keeping everyone fed and happy, organizing training, and settling disputes. All that junk." She took a sip out of a Nalgene bottle covered in faded stickers before passing it to Beckett.

"The Council is in charge," Beckett interjected. "The strongest of each Trinity. Lyra wants to meet you tomorrow morning during training. She tends to be a little...." he grimaced, "Intense."

Zara rolled her eyes. "Understatement of the year."

Willa scraped the last bit of stew out of her bowl and let it go. She wanted to know more, but there was only so much she could absorb in one day.

She smiled in thanks when CJ took her dish, slipping off her shoes and wiggling her toes against the warm fire. Her muscles dripped from her bones. She yawned as conversation swirled around her, content to listen to gossip she didn't understand and problems that were not her own.

A curvy girl named April was responsible for the guitar, the song soft and familiar. Her aura was a faint pink, like the inside of a shell.

Willa turned to Beckett before she could fall asleep. There was still one unanswered question. "How does training work?" she asked.

Beckett's pale cheeks showed the evidence of the flask he was sampling. "Caspian and Eden will teach you how to handle yourself in battle. I'll help you harness your power."

"So it's just the healing? Nothing else cool like flying or invisibility or...I don't know, seeing stuff that other people can't see?"

Beckett lifted an eyebrow. "Isn't being able to magically heal someone enough for you?"

She pressed her lips together. "Just checking."

April was singing now, an old sad song that Willa had listened to on her iPhone a million years ago. A song about winter and despair.

Zara had fallen asleep, curled into a ball with her head on CJ's thigh. Her tangerine aura traced the line of her body, a halo of color that only Willa could see.

She'd assumed the auras were a part of all this, but maybe she was wrong.

Beyond the flames and the frosted windows, she could see the black eye of the Umbra's sun. Somewhere in the streets below, monsters roamed.

· · · · ● · ● · · · ·

Asher flattened the wrinkled map on the dining room table, pressing the creases open with his fingertips. He'd studied it a dozen times in the past twenty-four hours, and still had no explanation for the familiar swoop of Tink's handwriting. No explanation that didn't taste like betrayal.

There was no way she could know the layout of the Central Park compound unless she had cobbled it together from fragments of their conversations. He'd told her about his time in prison, but only in pieces—secret words whispered as sweat cooled on their skin.

His stomach twisted. Their relationship had always been one of mutual needs satisfied, a business transaction he quite enjoyed.

The hard truth was, that Tink owed him nothing, but her deception still stung. They'd cobbled a life together. The shop and the band... hell, he had thought they had trust at least.

The front door opened in the foyer. He heard Tink stomp the snow from her boots as he traced a finger around the crude sketch of his former cell. He knew every brick. All 878 of them, including which ones grew moist when it rained. They tasted like earth and dirt, those bricks, cool against cracked lips.

Tink bustled into the kitchen, tossing her bag onto the already overflowing armchair and pausing to light the oil lamp. Her red hair seemed to glow as the lamp sputtered to life.

She jumped when she saw him. "Darkness Asher—why are you sitting in the dark like a serial killer?"

Beets. He'd sourced beets to dye her hair. They'd been a pain to track down, but Linda had saved him a few from the Market. He'd boiled them and strained the juices. Even held the pitcher as Tink rinsed, watching as the crimson dye circled the sink drain.

"What is this?" Asher said, holding up the map with two fingers.

"What's what?" Her eyes widened when they settled on the wrinkled paper. Asher listened to Donut's soft snores underneath the table and waited to see if she would lie.

The smile melted from her face. She slid into the chair across from him. "Asher..."

He couldn't look at her. "Tell me."

Tink took the map, smoothing the edges. "I joined the rebels," she said carefully.

Her dark eyes met his own with an intensity he didn't recognize. She looked like a different person, someone ambitious and driven.

"When?"

Tink shrugged, her white fur coat slipping from one bare shoulder. She didn't look like a revolutionist. She looked like a club kid. "A little less than a year."

Asher tried to calculate the number of times they'd slept together since then, stomach rolling. He tapped the crumbled paper. "This map. It has something to do with me."

She leaned forward, words urgent. "The Uprising has been gathering intel on the Compound for years. We have a plan to infiltrate—"

"Tink. Why would you get mixed up in something so stupid? So dangerous!"

Her eyes widened. She waved a hand. "There have been reports of something...unnatural out there. People getting killed. Taken. We think it might have something to do with the Compound."

"We?"

Tink sat back in her chair, her eyes sliding past his for the first time. The night before she'd come home long after Willa left in the swirling snow and it had been as easy as breathing to pull her underneath him. To press her into the mattress and use her body to forget.

He should be bothered that there might be someone else.

"You used me," he said flatly, aware of his hypocrisy and not caring.

Tink touched the back of his hand, her dark eyes filled with hectic fervor. "I knew you wouldn't understand! I did what I had to do. Don't you see? This is about what happened to Deliah. It is about our future—yours and mine and everyone's."

He stared at her hand over his. There was red dye still caught underneath her fingernails.

Asher stood, the chair screeching across the floor in protest. "Why didn't you just tell me?"

"Ash, I wanted to—I was *going* to, but you were so sensitive about your time in the Compound and then you promised Linda you wouldn't get involved and ..."

Asher grabbed his coat off the back of the couch. "Find yourself a new place to stay, Tink. I'm sure your new friends can help."

"You're being unreasonable," Tink snapped, pushing back her chair. "I know I should have told you, and I'm sorry for that, but...Darkness, at least think about it. You could join us."

He swiped the flask of apple whiskey out of her bag on the way out.

"Asher," Tink begged as he flipped up his hood. She was crying now. "We're family."

Outside, the wind howled, and cold bled underneath the doorjamb. Tink's red hair seemed obscene now—a joke told at a funeral. He wondered how much more this world could take from him.

Even after the Pulse, he'd believed *people* were the answer—that love could save them from the suffocating darkness. Now he wasn't so sure. Maybe things were hopeless after all.

"There is no *we* anymore, Tink. Just each of us alone in the Darkness."

Tink frowned. "You don't believe that."

He grabbed Donut's leash and swung open the front door. "I don't know what I believe anymore."

Chapter 23

A TRINITY VEST HAD magically appeared beside her hammock while she slept.

Willa stood on the small platform in her bare feet, hidden from the rest of the Healer's quarters by a gauzy curtain. A full-length mirror leaned against the scaffold, flanked by two wooden chests. Her backpack was propped against one of them, looking strangely out of place with the macrame keychain she'd made in third grade attached to the zipper. The only other thing in the small room was a coat rack that held a ripped denim jacket and a sword dangling from its scratched leather scabbard.

Zara snored in the second hammock behind her, one naked leg dangling over the edge. The girl had wanted to talk last night after the lights went out, but Willa had dropped into sleep like a stone. She'd been too tired even to worry about sleeping in a flimsy strip of fabric a hundred feet off the Triad floor. This morning though, she'd been grateful no one had been awake to see her barrel roll out of the hammock onto the platform.

The least she could do was try to keep her dignity.

Her new vest hung by the mirror, clean and pressed. It was beautiful closeup, even with the tattered hem. Willa traced the delicate filigree with one finger.

"The tailors brought it up for you last night," Zara yawned. She was sitting up, her purple mohawk flattened. "The vests are old—hundreds of years, apparently. The tailors weave any battle scars into the design with some sort of sewing magic. Each vest is a living piece of Trinity history blah blah blah…"

Zara swung her leg, sending the hammock in a slow lazy arc. She grinned. "That's what Beckett told me to say, at least."

Willa couldn't help but smile back. She slipped on the vest. The tailors had done their job well, the soft fabric draping perfectly along the outline of her body.

Zara stretched. "Well, now you look the part at least."

Willa studied her reflection in the mirror. Her hair was loose and there were dark circles under her eyes. She looked more like a Trinity than herself.

"How long have you been here?" Willa asked, waving a hand at the whole Triad.

Zara dismounted from the hammock with practiced ease. She was wearing a ratty white t-shirt and a pair of boy's boxer shorts. Willa had never seen anyone look less supernatural.

"Darkness, four years now," she mused, scratching her chest.

Willa did the math. Zara must have been a child when she had been Harvested—nine years old at most. The memory of Asher dying was still burned into Willa's mind. What sort of horror had Zara endured?

"Who do you...work with?" Willa asked, smoothing the edges of the vest.

"CJ and April," Zara leaned past Willa's shoulder, squinting at herself in the mirror. "We're the youngest Trinity."

Willa vaguely recognized the names. April had been the girl playing the guitar last night. CJ had taken her bowl. They were just kids.

She cleared her throat. "Who Harvested you?"

Zara frowned at a zit on her chin. "Caspian."

That lying murderous bastard.

Willa stared at the back of the girl's head. "How did...I mean...what happened?"

Zara reached for a small jar, dabbed some cream into her hand, and started to rub it through her purple hair. "He kidnapped my baby brother. Forced me to Hunt to save his life."

Willa hid her curled fists in the fabric of her vest. "I'm sorry"

Zara turned away from the mirror, her mohawk freshly spiked. "You've got it all wrong, new girl. Being Harvested was the best thing that ever happened to me."

"How is that possible?"

Zara shrugged on her vest, leaving it unbuttoned. The bandage on her upper arm was gone, rough stitches barely holding the cut closed. It looked like Zara had done it herself. Willa wondered why she hadn't let April heal it.

"I was four when the Pulse came," Zara answered. "By the time Caspian found me, I was starving and living on the streets with my mom. She was still a teenager herself and with two kids, she could barely keep us alive. She had to do things..."

Willa didn't need Zara's words to know the rest of her story. It was a familiar one.

Zara reached for her sword, cinching the belt around her waist. She should have looked ridiculous wearing weapons with pajamas, but somehow it was just heartbreaking. "The Triad has food. And warm beds. The people are good. Caspian saved me."

Willa didn't know how to accept that information. Caspian had taken her away from her life. He had lied and lied and triggered a gift that still tasted like a curse.

But she knew what the streets were like after the Pulse for the young and vulnerable. Knew what it required to save yourself in the broken wreckage of a world. So Willa just nodded and brushed her tangled hair into a ponytail. "What happens now?"

Zara grinned. "Now we get breakfast."

· · · ● · ● · ● · · ·

Eden watched Willa shovel another bite of pancake into her mouth from across the cafeteria. She'd come to breakfast with Zara, stalking past him without so much as a glance and taking a table as far away as possible. He was annoyed at how much it made him like her.

Eden remembered his first morning in the Triad. It had been like the first day at a new school only with much higher stakes. Willa, however, was laughing at Mae and drowning her second helping of pancakes in syrup.

Caspian did not appear to be as charmed by Willa's small act of rebellion. His fork scrapped his plate as he stabbed a piece of sausage and grumbled under his breath.

"You should have told her," Beckett observed dryly.

Eden glanced at him sideways and then looked away abruptly. The Healer was glaring at Caspian over his hot chocolate, whipped cream clinging to his upper lip.

"Wasn't my call," Eden said gruffly.

Beckett swirled his mug. "You have the emotional intelligence of a toddler, Caspian."

Eden nearly choked, hiding his coughing fit with a sip of coffee. Most of the Triad was terrified of the Golden Boy, but not Beckett. As far as Eden had seen, Beckett wasn't afraid of much.

A muscle in Caspian's jaw ticked. "I did what I had to do."

Beckett shook his head, "There is more to being a leader than being talented with a sword." He nodded at Willa, who was still pointedly ignoring them. "Betrayal is a rocky place to start."

Caspian set his cup down too hard, hot coffee splashed across his knuckles."What do you know, Fractured? You couldn't even keep your Trinity *alive*."

Around them, the murmur of conversation stopped. No one knew the details of how Beckett had been Fractured, just that it had been brutal and bloody. Eden tensed, but Beckett didn't need to be rescued.

"A quick temper isn't exactly the best quality either," Beckett observed mildly, plucking a piece of bacon from Caspian's plate. "Are you sure you're up for being a hero?"

Caspian watched Beckett munch on his bacon. Eden sent a warning down the bond between them. It wasn't like using words, but Caspian would get the message. He was a lot of things, but he wasn't stupid. Everything the Hunter did was calculated even when it was cruel. Starting a war with the most popular person in the Triad wouldn't do him any favors.

So he wasn't surprised when Caspian stood up abruptly. "I don't have time for this"

Beckett saluted Caspian's retreating back with his mug. Eden relaxed. The conversation around them resumed. A fight at breakfast wasn't all that uncommon in a room full of hotheaded warriors.

From across the room, Willa watched Caspian stalk off, but he didn't bother to look her way.

"I was surprised," Beckett said, his finger tapping against the table. "When Willa told me she didn't know about being Fractured."

Eden nudged a piece of pancake through his syrup. Quiet disappointment was Beckett's most effective weapon, but he had rarely found himself in its crossfire. There were all kinds of reasons for not telling Willa—urgency, loyalty, fear. But Eden knew Beckett wouldn't accept any of them.

"I didn't want to lie," Eden said, wondering when he'd stopped being a good person. If it was when he walked away from the crumpled body of his boyfriend, or some other less momentous moment—a quiet wearing away of his integrity.

He finally turned to Beckett, letting himself look completely. A few unruly curls fell across Beckett's forehead and he itched to brush them away, despite the Healer's furrowed brow. To push his fingers deep into the Beckett's hair, tilt his head back, and—

Eden glanced down.

His dead boyfriend had curly hair too, darker than Becketts and always untamed. It was embarrassing to know he had a type—quiet boys with intense eyes and fierce kindness.

Maybe things would be different between him and Beckett if he hadn't cradled Samuel's broken body that day. If he hadn't seen those same curls pulled straight, the tips heavy with blood.

"You owe her an apology," Beckett said quietly.

Eden nodded and gathered his plate. Anywhere was better than here, even if it meant apologizing to Willa.

Chapter 24

WILLA GLARED AT CASPIAN'S back as they worked their way through the crowded Triad floor. Eden had apologized after breakfast, fumbling over the words she'd likely never hear her Caspian say in a hundred years. She wasn't sure she was ready to forgive him yet, but her dance card was embarrassingly short.

Someone jostled her. A tall girl with white blonde braids that hung nearly to her wrists. "Hey, watch—"

The girl's eyes widened when they met Willa's and she muttered something indistinct before melting back into the crowd. Willa pressed a hand to her nervous stomach. The third pancake she'd had for breakfast sat in her gut like lead. It seemed like everyone in the Triad had come to see the new Trinity break in their rookie.

"Jesus, you'd think nothing exciting ever happened around here," Eden muttered.

Willa managed a weak smile, her hand on the pommel of her borrowed sword. It was gold, encrusted with rubies, and completely ridiculous—the kind of thing that should be hanging in the Natural History Museum under artful spotlights.

The closest Willa had ever gotten to swordplay was swinging a long cardboard tube and pretending it was a lightsaber, but she didn't think her limited Star Wars training was going to help today.

Willa hesitated just short of the large clearing in the center of the crowd, hoping the floor would open up and—

"Willa?" Eden asked his hand on her elbow.

"This is insane."

He gave her a wry smile. "Do you trust me?"

She didn't. But there was something about Eden that she liked despite everything. A hopefulness underneath his rough exterior that reminded her of Asher.

She stepped into the clearing. The hard floor was covered in a thick mat that bounced under her feet. Hanging on hooks along the windows were a wide variety of swords, vicious-looking daggers, and several weapons that Willa didn't recognize. The coffee in her stomach churned.

In the center of the clearing, Caspian was talking to two women in scarlet vests. Willa worried the shredded edge of her thumbnail as the Counselors approached. Was there some sort of salute or bow involved in this greeting? Was she expected to kiss someone's hand?

She glanced down at her bare feet. The purple nail polish Tink had applied weeks ago was hopelessly chipped. Underneath her ponytail, there was a tangle she hadn't been able to loosen with her fingers and she hadn't changed her underwear in days. Willa had never felt less prepared to receive some sort of dignitary.

Eden nudged her, and she looked up reluctantly.

The two women were physical opposites. The first was tall with dark brown skin and thick gray locks coiled on top of her head. She had a complicated aura, a mix of turquoise and peach that swirled softly when she moved. The woman held herself like someone who knew the length and breadth of their own power.

The second Counselor was pale and delicate with bird-like features. Her magnificent silver wings towered above them. She smiled when she stepped forward to greet them, but it was brittle. "Welcome Willa. I'm Counselor Lyra. And this is Ester. Our Healer."

Willa dipped her head awkwardly. Ester bobbed hers in return, wrinkled hands clasped in front of her.

"I trust that we have made you comfortable in your new home?" Lyra asked, raising her voice so it could be heard over the murmur of the crowd.

Counselor Lyra wore her beauty like a weapon. Her white blonde hair cascaded down her back, loose and soft. A trio of golden bangles jangling quietly on her thin wrists, the dark maroon of her aura a match to the soft bow of her lips.

Willa took Lyra's outstretched hand, raising her voice. "I am as comfortable as can be expected after your warriors nearly killed my best friend and then forced me to leave the only home I've ever known."

The crowd fell silent. Counselor Ester's lips twitched.

Lyra's hand tightened around Willa's like a vice. Her smile did not waver, but it took on a jagged edge. She pulled Willa close, pitching her voice low. "You're just a stupid girl. I will do what is necessary—torture, lie, kidnap, murder—to save my world. And yours."

"Lyra," Ester said, putting a hand on the Counselor's shoulder. Willa could tell it took all of Lyra's muster not to shrug it off.

"She's impertinent," Lyra responded smoothly.

Ester's expression remained impassive. "Yes, I can see that. And so are all of our best warriors." She turned her hazel eyes on Willa. "This young Healer does not know what she does not know."

"She will soon," Lyra snapped, spinning on her heel and striding away. Willa willed herself not to rub her bruised hand.

"She will soon indeed," Ester said quietly, her peach aura darkening to coral as she disappeared into the crowd after her leader.

Left alone in the center of the murmuring circle, Willa turned to Caspian, hissing through her teeth, "What the hell was that about?"

"Lyra has her reasons," Caspian said. There was a tightness around his eyes that Willa didn't like. "But none of this matters until you're properly trained. One crisis at a time."

Willa had never felt like doing something less. She looked desperately around the circle for a friendly face. This would be easier if Asher were here. If she could find his steady gray eyes in this sea of strangers.

Above, Beckett was wedged between Mae and CJ on a steel rafter, their feet dangling in the open air. Nearby, Zara stood on the edge of the circle holding a red and white bag overflowing with popcorn. She enthusiastically shoved a handful into her mouth and then waved at Willa with greasy fingers.

Willa huffed out a laugh.

Eden peered over her shoulder at Zara. "This is ridiculous. We won't get anything done with the peanut gallery watching."

"I feel like that girl in that 80's movie who showed up at her prom covered in blood," she muttered.

Caspian lifted his sword. "I do not understand that reference but we should—"

· · · · ● · ● · · · ·

Cold water lapped at Willa's feet. She gasped at Eden's unexpected transportation, the ice of his magic catching in her lungs. Her toes sunk into the cool wet sand. On the horizon, the reflection of the dark hole of the sun shimmered on the undulating black ocean.

"Jesus Christ, Eden" Caspian swore.

Eden chuckled and let go of her shoulder. "That will never not be funny."

They were on Coney Island. Willa recognized the broken shadow of the Ferris wheel on the boardwalk. The wooden skeleton of the Cyclone rollercoaster tangled with the stars.

She took a deep breath as the wind blew salt through her hair and peppered her face with sand. The stench of the Umbra was still there, but out here she could pretend that it was just the sea—fish carcasses and seaweed and the vast salty depths.

"Lyra isn't going to like this," Caspian observed, spinning in a circle with his weapon in hand, but there was no heat in his voice.

Willa opened her eyes. The beach was deserted, but Eden pulled an arrow from his quiver, nocking it. The silver tip gleamed in the moonlight, his eyes fixed on the boardwalk. "We couldn't train Willa in the Triad—too many gawking eyes."

To her surprise, Caspian nodded. "Agreed. But we stay alert."

And then Willa heard the sound of them, carried on the wind. The hiss and mutter of something that was not human; claws on splintered wood and the wet rattle of dying lungs.

"This seems like a bad idea," she whispered as the shadow figure of a Skotos slid between Nathan's hot dog stand and the abandoned ring toss.

Eden scanned the beach, the tide rushing over his bare feet. "Don't worry rookie—the Skotos can't hear us over the waves. We come here to practice alone sometimes. It will probably be fine."

Willa did not enjoy Eden's use of the word probably, but it seemed she had zero control of her destiny, so she just pulled her sword. It felt heavy and strange in her hand.

Caspian winced when she swiped it through the air. "Here—let me show you."

She let him, listening as he adjusted her stance. Nodding as Eden taught her where to place her feet. When their swords finally met, her mind was swirling with instructions she immediately forgot.

After thirty minutes, her muscles were trembling. After an hour she was grimacing every time Caspian's blade met her own, both from the pain reverberating through her shoulder and the sharp ring of metal over the quiet sand. Fortunately, she was too busy trying not to embarrass herself to look over her shoulder for anything monstrous. That was Eden's job. He stood knee-deep in the surf, bow in hand, keeping watch. He shouted instructions as they trained—keep her chin up, plant her feet, eyes open—until everything jumbled together and she was just trying to stay alive.

After two hours, she couldn't lift the sword. Her skin was slick with sweat and salt. Her arm felt like lead. "Enough," she gasped, the tip of her blade sinking into the wet sand.

She thought Caspian would protest, but he lowered his sword. "Enough."

Willa was wondering how she was going to lift her arm to put her sword away when Lyra and Beckett appeared on the beach beside them in a sudden gust of wind. Willa blinked the temperature plummeting so fast it made her teeth ache.

The pair took no notice. They were arguing. Beckett clung to Lyra's elbow, his aura bleeding from blue to black, his words caught in the roar of the waves. "—don't think this is necessary, Counselor. I beg you, please just let me—"

Lyra raised her hand to silence him, the wind lifting her hair like a pale flag. "It is done."

Beckett's eyes turned toward them, wild and frantic. Someone shouted as she followed his gaze over her shoulder. Willa turned toward the boardwalk, sword heavy in her blistered hand.

Zara was running toward them across the beach, her bare heels kicking up sand behind her. She was wearing the same ratty t-shirt from this morning, her vest fluttered like butterfly wings behind her. The sword strapped to her back was gone and a nightmare was chasing her.

It ran with a horrible shuffling gallop that made Willa's skin prick, the heaviness of its wet breath audible over the rush of waves behind them. It was a gossamer ghost—ragged flesh weeping from its bone as it swiped the air behind Zara, missing her by inches.

Caspian lifted his sword.

"Stand down," Lyra commanded, pointing at Caspian.

He froze, blade wavering. The Skotos was so close Willa could see the meaty flesh of its gray heart through the white bone of its ribs.

Caspian swung toward Lyra, mouth open in a plea that never came. She shook her head, her own sword still sheathed. Her words had not been a suggestion, but an order.

On the other side of Caspian, Eden had grown still, his bow held loose at his side.

Willa felt terror spiral out inside of her. She was going to see a girl die today and had no idea why.

Zara's eyes were wide as she ran toward them. Willa could see the pale flash of her empty palms. The Skotos roared, guttural, blood stippling its shredded lips.

"Lyra," Beckett pleaded, all color draining from his cheeks.

The Counselor turned to Eden. The Traveler stiffened, but his gaze never wavered from Zara and the nightmare beyond. The waves caught in the frayed hem of his vest, floating around him.

"Do your duty, Traveler," Lyra said gently.

Willa didn't have time to process what that might mean as Zara swept through their group, plunging into the ocean behind them. But Eden knew. His bow and arrow slipped from his fingers, drifting in the surf and he stepped in front of the Skotos.

The beast stopped, claws biting into the sand. The salty air became thick with the stench of rot.

Beside her, Beckett was screaming as the monster's milky eyes swiveled in Eden's direction. It growled—a horrible inhuman sound—and swung, its ragged claws catching him in the side.

Eden didn't make a sound as the blow lifted him and sent him tumbling through the air. There was only the rush of waves and then the heavy thump of his body hitting the wet sand.

Willa gasped, a shockwave of pain shuttering down the bond between them. Caspian lunged for the Skotos, but that was all Willa saw before she was running.

Behind her, the Skotos shrieked as Caspian's blade cut deep, but all she could see was Eden's body discarded on the sand, his wings curled around his shoulders like a silver coffin.

She fell beside him. He was breathing, but just barely, the skin around his lips turning white. Beckett collapsed across from her whispering ragged curses and prayers as his hands fluttered over Eden's body.

Willa pressed a hand to her mouth. The side of his skull was caved in, the bones around his left eye crushed, blood washing over his cheek in pulsing sheets.

Beckett's hands hovered over Eden's ruined face. He hesitated. Dimly, Willa was aware that the beach behind them had fallen silent once again.

"Help him," she begged, not yet understanding.

Beckett's fingers twitched, his mouth twisted in pain, but he didn't lay his hands on Eden. He lifted his eyes to hers, regret twisting the clear blue of his aura into something as black as pitch. Willa's heart thundered. She heard footsteps behind her as blood pooled in Eden's ruined eye socket.

Lyra's bare feet appeared beside them, her delicate toes painted the same silver as her magnificent wings. Willa did not look up, her mouth filled with bile.

"Healing Eden is your job, Willa," Lyra said softly, her voice light and musical and apologetic. And then Willa understood.

This horror had been a lesson. Another sick test.

She wanted to stand up and wrap her fingers around Lyra's thin neck. Wanted to scream at Eden. Wanted to run back to Asher and her life. But she had a job to do, she put her hands on Eden's broken body.

Her power waited in the darkness behind her eyelids, as constant as the beat of her heart. She reached for it, not knowing if it was even possible to heal such a severe injury. But the fear faded as light rushed over her. It was easier now as if this gift belonged to her. As if this was who she had been all along.

Willa wasn't sure how long she knelt there in the sand. When she finally opened her eyes, the tide was washing across her feet. Pain scaled the ladder of her bent spine, but Eden's breath was even, the ocean teasing his outstretched hand, copper lashes rested against his cheekbones, whole again. Healed.

Beckett sat on his heels, pale streaks cut through the blood on his cheeks. He looked bewildered. Caspian stood behind him, staring at Lyra, his aura a bruised nebula, but the Counselor's eyes gleamed as she watched the steady rise and fall of Eden's chest.

Willa bowed her head, exhaustion pressing between her shoulder blades. For a moment she thought these people might be good—momentarily seduced by magic and wings and whispers of prophecy. But she'd been mistaken. There was no good left in the world. Just shades of darkness.

Chapter 25

EDEN STARED DOWN AT his hands, willing them to stop shaking. He refused to lay down on the infirmary cot, perching on the edge while Beckett fussed around him. His fingertips were wrinkled and pale, grains of sand caught under the nails. He had no idea how long he'd been dying on the edge of the ocean.

His head still pounded despite Willa's healing touch and the IV antibiotics pumping into his body through the needle Beckett had stabbed into his hand. Lyra had requested his presence in the war room immediately, of course, and Eden was trying to figure out how he was going to make it across the Triad floor without vomiting.

"Fucking psychopath, that's what she is," Beckett muttered, tapping the IV bag for the tenth time.

Eden squinted up at him. Beckett wore a pair of tortoiseshell reading glasses. They'd slid down the end of his nose as he scribbled something on a clipboard. He looked like an adorable librarian. An adorable, furious librarian.

"I'm fine," Eden insisted, tucking his trembling, wrinkled hands underneath him. He wasn't fine. Willa had managed to Heal his shattered skull but the gash across his side was a different story.

Beckett's lips thinned. "Eden Samara, you are a terrible liar."

He tossed the clipboard on the cot and crouched. Eden gritted his teeth as Beckett moved his shredded vest aside, the fabric peeled away from the three deep claw marks across his ribs.

Beckett prodded the raw edges of the wounds gently, but Eden hissed, his fingers curling into fists under his thighs. Red streaks fanned out from the lacerations, reaching their tendrils eagerly toward his heart. Poison.

Skotos were filthy creatures that had been created specifically for destruction. Even the smallest cut or bite required modern medicine as well as a Healer's power.

Once the wounds were clean, Beckett reached for an antibiotic cream. His touch was warm and soothing as he applied the medicine—Healing while healing. Eden sighed his headache easing.

"You'll need to come back in the morning for some extra Healing and make sure to take the full round of antibiotics...but I think." Beckett's voice wavered. "I think you'll be okay."

Beckett's touch lingered as he examined his work. Eden shuddered, head bent, and told himself it was the pain.

"I'm so sorry," Beckett whispered, his brown eyes warm behind his nerdy glasses. "Lyra should never have asked you..."

"'Tis but a flesh wound," Eden teased, his chuckle turning into a ragged cough.

Beckett sat back on his heels. "Don't be an idiot."

"You seem to call me that a lot."

Beckett's lips twisted. "Yes, well."

Eden avoided looking at Beckett's lips by glancing up at the IV bag. It was almost empty. He pulled his vest closed, wincing.

"Why did you do that?" Beckett asked. "Why did you sacrifice yourself out there?"

Eden stared over Beckett's head at the distant war room where Lyra waited.

Because I'm worth more to the Triad dead than alive.

Because nothing has mattered for a very long time.

Because at least my life could save yours.

"I was following orders," he said instead.

Beckett didn't respond. He looked hollowed out, dark bruises forming around his eyes. Like someone who had almost lost something he couldn't afford to lose.

He reached out. For one brief horrible second, Eden thought that Beckett was going to put a hand on his cheek. But Beckett just touched the guitar pick that dangled in the hollow of Eden's throat. "Tell me about this."

There was sand in Beckett's curls, sparkling along the edge of his forehead. He smelled like salt water. Eden took the chain from Beckett's grasp as gently as he could, tucking it back inside his vest. "It belonged to someone I cared about. Someone I lost."

"Maybe you can tell me about him one day."

Eden thought about his dead boyfriend. He'd been a horrible guitar player, always insisted on coming over after school to practice while Eden slogged through algebra homework, much to the chagrin of his mother and their downstairs neighbor. Somehow those evenings always ended with them snuggled on the couch watching reruns of The Office and stealing kisses. It was one of the things Eden missed most about Before—normal moments eating cold pizza in the light of the refrigerator or sneaking cigarettes out of his grandma's purse. And loving someone.

There was sand on the Healer's lips too, small grains that caught the light. Eden pushed to his feet, willing himself not to sway. "Beckett. This thing between us...it isn't going to happen."

Beckett blinked up at him still clutching the antibiotic cream, cheeks blazing, but Eden didn't wait for a response. He fled, tucking cowardice and the night around his shoulders. There was only so much someone could stand to lose. The end of the world was no place for love.

· · • • · • • · ·

Caspian didn't like it.

He stood outside the war room curtain while Lyra debriefed Eden and concentrated on unclenching his fists. The Counselor didn't respond well to disrespect, but Caspian couldn't stop seeing Eden's crushed skull. Couldn't stop feeling the horrible silence down their shared bond and the chilling knowledge that he'd stood idly by while his brother was injured.

It wasn't uncommon to test a new Healer's abilities during training. Necessary even. But this had been extreme, and he had not been informed.

Willa slouched against the window next to him, her hood pulled up to hide her face. He didn't have to see her eyes to know what the day had cost her.

"Are you all right?"

She twitched at the sound of his voice. They'd barely spoken since the Harvesting.

He owed her an apology. For not telling her about the Fractured and a hundred other sins, but he'd been giving her space, which is the coward's way of hoping time would turn forgetting into forgiving.

Willa turned, her hood falling back a bit. Her dark hair was windblown from the salt air, eyes rimmed with red. "Did you know?" she asked roughly. "Did you know what they asked Eden to do?"

This was important. He could see it in the ridged way she held herself as if she were standing on a precipice.

Caspian stepped closer, holding out his palms as if he could show her his innocence. "I didn't, Willa. I swear on my sword. If I had—"

Willa lifted her chin, eyes filled with a terrible knowing. "Would you have stopped them? The Council? Would you have intervened if they *had* told you their plan?"

He froze. He'd made a promise to himself. A vow that he would never lie to her again. She didn't know about it. The promise was his alone—the only fraction of love that he could still offer.

"I would have volunteered myself in Eden's place," he responded honestly. "But I wouldn't have disobeyed a direct order."

Willa folded her arms around her middle. She was shaking, a faint tremor that shook her whole body. He had trained enough soldiers to recognize the symptoms of exhaustion.

"You should rest," he said, shifting closer still. "I'll talk to Lyra. We'll get this sorted out."

Willa nodded slowly but didn't move. He waited.

She met his gaze. He'd forgotten how beautiful her eyes were, even swimming with tears. "It's not what I thought," she whispered, waving a hand. "This place. It's...not what I thought."

Caspian hated himself at that moment. What Lyra had done on the beach was brutal and cruel, but she had a reason. Maybe even a good one.

It was a reason that Eden and Willa didn't know. There was dried blood on Willa's arm, the ghost of Eden's fingertips still curled around her bicep. Caspian wiped it with his thumb, smearing red across her skin. His team didn't know what they were fighting for.

"Willa, I am sorry," he said quietly. And meant it.

Tears cut a path down her face. "For what? What are you sorry for?"

Caspian sighed, running a knuckle down her arm. She smelled like sweat and the ocean. Like a girl who had fought and lost and deserved the truth.

"I shouldn't have slept with you." It wasn't exactly a lie, he told himself, more like information she didn't need. He regretted a lot of things, but that night on the hotel floor wasn't one of them.

Willa's brow furrowed. "No. You shouldn't have."

"I'm sorry about Asher," he continued, fingers circling her wrist. "And I should have told you about the Fractured. Willa, if I could have done it differently, I—"

"Your turn, Golden Boy," Eden interrupted, limping out of the war room, the heavy curtain falling closed behind him. His skin was the color of ash. He squinted at them through spiked lashes. Willa hurried to his side, and he leaned on her gratefully.

"I appreciate the assist out there partner," Eden said, his wink turning into a wince, his eye socket still mottled black and yellow.

Willa let out a choked laugh. "If you really wanted some attention, all you had to do was ask. There is no need to be so dramatic."

They shared a grin.

Caspian shoved his hands into his vest pockets, shifting awkwardly.

Willa waved in his direction. "Caspian here was just trying to apologize for being a world-class douche."

Eden lifted an eyebrow. "Oh, was he now?"

Caspian crossed his arms, wishing he had gotten a team that took their responsibilities a little more seriously. "There is something you both need to know."

Willa and Eden exchanged another glance. "This must be serious if he's going to reveal secrets," Eden whispered out of the side of his mouth. "Maybe it has to do with his hair. I've always wondered what product he uses to—"

"This *is* serious you idiots," Caspian snapped. He glanced at the curtain where Lyra was waiting for him. "Very serious."

There must have been something in his voice because they fell quiet. His jaw clenched.

Caspian rubbed a hand across his face, lowering his voice to a whisper. "A rift opened in London. The Triad couldn't defend it against the...onslaught. Everyone is dead—humans and Trinity alike."

"I thought that was just a rumor," Eden murmured.

"Lyra thinks New York is next."

Willa pressed her lips together. Caspian wished things were different for her, but she had arrived at the last chapter of a long tragedy. Eden was pale underneath his freckles, blood blending with the red of his hair as people swept past them on the busy Triad floor.

"I should have told you but Lyra..." he shook his head. "I should have told you."

"We've all been here before," Willa said quietly. "We know the world can end on a beautiful summer day. That you can be singing in the shower when planes start falling from the sky. There's nothing to do now but get ready."

Chapter 26

T INK WAS CROUCHED IN the shadow created by two Compound flood lights, her hoodie pulled up to hide the bright flash of her hair. The heavily guarded gate at the South end of Central Park was lit up like a surgeon's room and the air was filled with the growl of generators.

She never glanced his way. Asher had been following her for hours. For her safety, he told himself, it had nothing to do with betrayal.

Tink had been sleeping on his couch for the past few weeks, coming and going at all hours without a word. It turned out her friends at the Uprising didn't have a place for her to stay, a fact that gave him a sick satisfaction he wasn't proud of. She'd stopped trying to apologize days ago.

He should have been grateful that Tink wasn't around all the time—running into her in the kitchen or passing in the hallway was more painful than he'd like to admit. But he was tired of being left behind.

So he'd shadowed her. She'd been busy, disappearing into buildings he couldn't follow and talking to people he didn't recognize, but tonight had been different. Tink had come straight to this deserted corner, settling into a dark crevice with a clear view of the Compound and its heavily armed gate.

Asher had been standing in the alley across from her for hours, the cold bleeding underneath his jacket collar. Tink had his thermos with her. The battered green one he took to the shop to keep his coffee hot during a long work day. She sat, the ankles of her thigh-high leather boots crossed, and scribbled notes in a spiral notebook every time the guards passed.

He could have told her everything she needed to know about the Compound.

Asher knew the barbed wire fence was patrolled every ten minutes during the dayshift and every five after dark. That the soldiers came in alternating pairs and the gate was protected by half a dozen guards, including two snipers hidden in the surrounding buildings.

He'd watched the routine a thousand times from his cell.

It had only been possible to see outside if he stood on the empty shit bucket, his ragged fingernails digging into the ledge of the small window, but there had been nothing else to do, and it was the only way to see the sky.

Every once in a while someone would try to break into the Compound—a distraught parent or spouse of someone who shared his cozy prison. Which is how he knew about the snipers.

On the other side of the street, Tink chewed on her pencil eraser. The gesture was familiar, something she did when she wrote lyrics, hunched over her notepad while he worked on an engine. Asher hated that he knew that.

He would have told her everything if she'd asked. Even though it was something he'd rather leave behind; a nightmare in a life that was already filled with them. But she hadn't asked.

Tink pressed deeper into the shadows as a pair of soldiers patrolled the fence, the glowing tip of a cigarette visible through the darkness. Probably Mateo or Alex. Asher remembered the smoke that had clung to their uniforms when they'd stop by his cell for a casual beating.

His throat clenched. He shouldn't be here. Tink wasn't his responsibility anymore. He buried his hands in his pockets and—

An elbow caught him in the jaw.

Stars shattering his vision.

He spun, off balance, already fumbling for the knife at his hip. His attacker twisted his wrist sharply, and shoved him hard, a meaty forearm pinning him to the wall. The blade slipped from Asher's numb fingers, clattering to the ground.

Frank grinned at him around the damp end of a chewed cigar. "Well, what do we have here?"

"Let me go," Asher growled, digging at the cop's arm.

"You are a glutton for punishment, my friend." Frank's breath was sour, a cold sore crusting his top lip.

Asher grimaced. "I'll kill you."

The bastard laughed, pressing his forearm harder against Asher's throat. He clawed at the inky darkness.

Frank hadn't killed Deliah, but he'd been there, his knee driving into Asher's spine, pinning him to the ground while she bled into the dirt-packed floor.

"Let him go."

Tink looked tiny compared to Frank, but the Glock grinding into the back of the cop's skull was anything but small. Her hood had fallen back, her red hair a neon sign in the Compound's bright lights.

"This is none of your business girl," Frank sneered, pressing harder on Asher's larynx. Asher's feet scrambled for purchase, breath whistling.

There was a click as Tink thumbed back the hammer. "Don't tempt me you murderous piece of shit."

Frank's eyes narrowed, the whites cracked with red. Tink pressed harder. The bastard cursed and stepped back. Asher sagged, the rush of oxygen chasing away the shadows at the edge of his vision.

Tink's waved the muzzle of her gun. "Get on your damn knees. Hands behind your head."

She looked like a kid with a toy, but her dark eyes were hectic, her lips bloodless.

Frank spat at Asher's feet and did what he was told.

"Tink," Asher wheezed, clutching his side.

"You always have some girl saving your ass," Frank snarled up at him. "Not man enough to fight your own battles?"

Asher straightened, rubbing his bruised jaw. Frank had never been the picture of health, but now his skin was sallow and littered with pockmarks. His uniform hung loose where it used to strain against his ample stomach.

The muzzle of Tink's gun trembled but it never wavered from the back of Frank's skull.

"Just let her do it, boy," Frank sneered.

Asher frowned. There had always been hate burned into Frank's eyes, fueled by the fire of greed and power. But now they were empty. Dull.

"Get the hell out of here," Asher spat. "I never want to see your face again."

Tink's eyes snapped to his. "Asher."

Frank lumbered to his feet, cursing them as he fled, one hand holding up his belt.

Asher couldn't read Tink's expression as she watched Frank head for the Compound gate, finger still curled around the trigger. There were frantic red spots high on her cheeks and her eyes were hard. There was nothing of the bright girl he'd taken to his bed. The girl who made him laugh when there was no laughter to be had.

"There's no point killing someone who is already dead," he said.

Slowly, Tink holstered her gun. "You are too soft, Ash."

His chest ached. "You're probably right."

His hoodie swallowed her small frame. She wrapped her arms around her middle as he scooped his knife from the sidewalk. "Why are you following me?"

Because we used to be friends.

Because if things had been different, I could have loved you.

· · · · ●· ● · · ·

Eden turned the gift over in his hands.

On the other side of the Triad, Willa was curled at the end of one of the library's threadbare couches, head bent over a book. She played with the pages as she read, ruffling the corner with her thumb.

After the meeting with Lyra, he'd gone straight to his hammock, but it had taken him a while to fall asleep, haunted by the echoing sound of his bones breaking like dry sticks. He'd woken ten hours later with a dull headache and darkness still pressing against the windows.

The Triad was silent as a graveyard, the fiery eye of the black sun glowing off the ivory floor as he crossed to the library.

"What are you doing awake?" he asked when Willa looked up from her book.

She lifted a steaming cup of hot chocolate. "Couldn't sleep."

Eden nodded, recognizing the haunted look on her face from his own reflection. Insomnia was a common problem in a world where nightmares were real.

He sat at the other end of the couch, propping his legs on the coffee table. Willa was wearing pajamas featuring tiny llamas wearing Santa hats. She dog-eared the page and closed her book, waiting.

Eden cleared his throat and pushed the package across the couch. He'd wrapped it in the cleanest newspaper he could find, folding the paper like origami instead of searching for tape. "I got you something."

Willa stared at the package as if it might contain a nest of tarantulas. "You did what?"

He huffed and nudged the gift closer. "Just take it."

She put down her cup and picked up the package, turning the large snowball of paper over in her hands. "If you wanted a favor, you could have just asked," she teased. "No need to ply me with—"

Willa made a soft sound as the paper fell away.

The Polaroid camera was old, but he had oiled the stiff leather strap and wiped off the dust as best he could. He'd found it in an old man's apartment wedged between a dusty stack of books and a rotting bag of dog food. Willa cradled the camera in her hands as if it were something fragile and precious.

"I know it's not the same as your Nikon," he started, desperate to fill the silence. "But I thought this might be a decent substitute. There's no darkroom here so I thought—"

"Eden." Willa ran a thumb over the cracked strap.

He resisted the urge to squirm. The words he needed to say were caught in his throat like glass. Hard words like *I've been an asshole.* And: *I don't deserve your kindness.*

Words like: *Thank you for saving my life.*

Instead, he shrugged, "Consider it an apology for trying to kill your best friend. That definitely wasn't cool."

She laughed, the sound so unexpected and bright he couldn't help but smile. Eden knew he didn't need to say all the hard words out loud—not with Willa. It was hard not to fear someone who could carelessly root around in your secrets as if they were no more than scraps of memories locked away in a forgotten attic. He'd meant to ask Beckett if Willa was normal. Eden had never heard of a Healer that could read emotions like a fortune teller examining the lines of your palm.

Eden blinked as the camera flashed. It whirred quietly, dispensing a small familiar framed rectangle. Willa smiled, pinching it between two fingers at the corner.

"Can I ask you something?" she said, shaking the Polaroid gently.

"Ask away."

"How do you survive this place?"

He rolled his head in her direction. "What do you mean?"

Willa stared at the picture developing in her hand. "I'm used to depending on just myself." She shook her head. "But here...how can we work together if no one trusts each other? If everything is lies and secrets?"

He picked at a loose thread on the couch arm. "I guess it's just like the real world. Eventually, you have to trust someone."

Willa bit her lip, something like regret flickered across her face. She held up the Polaroid so he could see. It was a good shot despite the low light in the Triad. She had managed to capture him, his drawn face and bruised eyes framed by white. Bitterness caught in his throat. He hadn't always been like this.

"Why don't you run?" she said.

Eden knew what she was asking. His wings felt like an amputated arm when they were confined to his skin. His gift was freedom—and yet here he was, glass and responsibility pressed around him like a cage.

He thought of Beckett. The Healer had been waiting outside his quarters when he'd gotten back from the war room. Eden hadn't been able to look at him. Not when Beckett helped him into his hammock or when the Healer's fingers brushed the hair from his forehead. There was too much between them.

"By the time I was able to leave the Triad, it was too late. This place...the people..."

He didn't know how to finish the thought, but Willa seemed to understand. She ran one finger absently over the camera in her lap. "Lyra informed me that the last step of my Initiation would be in a few days."

Ah.

Her insomnia was suddenly more clear. It was a tradition that every recruit had to be initiated by the most skilled Hunter before they could go into the field. And right now that happened to be Caspian.

Willa would have to fight him in front of the whole Triad to prove her capability. The only way to win was to rid Caspian of his weapon. A hard task on any day. Normally the Initiation would be held after months of training. Or even years. But things were different now.

"Someone like Caspian can always be beaten."

Willa scowled, tucking her feet underneath her. "What's that supposed to mean, Yoda?"

"Caspian is an arrogant prick. You can use that against him. He's stronger than you and faster than you and better trained than you—"

"This is very helpful," Willa grumbled.

He grinned. "But you are smarter than him in all the ways that matter."

Willa drained the last bit of her cocoa, wiping the chocolate off of her lip. "Is that how *you* beat him?"

Eden winked, his grin widening. "Hell no. I punched him in the face and dropped him forty feet onto the training mat."

Willa snorted.

"You'll be okay," he said, and meant it.

Willa fidgeted with her empty cup. "I need a favor."

He raised an eyebrow.

"Can you take me to see Asher?"

Eden let out a hard breath. "Now?"

Lyra would not like it. Rookies were supposed to stay in the Triad. It was a way to detangle them from their former lives.

Willa tucked a stray hair behind her ear. "I need to see him."

Eden understood the need to be near someone who wasn't yours. Someone who smoothed the rough edge inside your heart so he held out a hand, ice whispering beneath his fingertips. "I promised I would take you home whenever you needed Willa, and I intend to keep my word."

Chapter 27

THE SUN HAD JUST broken the horizon when they arrived in her world. Willa lifted her face to catch the warmth, the golden light of morning dancing behind her eyelids.

"It never gets old," Eden said, squeezing her shoulder before letting go.

She took a deep breath. The air smelled sweet, like wet pavement instead of rotting flesh. "How do the Fractured stand it?" she asked. "Being trapped in the dark forever?"

Eden grimaced, and Willa knew he was thinking about Beckett. "God, I don't know."

At the end of the block, Asher sat on the stoop of a crumbling brownstone she didn't recognize, his hands hanging loosely between his knees. His head was down, a black beanie pulled low over his ears. Donut was curled on the sidewalk by his feet and a silver thermos sat by his hip.

"You have fifteen minutes, Celadon," Eden said, before taking off in a gust of wind and disappearing between two buildings.

Asher didn't look up at her as she approached. There was a crumpled paper in his hand, which he kept unfolding and refolding, the creases darker than the rest of the paper. He looked thinner than she remembered, his cheekbones more defined underneath the scruff of his beard.

Willa tucked her hands into her vest pockets, wondering for the first time what had happened while she had been off becoming a warrior princess. She wondered if something fundamental had broken between them.

Asher finally lifted his head, the gray storm of his eyes both familiar and strange. He didn't smile.

"Hey," she said softly, suddenly unsure.

Donut lifted his head, pink tongue lolling out.

Asher lifted his boot, freeing the leash as the dog barreled toward her. Willa crouched, enveloping the big mutt as he covered her face in slobber. She laughed, the sound bursting from her like a champagne cork—bright and sparkling.

Donut's breath smelled vaguely like wet garbage, but she buried her face in his fur anyway. He was soft and warm and so familiar it made her eyes water. She could have stood there forever, letting her fear and worries soak into his wiggling body, but they didn't have forever, so she stood, keeping one hand on his furry head. He leaned against her knees, still shivering with excitement.

"Thank you," she said to Asher, aware of how inadequate those words were.

Asher gave her a smile that was shaped like a lie. "He's not the worst thing in my life."

Willa shuffled around the quivering dog and settled next to Asher on the cold step. Donut licked her fingers and then flopped down on her feet. His fur was silky and soft. Even his long tail, which swept back and forth through the melting snow, was free of tangles.

Her throat burned. Asher had taken care of her dog. He had loved this small piece of her heart while she was gone even though he was angry.

Willa touched the back of Asher's hand. His fingers stilled on the creased piece of paper. A half-eaten sandwich sat on the step next to him as well as a thick wool blanket.

"Have you been here all night?"

Asher stared down at their hands, dark lashes hiding his seawater eyes.

"Why are you here, Willa?"

She tensed at the sharpness in his voice, but then he turned his palm up to capture her fingers. Grease was caught in his nails. He ran a thumb across her knuckles as if he couldn't stop himself.

Willa swallowed and looked around the empty street, searching for something to say. They were somewhere on the Upper West Side, an area usually swarming with drug dealers and prostitutes. "I was going to ask you the same thing," she said, trying to keep her voice light. "What are you doing in this neighborhood? Selling drugs? Trolling for a new girlfriend?"

Asher stiffened and pulled his hand away. "You don't get to show up here and start asking questions. Not after all this time."

Willa picked at the frayed hem of her vest. Her stomach ached. "Fair enough."

Asher's lips were tight as he stared down the street. Donut snored softy. Willa wondered what the hell she was doing here.

"What's it like?" he asked, after a long minute. "The Umbra?"

The sun was warm on the part of her hair as she considered what to tell him. "It's dark," she said finally. "The sun never shines."

Asher glanced over. "Is it terrible, then?"

The dark fringe of his bangs was caught in his eyelashes. He was badly in need of a cut, his hair curling at the edge of his collar. She shrugged. "Not all the time. There are some good people there."

Asher looked skeptical. "And Caspian?"

Willa huffed. "Still an ass. But..."

She squinted as the light bounced off the shattered windshield of an abandoned Volvo. She didn't want to talk about Caspian. Not with Asher. So she said, "I have to fight him soon—some sort of stupid Initiation. To prove I'm worthy of being a part of their weird warrior cult."

Asher raised an eyebrow. "Good luck?"

Willa laughed. "Yeah, I don't think it's gonna go well either."

Asher tapped the folded piece of paper on his knee, and Willa realized it was the map she'd found—the one with Tink's handwriting.

"So you're okay?" he asked.

She wasn't okay. Her body still ached from the fight on the beach. The world was about to fall apart. She missed him.

Willa traced the bruises still yellowing on her knuckles. "I'm okay."

Something flickered in Asher's eyes. The gulf between them yawned deeper. "You'll have to tell me about it sometime."

"I will."

They both knew it was a lie.

Asher hunched his shoulders. His hoodie swallowed his lean frame. She wanted to ask him how he really was, but there wasn't time.

"I came to warn you," she said, tugging the elastic out of her braids and brushing them out with her fingers. Her hair fell in waves around her shoulders.

Asher watched, his aura darkening. It looked like he hadn't shaved in a week, the usually crisp lines of his beard had become scruffy. "About what?"

There are monsters, Willa thought. The kind that crawls out of your nightmare and follows you into the light of day.

Asher shoved his hands into the pocket of his hoodie, leaning forward as if he were trying to fold into himself. "Just tell me, Willa," he said, addressing the pavement between his boots.

She tucked hair behind both ears and then pulled it out again. "There is something bad here. Something unnatural has escaped from the Umbra. It will kill you, Ash. Hell, it might kill everyone."

She cleared her throat. "I need you..."

He looked up sharply, the heat in his gaze causing her to stumble over the truth in those three words. His eyes found her mouth, burned there.

Shit.

She wanted to lean forward and taste the sunlight that cut across his lips. Wanted to see if the tension that coiled in her chest when he looked at her would ease if she just...

"I need you to be careful," she rasped, certain he could hear the thunder of her heart.

He didn't answer. His teeth scraped his bottom lip so slightly that she wouldn't have noticed if every molecule of her body hadn't been paying attention to his.

"I miss you," he said finally. "It is too quiet at the garage and Tink—"

A door opened across the street.

Asher's head whipped around, one arm pushing her behind the concrete banister and out of view. He put a finger on his lips as a familiar figure slipped out of the rusty door at the end of the street.

Tink wore a nondescript leather jacket, but Willa immediately recognized the red hair peeking out from her bright pink beanie. The pouf on top was nearly the same size as her head. She smothered a smile. The girl was dreadful at going incognito, but her fashion sense was always on point.

Beside her, Asher tensed. Tink was not alone.

An older boy was with her, his long hair dyed the same bright red shade. As they watched, he wrapped an arm around Tink and kissed the top of her head. An automatic weapon was strapped to his back. It was not the sort of gun someone used to defend themselves. It was for something else entirely.

"What's Tink gotten herself into?" Willa murmured, as the pair ducked out of sight.

"Nothing. It's...nothing." Asher ran a hand through the mess of his hair. "I was just confirming something I already knew." He stood and started to gather his stuff.

"Is this about that map?" she asked, as he slipped on his gloves.

"Nothing you need to worry about. Anymore." He clicked his tongue. Donut stood slowly and stretched.

"Don't be an ass."

A muscle ticked in Asher's jaw. He looked at Donut instead of her. "Tink was using our relationship to get information about the Compound. They're planning some sort of attack on Central Park. I don't know—she didn't exactly give me the details while I was kicking her out of my bed."

"Darkness, Asher."

He wrapped Donut's leash around his wrist to reel the dog closer.

The sun was warm on the back of her neck, but Willa shivered. "How can I help?"

His eyes were unreadable as he pulled up his hood. "I think you've got enough to worry about these days."

"Asher," Willa started, but he was already turning away. Donut resisted, but Asher tugged the leash and the dog fell into step, glancing balefully over his shaggy shoulder. The words she wanted to say pressed against the back of her teeth. But he was right.

She felt Eden land behind her, the wind picking up the edges of her long vest. Asher's was a vortex of indigo, silver scattered across it like stars.

"Ash." She said it so quietly that there was no way he could have heard, but he turned anyway.

He smiled, small and tight. "I'll see you around, Robin."

Willa squinted into the sun as he disappeared around the corner, Eden's hand bleeding frost into her skin.

· · · · ●· ● · · ·

Willa cooled her sweaty forehead against the window and stared up at the jagged scar that cut between the stars and the black sun. The new rift had opened a few days ago, throwing the whole Triad into panic. Although this one hung too high for Skotos, its sudden appearance was proof the Umbra was running out of time.

Something moved inside that horrible slice of broken sky—shimmering, undulating stardust. It should have been beautiful, but it filled her with dread.

"Try not to look directly at it," Eden said quietly. "It will just make you sick, like reading in the backseat of the car. Your mind isn't designed to process the movement of time."

Willa slid down the glass next to him, stretching out her aching legs. Caspian rolled onto his stomach from where he had been sprawled on the training mat. He propped his chin in his hands, sweat dripping down his temple. "You're finally getting better with the sword," he observed, pointedly avoiding any discussion about the rift or its deadly implications.

It was as close to a compliment as he'd offered in weeks even though it was a lie. She was shit with the sword. She was also clumsy with the bow and flat-out terrible with throwing stars.

"I mean, you managed not to shoot the Traveler who was sitting in the library during our archery session today," Eden offered, running the guitar pick back and forth across his chain. "So that was good."

Willa threw her sweaty towel at Eden. "Screw you."

He laughed and leaned back against the cold glass. The boys had disposed of their shirts halfway through training. Willa, who was trapped in a damp sports bra, was simultaneously jealous and not mad at the view.

Eden was built like a swimmer, with broad shoulders and a narrow waist. A Fractured tattoo peeked out from the hollow of his hip. Willa had never seen a full Trinity with the familiar crescent tattoo. She made a note to ask him about it sometime.

Caspian was all rippling golden muscle. He pushed up on one arm, shoulders flexing, and took a long pull from his water bottle. Mesmerized, Willa watched droplets leak from the corners of his mouth and drip onto his broad chest.

Mother of Darkness, give her strength.

Impulsively, she tugged at Caspian's bond with her mind. His head shot up, eyes narrowing at the flash of heat.

Eden's eyes slid toward her. "Should I leave?"

Oh god.

Willa blushed.

"Yeah, no secrets," Eden muttered, unfolding himself from the ground. "This should be fun."

Willa had a sudden, terrible flash of kissing someone while these two idiots watched from their supernatural perch on her shoulder. "Um, how far exactly does the 'bond' thing extend?"

Eden snorted. "Dear god, I hope not that far. I have no desire to see what Caspian is like in bed."

Caspian stroked his rippling abs. "Oh, don't lie. You'd love to get a little taste of this."

"I just threw up in my mouth a little," Eden shot back, gathering his things. He arched an eyebrow in her direction. "I'll leave you to it."

She couldn't miss the warning that Eden tossed down the bond as he walked away. Willa gave him the finger with her mind, unsure if it would work, and felt the bond shimmer with laughter. Asshole.

"He doesn't approve," Caspian said mildly. He'd rolled onto his back, leaning on his forearms. He managed to look like a model who'd been misted with fake sweat. Meanwhile, Willa felt like she'd just tumbled out of a washing machine.

She reached for her Polaroid. Caspian didn't look away when the camera flashed. He was used to being the center of attention, even in the frame of her lens.

"Do *you* approve?" he purred, his glacial eyes raking over her.

Somewhere along the way, she'd started to forgive him. It was unconscionable. The camera whirred. She was clearly a horrible person. But betrayal was never quite so black and white as it first seemed. Over his shoulder, the nauseating flicker of the rift roiled in the sky.

It turned out Caspian had reasons.

Maybe it was an exhausting lifetime of bitterness that made her soften. Or maybe it was just the memory of his mouth and the rough certainty of his hands. She was only human.

Chapter 28

WILLA TRIED TO IGNORE the finger poking her relentlessly in the side, but the movement made her hammock swing lightly. She grumbled and covered her face with her forearm even though there was no real sun in this godforsaken place.

The evil finger turned into a foot and became more insistent, causing her bed to swoop violently. She tried to shift away, but dull pain rippled down the column of her spine. Willa groaned and peeled open her eyes, glaring up at Eden. "What the fuck?"

"Looking stunning as usual, Celadon."

She gave him the finger and then wiped the drool from her cheek with the back of her hand. Across from her, Zara was still snoring loudly in her hammock.

Over the past few weeks, sleeping in a strip of cloth a hundred feet off the ground had grown on her. Something was soothing about the way it curled around her sore body. There were other things about the Triad she didn't hate. Warm baths, nights around the fire, and the extensive library. Yesterday, the kitchen had slaughtered a wild pig, roasting it for hours over glowing coals and driving everyone crazy with the unctuous smell. At dinner, she'd licked the fat from her fingers, washing the pork down with a spiced mead that Beckett had been brewing in his room.

Even Caspian was thawing, joining the group around the fire and shaking his head at Eden's relentless teasing. He'd sat next to her last night, their shoulders brushing as they listened to April's newest song. She'd fallen asleep like that, her head tucked between his arm and the cushions.

"I think you're gonna wanna fix that rat's nest you call hair," Eden observed.

Willa rolled her eyes. "It truly is a delight to have you wake me up in the morning."

"Oh, it is my pleasure, darling."

Her whole body ached from training. She had a fist-sized bruise across her ribs and she'd brutally wrenched her elbow when Eden had caught her awkwardly during a practice fall. At some point, she'd chipped a tooth.

Still, she ignored Eden's outstretched hand and crawled onto the platform. He chuckled as she rolled onto her back, nudging her with his toe. "Why don't you just heal yourself?"

She struggled to a sitting position, wincing as her rib shifted. "Beckett said it was cheating."

Eden sat down on her wooden chest and crossed his arms. "I realize that everyone thinks Beckett walks on water, but he doesn't know everything."

Willa managed to push herself into a standing position without too much undignified groaning. "What the hell is the deal with you two anyway?"

He was silent for a beat. "What do you mean?"

She put two knuckles into the small of her back and stretched. "Don't be dense. Beckett has a thing for you, but you avoid him like the plague. What's that about? Old lovers?"

Eden's lips thinned.

Willa linked her fingers above her head, trying to work out the knots in her shoulders. "He's awfully cute," she teased. "Don't tell me you didn't tap that."

Eden sneered.

She stroked her chin, pretending to consider. "Not boyfriends then. Is there some sort of stupid Triad rule about dating? Oh Darkness, don't tell me sex is taboo around here because if it is…"

"This is none of your goddamn business but no, it's nothing like that."

He had gotten a haircut recently, the sides shaved close but the top still falling over his deep green eyes. Eden was handsome in that ethereal way only a redhead could be, all pale skin and freckles. He could have anyone he wanted, including Beckett.

Especially Beckett.

Willa gripped one elbow, stretching it across her body. "So it *is* *something* then," she mused. He stared out the window, jaw tight. Eden was always up for some friendly ribbing, but not, it turned out, about this.

Without thinking, she touched the connection between them, feeling the undercurrent of sorrow that Eden hid beneath a wicked tongue. He glanced up sharply. "Stop that."

Willa flushed. Beckett had taught her that it was extremely bad form to tap into your Trinity's connection unless it was absolutely necessary. Using the tenuous thread between them for everyday curiosity was akin to seeing someone naked. It was intimate and invasive.

"Sorry," she mumbled, stretching down to touch her toes so she wouldn't have to look at him.

Eden sighed. "Listen..."

Willa swung her arms up in a sun salutation, trying to think peaceful thoughts as her muscles loosened. Eden stood. "This isn't a damn high school. We are fighting for our lives here. Some of us have...lost people." He shook his head. "There is no time for a fucking relationship."

Willa brought her hands down into the prayer position and lifted one foot to rest against her inner thigh. She tightened her core and breathed.

Eden turned to the hanger where her vest hung, cleaned and pressed by some Fractured tailor in the night. He pulled it down, straightening the already crisp hem. "You'd be wise to stay away from Caspian. That will only end in disaster."

Willa swayed and lost her balance. Eden smirked and held out her vest.

She wanted to tell Eden that there was nothing going on between her and Caspian—that his betrayal had crushed any hope of a relationship. But that wouldn't be entirely true.

He was an asshole, but he was such a sexy asshole. If they were going to be stuck together, what would be the harm in...indulging?

"Sex is just a release. It doesn't have to mean anything," she insisted, snatching the vest from Eden's hand. Nothing had happened yet, but there had been flirting and she knew how it made her look.

"At what cost?" Eden shot back. "Pain like that isn't worth a quick screw, Willa. Darkness, you don't even *like* him."

She crossed her arms. "Thank you for your advice, Saint Eden. Haven't you ever been with someone just for the sex?"

Eden headed toward the opening in the small privacy curtain. "You two are a train wreck. Get dressed."

She scowled and shrugged on her vest, staring at her reflection. Her time in the Umbra was starting to show. She'd gained weight from the steady diet of actual food and her skin seemed to glow despite the lack of sun. Her arms were showing definition, and she could do more than two push-ups. She looked good. Healthy. Almost happy.

Willa raked her hair into a tight bun. This was no time for vanity. Rumors were circulating that an organized attack on the Skotos was imminent. The last member of the London Council was arriving today and then the mission would move forward.

She strapped on her sword, tucking her gun into her waistband. Eden was right, of course, she had more important things to worry about than a stupid boy. Like the end of the world.

And today's Initiation.

"You know," she said as she ducked out of her room to where Eden was waiting on the narrow rafter. "We wouldn't even be having this conversation if I was a dude. You'd be high-fiving me about my manly conquest."

It was Eden's turn to roll his eyes. "I'm just not too excited about being caught in the middle of your inevitable breakup and the eternity of snarky remarks I will have to endure for the rest of my goddamn life."

Willa punched him on the shoulder. The sweet smell of maple syrup drifted up from the cafeteria tables and her stomach rumbled in response. She looked at Eden expectantly, but his attention was on the long community table below them.

Beckett was straddling the bench next to a Traveler she recognized—Trevor. They had trained together with throwing stars a few days ago. He'd been rubbish at it, but she'd seen worse. Nice guy; smart and funny.

They watched Beckett laugh and rest his hand on Trevor's thigh. Eden stiffened. Somehow, Willa didn't think casual was something her new friend could handle at all.

She cleared her throat. "Anytime you want to get out those wings so we can get breakfast would be awesome. I think I smell sausage."

Eden didn't comment on the little scene below them, shuddering as his wings slid through the slits in his vest, the sharp tips slicing through the skin of his shoulder blades. Willa couldn't help but wince even though she'd seen it a hundred times.

It was magic, plain and simple. There was nowhere in the human body for those wings to be hiding and yet they emerged fully formed and impossibly grand. Weeks ago, he'd called them during a training exercise, and Willa had seen the ragged wasteland of his bare back for the first time. Two jagged scars ran the length of his spine, thick and red. There had been no time for finesse that time as his wings tore through those scars, separating the muscle like a surgeon's knife, blood sliding down his back. She wasn't sure how something could be so horrible and beautiful all at the same time.

"It's okay. It doesn't hurt when I do it slow," he said, flexing his wings. "I'm used to it."

"I don't know how you possibly could be."

He shrugged, the way boys did when they were trying to dismiss things that really mattered. "How do we stand anything really?"

Willa didn't respond as he gathered her in his arms and dropped lightly into space. She knew it should start to feel normal, but the rush of falling—of flying—never seemed to get old. Eden took his time, looping lazily through the air. Willa breathed her healing energy into his ravaged muscles as they glided toward the floor. He would never ask for her help, but that didn't mean she couldn't give it.

Caspian looked up as they landed in the dining area. "About damn time," he snapped, shoveling the last bite of waffle into his mouth.

Eden snorted. "Relax, Golden Boy, we have plenty of time before the Initiation."

Caspian's gaze flicked to Willa. "You should have trained this morning instead of sleeping. I'm not going to go easy on you, just because we are Trinity."

Willa sat down, pretending his words didn't hurt. They'd been getting along lately—civility sliding slowly back toward a tentative friendship.

"You're an idiot if you don't go easy," she said mildly, accepting a plate from Mae, who smiled at her grimly. "Your success depends on my success."

Caspian pointed at her with his coffee cup. "That's where you're wrong, Celadon."

"And why is that?"

He stood. "Because if I'm going to take a rookie into the field, then I'm going to be damn sure that she doesn't crumble at the first sight of real danger." He stalked off, calling, "I'll see you soon Healer. Try not to embarrass me."

"Asshole," Eden muttered, sliding into Caspian's vacated seat.

Willa stared at her breakfast. She wasn't as hungry as she had been a minute ago.

"I can see what you see in him," Eden said, nodding at Caspian's retreating back. "He's a real sweetheart."

Willa stabbed a bite of French toast with her fork. "Oh, shut up."

• • • ● • ● ● ● ● • •

"Come on, you hairy beast, it's the middle of the damn night. Just pee already."

Asher sighed and pulled his beanie over his freezing ears as the dog tangled himself around another lamppost and sniffed a pile of gray slush.

The garage was quiet without Tink and Willa. Grayson had stopped by once to find out what was going on with the band, but there wasn't much to talk about. There was no band without Tink.

He'd been fine until Willa had shown back up a couple of weeks ago. Or at least that was the lie he'd been telling himself. She was a horrible friend, moody, and prone to rash decisions. But the world seemed hollow without her.

Asher jingled the leash. "Anytime today, Your Highness."

Donut huffed and lifted his head, staring at nothing. Asher flipped up the collar of his jacket. It hadn't snowed in weeks, instead the weather had degraded into a perpetual gray. It was the armpit of the year and it matched his mood just fine.

Asher squinted down the empty street, following the dog's gaze. He should have brought some treats to help the process along. A piece of jerky or—

Donut bolted.

Asher yelped, almost losing the leash as it nearly wrenched his arm from its socket. He cursed while Donut dragged him to the end of the block, coming to an abrupt halt in front of a pile of trash.

"Stupid freakin' dog," he muttered, rubbing his shoulder as the dog nosed happily through the rubbish.

He glanced down the nearby alley. Not a sliver of moonlight penetrated the blackness. A chill pricked the back of his neck. For the first time in weeks, he thought about Willa's warning and glanced down at his gray sweatpants. When he'd woken to Donut's hot dog breath in his face, it had been all he could do to just roll out of bed. No pockets; no weapons. Brilliant.

Something chittered.

Donut looked up from his investigation of a pigeon carcass. The sound came again. Strange and quiet. A soft scratching that made Asher's flesh crawl, like teeth gnashing together.

The dog growled. The noise stopped abruptly. He held his breath, listening. Maybe it was just a rat skittering along the wall or a piece of trash blowing in the wind. He desperately wished that he'd bothered to tie his bootlaces when he'd shoved them onto his feet and shuffled down the stairs.

Then a new sound. Tapping against the pavement. *Tap.*

Tap. Tap.

The sound was deliberate, like Morse code.

Asher took a step back. Donut growled again, a low rumble. When the quiet scrape came again, it was accompanied by a gurgling breath, as if whatever was coming toward them was trying to breathe through thick mud. Asher had no idea what could make a sound like that, and he didn't particularly want to find out. Donut seemed to agree, his tail disappearing between his legs, as Asher slowly started to back away.

Tap.

Another wet breath. Closer.

Tap.

He wanted to run. Every nerve in his body was telling him to run. But he wasn't about to give his back to the horror that lurked in the dark. Asher took another slow step back.

It whispered.

The sound didn't come from the yawning black maw of the alley, but from inside his own mind. His body stiffened at the invasion. He bent, clutching the sides of his head as if he could exhume whatever was invading his mind with his fingertips.

The voice murmured again, and visions flooded hin: Deliah limp and bleeding in his arms, Tink naked and writhing underneath a faceless man, Willa falling and falling until the concrete rushed up to meet her.

Asher gagged and the leash slipped from his loose fingers.

Donut darted away, disappearing into the darkness. Asher didn't blame him—he desperately wanted to follow, but the voice was a grenade inside his consciousness, obliterating his control.

The moonlight shifted and a nightmare slid out of the shadows.

Asher fell to his knees.

It was a rotting corpse, its flesh a thin membrane that hung from its bones in wet sheets. Vertebrae broke through the skin of its hunched back, a morbid ladder of gristle and bone. It leaned against the wall, leaving a trail of foul wetness on the brick as it shuffled closer. Asher could smell it—a putrid, dead smell that made him retch.

He should run. Should get off the cold ground and save his own damn life, but he was frozen—afraid that his mind would unravel completely if he looked up into its face.

"Look," the voice purred inside his head. Asher shuddered. It was more than a suggestion. The command wrapped around his brain. So he looked.

If he had been in control of his own faculties, he would have screamed. The creature had a skull for a face, sharp cheekbones cutting through its tattered flesh. Its eyes were the same milky white as its skin, shot through with a scarlet web of broken blood vessels, and when it smiled, bloodless lips stretched grotesquely over black teeth.

Something in Asher's mind let go at the sight. He scrambled backward, babbling prayers to whatever god would listen.

"Your life is mine now," the creature whispered. The words echoed inside Asher's head like a funeral bell.

He needed to stand up, but the words sank into the crevices of his brain, telling him to surrender in a voice as gentle as a lullaby. He turned his head and vomited onto the pavement. Bile burned in the back of his throat, sharp and tangible.

This wasn't a nightmare. This was real. He spat, arms trembling as he tried to hold himself up.

"No one is coming to save you," the monster sang.

Asher sank to his elbow, despair settling like a heavy blanket on his shoulders. He believed it. Not because it was a curse whispered by a monster, but because it was true. No one would care if he died. He was alone again.

"You are insignificant," the creature sighed, close enough now that Asher could smell the carrion on its breath. He rolled onto his back, hot tears pooling in his ears.

The thing crawled up the length of his body, the loose curtain of its skin brushing his arm. Asher shivered in revulsion. The monster licked its cracked lips with the pink meat of its tongue, leaving behind streaks of blood.

Asher looked past the creature's ruined face to the small patch of night visible through the clouds. The stars gleamed, steady and familiar.

He was going to die in an alley after all. It was funny really. As if death had been waiting here to collect the soul Willa had snatched away.

The creature's carrion breath washed over his face. Asher pressed his palms into the cold concrete and thought of Willa. He'd kissed her that first day in the convenience store. It had been just a light brush of lips, but she had stiffened in his arms. He had felt it too—a sizzle along his nerves he couldn't seem to shake.

He hadn't even known her then. Hadn't known the way her chin jutted out when she was lying or the spots of color that appeared on her cheeks when he stood too close.

Above him, the thing paused.

"What's this now?" the nightmare breathed, leaning closer.

As soon as those horrible blind eyes rolled in his direction, Asher knew he had made a mistake. His muscles seized, agony rolling through him as the creature probed his consciousness with the ruthless scalpel of its mind.

Asher tried to hide her.

Despite the pain shattering underneath his skin, he tried to hide Willa behind other memories, but the creature drew her out, a mental bloodletting: Willa with grease on her face as they changed a radiator, the feel of Willa's healing hands on his ribs, Willa falling into the snow dusted sky.

The monster released him, and Asher gasped, his body sagging back to the ground, pain rippling across every nerve.

"So..." the monster mused, "your life might not be useless after all boy."

Asher pressed his cheek to the pavement. It would be better if it was over now.

A few feet away two yellow eyes met his from underneath a dumpster. Donut whined, high and quiet—a silent witness.

Fresh tears blazed down the side of Asher's face. Donut inched closer, his wet nose just visible. Asher stretched out a hand, palm cupping the moonlight.

The monster above him chuckled. And took his mind.

It was a tidal wave of pain.

The compulsion washed over his consciousness, stealing his identity until there was nothing left of Asher—only a nightmare wearing the face of a boy with Al's Auto Parts stitched onto his pocket.

Chapter 29

SWEAT DRIPPED DOWN WILLA'S spine as she struggled to hold the sword steady.

Caspian slid to the left on the training mat, his steps light and impossibly graceful. "You tired already, Celadon?"

Willa scowled, realizing a fraction too late he was trying to distract her. Caspian lunged. She met his sword, the vibration running down the length of her arm as he leaned against the blades.

She gritted her teeth and held her ground, wishing she had any other weapon. It had only taken Caspian moments into the Initiation to nearly disarm her; managing to take her gun and the hidden dagger in her boot before the crowd had even settled.

That had been hours ago. Or minutes. She couldn't tell.

Her muscles felt like water as Caspian pushed the edge of her own sword closer to her face. He was toying with her, testing the limits of her ability.

"Now, you're just showing off, you arrogant bastard," she hissed into his smug, handsome face. Her palm slipped, and he darted forward to kiss her on the cheek before spinning away.

Ass.

Willa backed away, breathing hard. It wouldn't be so humiliating if this was just another training session, but the whole Triad was here. She could feel their eyes boring into the back of her skull, the circle of their faces a blur as she retreated.

Mae stood next to Zara, arms crossed, eyes intent. Beckett was there too, leaning back into the circle of Trevor's arms. Eden watched from his perch high above them with the other Travelers.

Willa wiped her damp palm along her vest. How the hell had she gotten herself into this?

Caspian strolled across the circle, unconcerned about his exposed back, showing off for the crowd. The rules were simple. Disarm your opponent. The first without a weapon in their hands was the winner.

Willa cursed. Hunters had heightened senses. Travelers had wings. All she could do was heal a paper cut slightly better than a bandaid. She was a talented nurse, for Darkness's sake.

She wiped her hair out of her face with her wrist and tried to remember her training as Caspian turned. She watched his hands and the ice of his eyes for any hint of his next movement—a twitch or tell that could help her. Warn her.

But there was nothing.

So Willa attacked, trying to catch him off guard. She might as well have been moving through mud. His sword met hers easily, blades screaming. Caspian tutted as he twisted the flat of his sword. The sharp movement wrenched her wrist, and Willa cried out, barely managing to hold onto her weapon.

The pounding of her pulse drowned out technique and training—she was just trying to stay alive. Caspian circled her slowly, a predator.

The Council looked on, still and silent on the edge of the crowd, their scarlet hoods pulled up to hide their faces. There were three of them now, the last had arrived from London just before the Initiation. Willa didn't need to see their eyes to feel their judgment.

The blister on her palm had burst, blood and pus smearing the grip of her borrowed sword. The Council's disappointment in her—everyone's disappointment—filled up the space around her lungs. The only reason she was still standing was Caspian's pity. The truth burned.

Caspian darted forward, three quick jabs as if testing her resilience. Or the smoothest path to her defeat. Willa grunted and managed to parry. Eden was right. There was no way she could beat Caspian with a sword—not even with *years* of training.

"Do you give up?" he called.

Yes, Willa thought. *I give up. I'm not strong enough.*

Yet despite everything, Willa could feel the quiet confidence down Eden's bond, a direct contradiction to the doom she read in Caspian's eyes. She wanted to look up. To find him in the crowded rafters and ask why in holy hell he believed in her.

Willa tightened her grip. She might not be talented or special or a fucking key, but she was no coward. If she was going to go down, she could at least give them a show.

So she stepped forward, taking the offense for the first time since the whole mess had started. Caspian raised an eyebrow.

"Why don't you take off those kid gloves you've been using," Willa called. "Afraid I'll embarrass you, Golden Boy?"

Surprised laughter rolled through the crowd. Caspian's mouth thinned, aura blackening. And then everything about him changed.

His gaze sharpened, nostrils flaring. Everything about him became more clear. More true. Willa realized she'd never seen Caspian use become a true Hunter—the humanity drained out of him and he stalked forward.

She stepped back involuntarily but a dozen hands pressed against her spine, pushing her back into the circle.

She was about to lose. Spectacularly. Relief ate through her fear. This was almost over. These supernatural warriors would realize their mistake and take her back to her big stupid dog and empty apartment. Back to Asher.

Except.

Caspian had taken something from her. He had chipped a sliver from her already weary heart. Taken something with his lying eyes and clever mouth. And she had a chance to hand him back a piece of her pain.

Willa lowered her sword, blocking out the crowd's murmur. It was suicide to leave herself exposed—a lamb lying down in front of the lion, but she reached for Caspian's bond and found it pulsing just below her sternum, swollen with triumph.

She forced herself to remember the taste of Caspian's lips in that dark hotel room. The sound of his muffled gasp and the feel of his calloused fingers. She knew he still wanted her, even now, so she gathered that heat and thrust it down the bond toward him, twisting desire into a weapon.

He staggered. Even from a distance, she heard the ragged intake of his breath and saw the end of his sword wavered.

The crowd went quiet.

For a moment, he was still, emotions rippling through his aura. Want and Anger. Betrayal and Guilt.

When Caspian looked up, his eyes were a wasteland. "So that's how you want to play it, love?" he purred, lifting his blade.

Willa retreated, the tip of her sword dragging the ground as Caspian prowled forward, teeth bared in a mockery of a smile. She had miscalculated.

There was no mercy on his face now. He came impossibly fast, his weapon a whirlwind. Somehow she managed to deflect the first attack, barely in control as she slipped away with a breath to spare. She narrowly got her sword up before he was on her again. The clash of blades made her teeth ache. Desperately she swung, wild and wobbly, and Caspian swept her feet out from under her in one fluid movement.

Her teeth clicked when she hit the training mat, the air whooshing from her lungs. Silver glinted in the rafters above her head, the distant Traveler's wings indistinguishable from the stars dancing in front of her eyes.

Caspian pointed his sword at her chest and then flicked his wrist, the blade grazed her cheek in the same place he'd kissed just moments ago. It stung, and Willa could feel the blood welling to the surface.

His face was stone. "You aren't ready, Willa. Maybe you never will be." He drove his sword into the mat, leaning on the hilt as he leaned close. "But if you want to fuck, I'd be happy to oblige."

"Never again, you self-righteous asshole," Willa gasped.

Caspian let his gaze flicker to her lips. For a second, she thought he might kiss her. Right here in front of everyone. With the heat of battle and the prick of desire still dancing across her skin, Willa wasn't sure she would stop him.

His gaze lifted back to hers knowingly before he straightened, raising his voice to address the crowd. "This Initiation is over. The Healer is unworthy."

Caspian yanked his blade from the mat and strolled toward the three Counselors. The Triad floor burst into conversation. From her place on the floor, Willa could see money and goods trading hands. Her cheeks burned, knowing no one in their right mind would have bet on her.

The crowd started to drift away, but the Council remained unmoved.

Willa rose silently, leaving her weapon behind. She hugged the edge of the loose circle, her steps light, keeping in Caspian's blind spot as he cleaned her blood from his sword. The press of a hundred eyes followed her as she slipped passed Mae, smoothly slipping the girl's gun from her holster.

Not a messiah or a key, but a thief.

Willa barely registered Mae's shock, her eyes on the back of Caspian's golden head. She thumbed off the safety, passing the silent Council as he started to turn, alerted by the murmur of the Triad.

Caspian froze when he saw the empty place where she should have been. Willa planted her feet but he was already moving—faster than she thought possible—his hand a blur as he reached for his sword.

Her finger jerked on the trigger.

The bullet hit the Caspian's blade like a bell being broken. He cried out as it shattered, the pieces pinwheeling through the air.

He pulled the throwing daggers from his waist before the shards had even landed and they lifted Willa's hair as they passed, embedding in the pillar behind her. She breathed, the muzzle smoking.

The circle was silent. Caspian stared down at his bleeding palm as Eden landed lightly next to her.

It was over. Willa tucked Mae's gun into her waistband with shaking hands.

Caspian clenched his hand and smiled, humanity bled back into the ice of his eyes. "She's ready."

Eden grinned. "Hell yeah, she is."

At the edge of the circle, the Council stepped forward.

It was the beginning of something, and Willa tried very hard not to imagine what the end might look like. The muzzle rested against her back, burning.

· · · · ·· · · · ·

There should have been cheering or a burst of conversation, but the only sound was the bright sing of Travelers' wings as they took flight, a flock of silver starlings. Willa tried to straighten the wrinkled edges of her vest as the Council drew closer. Even Caspian wiped the moisture from his upper lip.

She was absurdly pleased she'd made him sweat. If it had been a real battle, she could have put that bullet between his eyes. Caspian cupped his bleeding hand behind his back. It would be a long time before she could forgive him, but Willa felt balance restore itself between them. A balance she could live with.

The Council stopped in front of them. Ester came first, her dark eyes smiling. "You've done well, Willa Celadon."

Lyra tipped her head, her gaze shrewd. "Congratulations, Healer."

Willa thanked them, already calculating how many moments she was from a warm bath, but Lyra turned to the last hooded Counselor. "Willa, I want you to meet the New York Triad's Hunter. This is—"

The stranger stumbled forward, a strange movement considering the formalities, her hood falling to reveal thick dark hair and a wide expressive face. The woman was shaking—not small tremors, but violent convulsions that shook her whole body. Her eyes were wild, fixed on Willa's face as if she had seen a ghost. Her Fractured tattoo was a dark crescent across her left cheek.

Willa's smile faded.

The woman's aura was a dark flame of greens that matched her eyes, juniper and chartreuse. Wrinkles bracketed her mouth, a strange contrast to the sunburst of laugh lines at her temples. It made her look young and old at the same time, as if life had worn down her happiness prematurely.

"Willa?" the woman breathed.

No.

"Liliana, what the hell is this?" Lyra demanded.

The name was a gunshot. Willa stared at her dead mother. At the curve of her ear, and the unusual shade of her eyes. Stared at the consultation of freckles that sat in the hollow of her throat and her long elegant fingers. The memories rushed back, a brutal assault: her mother singing in the kitchen wearing frayed jeans, gentle hands lifting her from the bathtub, ballet lessons, and bedtime stories. They were more dreams than reality. Lullabies she told to put herself to sleep.

Her mother lurched forward, pulling Willa down to the mat, her dark red vest swirling around them like blood. Willa couldn't speak. Her life had fallen into place and splintered into a thousand pieces in a matter of moments.

Liliana's hand fluttered around her, touching Willa's cheek and her hair and the curve of her elbow, as if she were some sort of precious thing. "My daughter. You are here. Finally, you're here."

Willa captured the fragile bird of her mother's hands and pressed them to her chest where numbness was already stealing into her heart.

Chapter 30

THE BOY WHO USED to be Asher stood over the body of his ex-girlfriend and watched the growing puddle of blood saturate the tips of her red hair.

Tink had told him everything in the end.

He stepped over her corpse. She'd revealed the location of her friend's little hideout when he'd broken her index finger. It had taken a little more to get the names of their leaders, but she had given in before he took her eyes.

The attack planned on the Compound was a minor nuisance compared to the much larger problem of the Triad. The humans were barely more evolved than feral animals, but the Trinity had proven to be more difficult to eradicate.

He grinned, blood in his teeth. The Triad and the human uprising were planning an attack together. It was excellent news. Two silver-winged birds. One stone.

The boy who was not a boy squinted out the kitchen window at the rising sun. Even in this stolen husk, he hated traveling in the day. The light burned. Once the blanket of night settled, he'd return to the others.

The Asher-shaped thing knelt beside the body, oblivious to the blood soaking into his jeans. Her hands had fallen at her sides as she died, the fingers curled gently, perfect crescents of the boy's skin caught underneath chipped nails. She'd fought, the pathetic little thing.

The Asher-thing ran a finger through the thick pool of the girl's blood. It was warm, her heart still busy pumping out the last of her life. He rubbed her blood across his gums.

The boy howled inside his mind.

The monster frowned. It was the second time he'd felt the human struggle. Most humans simply surrendered—the horror of being invaded too much to bear. This one's resistance was an unexpected complication. He sat back on his heels as the boy shrieked and considered the dilemma.

Perhaps more horror would silence him.

The Asher-shaped thing pressed his hands to the floor, blood squelching through his fingers as he bent to drink from the puddle. The copper taste of the dead girl burst on his tongue, bright and warm.

The boy's howls turned to sobs.

The monster drank.

· · · · ●· ● · · ·

Her bath water was getting cold. Willa lifted her foot from the porcelain tub and examined her wrinkled toes. There was a deep purple bruise along her left shin and no skin on either knee. The shallow stab wound beneath her ribs looked like it needed a half dozen stitches. Willa winced and sunk deeper into the tub.

It had taken two changes of water to get her clean. The humid air trapped in the curtained bath corner smelled like eucalyptus and lavender. The washroom girl, a pretty Fractured Healer with violet eyes, had gently wiped the blood from Willa's cheek with a soft washcloth.

The last time someone had given her a bath she'd been three years old, standing in their tiny apartment bathtub with rubber duckies and a windup tugboat drifting around her feet. The hands helping that day had been her mother's.

Willa closed her eyes, hoping the steam would hide her tears. It was past time to get out. Her hair was so clean it squeaked, and the scabs on her knees were starting to stiffen, but she had chased off the washroom girl twenty minutes ago.

What she really needed was a hot meal followed by three days of sleep, but the Triad floor would be filled with people with their whispers and eyes, so she was hiding in the bathtub like any self-respecting girl until she could face the fucking train wreck of her life. Willa sunk further into the tepid water, bubbles tickling her nose.

Her mother was alive.

A woman she could barely remember. The woman who had poured her Honey Nut Cheerios and chased away the nightmares. The woman she had mourned and left behind.

Her mother belonged to the past. Willa had no idea what to do with the living, breathing stranger waiting for a heartwarming reunion in the Triad.

"Are you planning to hide until you dissolve into the bathwater?"

Willa jumped, splashing water from the tub. She glared at Caspian, who leaned against a nearby pillar.

"What the hell are you doing?" she demanded, gathering the remaining floating bubbles in a vain attempt to cover herself. He shrugged, eyes skimming lazily down her submerged body.

Caspian was dressed in a plain white t-shirt and loose drawstring pants. Steam tangled with the mellow throb of his aura. His feet were bare. He looked clean, safe, and delicious.

She scowled. "Go away."

Caspian chuckled.

"I'm not in the mood." She tried not to shiver.

"Yeah, I gathered as much," he said, picking up her towel before reaching between her ankles to pull up the drain.

"Hey!" she said, kicking at him halfheartedly.

Caspian dodged her easily and held out a hand. "Up."

Willa stood with a huff, crossing her arms over her chest, but for once Caspian wasn't looking. He wrapped the fluffy white towel around her shoulders and helped her from the bath. She snatched her hand away as soon as her feet touched the cold marble, but he didn't comment, perching on the edge of the tub while she scrubbed at her hair with another towel.

"You tried to kill me," she said finally. That wasn't exactly true but she was feeling dramatic.

"Come here."

She eyed him nervously. He let out an exasperated laugh and pulled her into his arms.

"Caspian..." She put her hands on his chest but couldn't convince them to push him away. They weren't lovers. Hell, they were barely friends. But she had left Asher behind, and there was no one else.

Willa pressed her forehead to his shoulder. Caspian's fingers rested loosely on the back of her neck. The drain gurgled.

"She wasn't there when I needed her," she whispered, wishing her words weren't so small.

Caspian made a shushing sound, lifted her chin, and kissed her. It wasn't like any other kiss they had ever shared, so light that it made her shiver. He pulled away, eyes serious. "You have us, Willa. Eden and I are your family now. Always."

Willa searched his handsome, lying face and found only fierce protectiveness. She touched the purple bruise on the bridge of his nose and—

Someone outside the curtain cleared their throat. "Uh, still out here guys," Eden called.

Willa made a sound of dismay and wiggled away from Caspian. He let her go, his face unreadable. "Go the hell away, Eden," Caspian hollered.

"Oh, I would love to, believe me," Eden responded dryly. "But we've got shit to do, and the Council isn't going to wait while you two paw at each other like teenagers."

Caspian rolled his eyes.

Willa tightened her grip on her towel, trying to look as dignified as she could while being mostly naked. "You can go now," she said primly, pretending that she hadn't kissed him in a moment of supreme stupidity.

To her surprise, Caspian just nodded and left without anything more than a smoldering glance.

Willa sighed, slipping on her clothes. She was the dumbest girl who ever lived.

She ran her fingers through her wet hair, wishing there was some sort of portal back to her little hammock. What was the point of magic if you couldn't use it to avoid awkward social situations?

When the magic didn't come, she stepped out of the bathing room where Eden waited clutching a plate in his hand. He thrust it in her direction. "The kitchen was closed, but I made you something to eat."

She took the sandwich gratefully. Eden had taken the time to warm up some roasted pigeon meat, tucking it between two fluffy slices of sweet bread. Her eyes pricked at the small kindness. "Thank you," she mumbled around a mouthful.

Eden smiled tentatively, his wings ringing like distant bells behind his shoulders. Caspian cleared his throat, shifting awkwardly.

"So your mom's alive—that's a kick in the balls huh?" Eden blurted.

Willa nearly choked. Caspian glared at the Traveler, who just grinned and thumped her on the back.

She tried to smile at the teasing, setting the sandwich back on the plate. It suddenly tasted like sawdust. "I don't know what to do."

Eden shrugged. "Sometimes when you don't know what to do—the best thing to do is nothing."

She nodded. It was as good a plan as any.

Chapter 31

C ASPIAN STRODE ACROSS THE Triad floor in full battle gear, ignoring the way the other Trinities parted for him. A cute blonde Traveler glanced up from her book as he passed, blushing when he winked.

He felt good. Yesterday, he'd been worried Willa wasn't ruthless enough to complete the Initiation. It happened. A Trinity who couldn't finish the process languished on the sidelines. Sometimes for years.

It was a fate he could not endure. Not now, when so much was at stake. So he had pushed her.

Attitude was critical during battle. People thought it was skill or weapons or teamwork, but that was bullshit. Emotion marked the slim difference between life and death. Fear was best; the instinct to survive was the most powerful motivator, but fear didn't work in the Initiation ring. Willa knew he would never really hurt her. so he had used the intimacy between them, taunting her pain and loneliness until rage had risen and swallowed her uncertainty. And it had worked. His team was finally complete.

Caspian stopped in front of the war room's curtain. Everyone important had been summoned this morning. It was early, the smell of coffee just starting to permeate the air, but he'd been eager to get started. There were worlds to save and he intended to be on the front lines.

He reached for the curtain but raised voices stilled his hand. It was the kind of hushed shouting people did when they were arguing about something important—something that was a secret.

Caspian glanced over his shoulder. He should announce himself. Whatever the Counselors were discussing was above his rank, but after what had happened with Eden...he didn't want any more surprises. So he loosened the tight fist around his power.

The Triad became a cacophony. He could hear a hundred heartbeats and the whisper of book pages as clearly as if they were happening within the confines of his own skull. The rest of his senses sharpened too, the deafening noise mingling with the tang of sweat and the citrus polish they used to keep the marble floor gleaming. The faint brush of air on his skin was like sandpaper.

During battle, he barely noticed his heightened senses but in quiet moments like this, it was overwhelming. His head started to throb. Caspian ignored it and focused. The voices behind the curtain sharpened. He held his breath.

"—will be fine. " Lyra was saying, her voice calm.

"I just got her back," Liliana fumed. "It was my job to clean up the slaughter in London. I know what it looks like to lose a whole Triad. This is too dangerous."

There was a pause. Caspian wished his power included seeing through walls.

Lyra's voice was unruffled. "She is Trinity, Counselor. Caspian and Eden are our most promising fighters. Your daughter will be fine."

Caspian glanced again over his shoulder at the girl he'd winked at, but she was busy with her book again. There were no secrets here, just a protective mother worried about sending her daughter into her first battle. It was bad manners for a Hunter to activate his power in the Triad. He'd accidentally overheard enough forbidden love trysts to understand the purpose of this unspoken rule. Privacy was hard to come by in a place where people could travel anywhere and hear every whisper. He shouldn't be spying.

"I know she can handle herself," Liliana snapped. "But the Skotos are a new kind of monster now. Darkness Lyra, we lost this war eight years ago. Sending *anyone* out there is suicide."

Caspian leaned closer, nose brushing the curtain. There was a terrible certainty in Liliana's voice. As if their future was already written.

"Are you suggesting," Lyra responded, her voice like ice, "that we hide in the Umbra like cowards? That we just let humanity fend for themselves?"

"Cities are falling," Liliana argued. "Thousands are already lost. When is it time to leave the humans to their own devices?"

Caspian stiffened. Her words were treasonous. Protecting the world wasn't just what the Triad *did*, it was who they *were*. To suggest otherwise was...

"We will suffer great losses, it is true," Lyra countered wearily. "These rumors about the Skotos' increased consciousness are circumstantial at best. We must strike while we are still strong enough to do so."

Caspian edged closer, but the rest faded into words even he could not hear.

He didn't understand. The Skotos were animals—vicious and deadly, but nothing more. It was in their nature to be ruthless.

But there had been rumors. Murmured tales told around the fireplace about a horrible *knowing* buried behind the Skotos' milky eyes now. Caspian shook his head. It wasn't possible. Animals didn't just *change*. Rabbits didn't sprout wings so they could catch better food.

Rapidly approaching footsteps interrupted his thoughts and he jumped back just as Lyra swept through the curtain, nodding at him sharply as she passed.

He waited for a beat before peeking into the dim war room where Liliana was still hunched over the massive wooden table that dominated the space. It was a mess, papers and discarded coffee mugs strewn haphazardly across its worn surface. A sword encrusted with emeralds was being used as an expensive paperweight.

Liliana's body curled in on itself as if trying to protect the soft underbelly of her heart. She looked defeated and small. It just seemed strange for her to look that way after she had gotten her daughter back from the dead.

"Oh God," Liliana breathed, not seeing him. "Why have you given me back my daughter after all this time? I do not deserve this kindness. Her face is a gift I am too ashamed to bear."

Caspian had done awful things. He'd pushed Eden's boyfriend from a roof. Had tasted Willa's skin with lying lips. Had killed and killed and killed. But no guilt could match the torment he heard in the Counselor's rough voice. He let the curtain fall, reeling in his power until the Triad was once again a hollow vacuum of sound.

· · · · · ● · ● · · ·

Willa stared at her steaming coffee cup as her dead mother called the meeting to order. She was numb, her muscles still ticking like a tired engine, but Beckett had forced the mug into her hand when she entered the war room, and she was quite sure it was the only thing keeping her upright.

Last night her body had begged for sleep, but her mind had been a river after a storm—swollen and churning. At least everything she had been through had earned her a sympathetic seat at the table. The rest of the room was full—standing room only.

Eden leaned against a window, half hidden in the crowd and pretending not to watch Beckett and Trevor talking quietly at the table. Caspian had positioned himself at Lyra's right elbow. Across from Willa, Zara was using one of the ancestor's swords to clean the mud from her boot tread.

Willa forced down a sip of coffee and tried to look normal.

Her mother was wearing the deep red vest of the Council, her dark hair peppered with gray and pulled into a tight bun. She barely resembled the smiling woman in the Polaroid Willa had kept under her pillow for years. Time and training had erased Liliana's soft edges. An emerald-encrusted saber was strapped to her hip, the familiar Fractured tattoo curving along the top of her cheekbone.

She looked strong now that her tears had dried, her eyes sharp as they scanned the crowd. Willa registered for the first time that her mother was a Hunter—*the* Hunter, actually. The small collection of memories she had of Liliana were water-swollen pieces of a moldy puzzle. The picture was still there, but the details had changed and distorted. This woman was a stranger.

She could feel the weight of her mother's gaze and took another sip. They had shared a tight smile when Willa entered the crowded room, but she wasn't sure what was supposed to happen next. Should she wave? Go over for a hug? Make small talk?

Her overstimulated brain couldn't work out the answer, so she opted to stare into her mug. Willa rubbed the center of her forehead and tried to focus on the meeting. There were far more important things happening than a resurrected mother.

"Largest rift has formed in Central Park," Liliana was saying, pointing at the Metropolitan Museum of Art on a rudimentary map of the City. "Everything that is happening in New York also happened in London just before the final invasion. An unusually quiet Umbra, increased Skotos activity, and reports of newly formed rifts are all warning signs. It's like the tide pulling away from the shore before a tsunami. We need to proceed with extreme caution. If we deploy all of our—"

"Thank you for your intel, Counselor," Lyra interrupted, rising from her seat.

Willa didn't know much about Trinity politics, but she knew a dismissal when she heard one. Liliana muttered something under her breath and Willa found herself biting back a smile. At least they agreed Lyra was a class-A bitch.

Lyra lifted her chin, delicate hands folded in front of her. "We will attack first thing in the morning. Counselor Liliana and Counselor Ester have been busy the past few weeks recruiting Trinity from the other Triads to assist. They arrive tonight. Please welcome them." Her gaze swept the room. "If we eliminate the Skotos in one big sweep, we will win the war. To give us the greatest chance for success, we have allied with a rebel human group."

Willa held onto her coffee as the room erupted with angry voices. Eden pushed off the window, frowning at the back of Caspian's head. She didn't exactly understand what the commotion was all about, but she agreed with any argument that involved not fighting monsters.

At the head of the table, Lyra waited. Her lips were painted blood red to match the scarlet of her vest. The candlelight shimmered across the arches of her cheeks. Willa wondered what kind of woman brushed highlighter across her face before going to a war meeting.

A chair scraped across the floor and the hubbub died as everyone turned to Beckett. He smoothed the front of his vest. "Counselor Lyra, with all due respect, humans are unprepared for an enemy of this magnitude. It will be a slaughter."

Lyra nodded, as if she expected this response. But it was Counselor Ester who rose to answer. She held her body gracefully, like a dancer. Or a warrior.

Ester put a hand on Lyra's shoulder, her warm eyes taking time to land on each face. "I understand your concern. The Triad has spent centuries protecting humanity. We've fought and died in the darkness. I have seen the blood of the London Triad drain into the sewers. If we don't fight now, we will die—Trinity and human alike. It is time for us to stand together."

Liliana caught Willa's eye, her aura nearly swallowed by black. She could read the regret in her mother's eyes as clearly as if Liliana had whispered them in her ear.

Her mother rose to stand next to Lyra and Ester. The Council's decisions had been made. The air went out of the room. Beckett lowered back to his seat, clutching Trevor's hand. Zara stared at the ancestor's sword in her lap. The zit on her chin was starting to scab over. She was thirteen.

Willa stayed in her chair as the meeting ended, not bothering to listen to plans she wouldn't understand as the crowd filtered away. Eden hesitated in front of her, lifting an eyebrow. She gave him a half smile as Liliana started toward her. Whatever this was, she had to see it through.

Eden nodded as if she'd spoken and left her alone with her mother.

Liliana took the chair beside her, perching on the end awkwardly as if she didn't know what to do with her body. She cleared her throat. "Are you okay?"

Willa fiddled with her coffee mug. The last time she'd been okay was in Asher's living room. "Liliana, " she stopped. Her mother's name tasted foreign in her mouth.

Liliana's lips twisted. She was still wearing her wedding ring—a modest silver band with a single diamond and two chips of emerald.

"I wish I knew the right words to fix this," she sighed, spinning her ring with her thumb—a familiar movement that made Willa's stomach hurt. "Baby, you have to know, there was nothing in this world that I would have chosen over you. When I became Fractured I was devastated. I tried—"

"I was alone," Willa interrupted. Her mother had been a prisoner here. The grown-up part of her understood, but Willa didn't know how to forget the endless lonely nights or forgive the hollow of starvation.

Liliana's eyes shimmering. "I know. If there was a way to reach you, I promise you I would have."

She reached over and squeezed Willa's hand. "But you are strong and fierce. My beautiful daughter. You are the key in the door. A piece of hope!"

Willa stared at the black sun over her dead mother's shoulder. She missed Asher. Missed the quiet way he had of not needing her. She pulled her hand away gently. "I didn't become who I am *because* of you, Liliana. I became this despite you."

Chapter 32

E DEN RAN THE EDGE of his arrow across the sharpening stone and
pretended he didn't know Beckett had stepped into his room. He didn't
have to turn around; every nerve in his body sparked to attention.

"Eden?"

Eden dabbed a bit of water onto the diamond stone and tried to ignore the
way Beckett's voice skittered across his skin. It was barely morning, the smell of
coffee weaving up to the Traveler's quarters which were tucked into the highest
rafters of the Triad.

Caspian had already been to see him about today's mission. Yesterday they
had just been children playing at being soldiers. Today they'd go to war.

"Eden," Beckett repeated, a little more impatiently.

Eden ran the arrow's sharp edge across the stone one more time, the
movement comforting and familiar. He arranged his expression into casual
disinterest before he turned.

Beckett's cheeks flushed.

Eden cursed silently. It was so early he hadn't changed yet, his loose pajamas
low on his hips and his chest was still bare. Standing half naked in front of the
man you wanted to take to bed was a decidedly bad decision, so he straightened
his spine, slipping on false arrogance like armor. A trick he had picked up from
Caspian.

"You look...rested," Beckett stammered, his gaze flickering down Eden's
body.

Beckett might as well have touched him. Eden's skin tingled.

The Healer's curls were a wild riot around his head, and Eden wondered what they would feel like between his fingers. "What can I do for you, Beckett?" he asked, keeping his hands busy by slipping the arrow into his quiver.

Beckett fiddled nervously with the hem of his vest. "I just wanted to...check on you. Are you ready for today?"

Eden shrugged, pretending the question didn't matter. Pretending that having someone who cared didn't change everything. Beckett must have seen because he stepped closer, reaching out to touch Eden's arm. It was an innocent gesture, a friend comforting a friend. But Beckett's fingertips seemed to burn. He couldn't tell if it was because of the Healer's power or his own overwhelming desire to taste the boy's skin.

Darkness damned, he couldn't do this right now.

He shook off Beckett's hand, shrugging on his vest. "I'm surprised you bothered to stop by, was Trevor busy?"

Beckett stiffened. "Don't be an ass, Eden. It doesn't suit you."

"Shows how little you know me."

The Healer flinched. Regret was a sharp barb, but he schooled his features into bland disinterest as Beckett glanced at the door.

"I think I know you better than you'd like to admit," Beckett said, worrying his bottom lip. His utterly kissable bottom lip. Eden sent a silent prayer to whatever god might be paying attention for Beckett to stop immediately so he could think straight.

Desperate for this moment to be over so he could get busy dying Eden said, "Well, I'm fine. Is that all?"

"You have no right to be rude, Eden. Not about Trevor. You had your chance and..." he stammered, heat blazing on his cheeks. "And you didn't want me."

Nothing could have been further from the truth. Eden pressed his hands against his thighs to stop himself from dragging Beckett closer.

The Healer had a freckle that teased the corner of his mouth, normally hidden inside the curve of his dimple. Eden wondered idly what it would taste like, what Beckett would do if he leaned forward and brushed that tiny mark with his lips.

Beckett's eyes widened and he swayed forward a fraction. It shouldn't have been perceptible, but Eden's body noticed. He sucked in a breath. Maybe he should say yes. He should be able to have this. Should be able to take what he wanted just once. It wouldn't *mean* anything.

That was a lie. If he slept with Beckett, his heart would never recover.

"You need to step back," Eden whispered roughly.

Beckett's lips parted, doubt warring with desire in his dark eyes. Eden had never wanted anything more than to dip his head and capture Beckett's mouth. To swallow the soft sound of surprise and drag him to the floor until the world narrowed to just the two of them.

But he didn't.

Because he had lost before. Because for a short time, he had found happiness in the arms of a boy who had loved him. Had found light in the never-ending darkness. And it had been enough. Hell, it had been everything. But the absence of that light had left a bleeding, gaping hole in his chest, and Eden wasn't sure he could survive it again. So he didn't move.

But Beckett did. Determination flickered across the Healer's face as he stepped closer.

Eden went still when the warm line of Beckett's body pressed against his own. His fingers curled around Beckett's shoulder. He meant to push him away but suddenly it felt as if the Healer was the only thing anchoring him to the world. "Beckett," he begged. "I can't."

Beckett didn't answer, his wandering fingers sweeping across Eden's cheekbones and across his bottom lip. The wanting stretched out forever, the two of them suspended in the purgatory between the haunted past and the doomed future.

Still, Eden shook his head, and after an endless minute, Beckett retreated.

"I don't understand you," he said softly.

Eden slid his hands into his pockets so Beckett couldn't see them shaking. "I have to go."

There was desire in Beckett's dark eyes but also something haunted. His Fractured tattoo stood out on his cheek, a constant reminder that he was a prisoner.

He smiled and there was so much sadness in it Eden almost strode back to him. Almost gave him what he wanted. Anything to smooth that expression from his face.

"Don't die," Beckett said quietly.

Eden swallowed the words that clamored at the back of his throat. "I'll try."

· · · · ● · ● · · · ·

The boy who used to be Asher stood in the shadow of the Metropolitan Museum of Art. The statuesque building was a charred husk of what it used to be, the walls inside had been stripped of their riches long ago. Now it was just a gravestone of the past.

The monster didn't know this.

But Asher did. And the creature accessed those thoughts as easily as flipping through a rolodex.

The boy used to come here when a new foster home wasn't working, skip school, and jump the subway turnstile until he found his way back to this place. The boy found comfort in getting lost amongst the cold marble statues and the bustling tourists. As if this building were home. As if he weren't lost.

But the nightmare didn't care about those memories, searching instead for the map etched into the boy's mind. Accessing memories of the way time had eaten into the quiet beauty of the museum, leaving behind collapsed roofs and the soggy ruins of masterpieces.

The monster stood in the center of 5th Avenue and watched a girl move aside a sheet of rotten plywood, slipping inside the museum without a glance at the street behind her. She could have been any street urchin except that her hair was the same shade of red as the dead one on the boy's kitchen floor, the color peeking out from a Yankee's cap.

This area of the city was almost abandoned because it was too close to the Compound, so the girl didn't see the not-Asher standing in the middle of the street, despite the sunlight stretching across his feet. Didn't look over her shoulder to see the army of Skotos hiding in the shadows.

The monster could hear them—his brothers—the muffled click of their claws and the wet suck of their lungs. The human rebels would not go without a fight, but they were young and stupid and so they would die drowning in their own blood.

They did not know that they had already lost.

The boy trapped inside his head was quiet now. Quiet even as he gave the signal, standing aside as his brothers swept past, the sweet perfume of rot trailing behind them. The monster smiled as screams drifted from the grand museum into the morning sun.

Even then, the boy's voice was silent.

Chapter 33

"It's not as scary as it looks," Mae offered as Willa peered over the edge of the Traveler's launching platform. The terrace was attached to the outside of the building, so high in the air she could feel the subtle sway of the building. An empty window gave the Travelers easy access from the inside of the Triad. There was no railing, just tuffs of clouds and the dark city stretched out before them.

Willa eyed Mae's wings, the razor-thin feathers curving around the girl's shoulders like a cloak. "Not comforting coming from someone with wings," she retorted.

Beckett chuckled and strapped a thin, wicked-looking sword to his back. It was the only weapon he wore and it looked strangely out of place on him, like Mother Teresa with a machine gun.

"Don't lie to her, Mae," Zara interjected from where she was stretched out on the platform ledge, one leg dangled over the fathomless drop. Her face was tilted up to the black sun, eyes closed as if she were basking in the light. "It's gonna be a shit show."

"Zara," Beckett scolded, nudging her in the hip with his toe until she squirmed away.

Willa tried to smile despite her intense desire to vomit. They all seemed so relaxed.

Eden munched on a piece of bacon as he spoke to Caspian and Lyra. Willa checked the chamber of her gun for the fifth time since breakfast and tried not to look terrified. It was her first time in the field. The first time other people's lives would depend on the choices she made. What if Caspian was right? What if she *was* a coward?

She bit her lip and wondered if it was possible to get fired from being a supernatural warrior. Maybe the severance package was good—free health care and unlimited Traveler flights to the Bahamas. Willa suppressed a laugh as Caspian and Eden made their way toward her across the crowded platform.

The whole Triad was here. There were newcomers too. Willa could hear the lilt of a South African accent mixed with the sharp snap of German. A wide-faced girl sat cross-legged on the edge of the platform, a pink flower tucked behind her long black hair. Two French boys leaned against each other, talking quietly. It reminded Willa of the city Before—filled with a hundred different languages and faces.

"I feel like I should stop asking if you're okay but I can't seem to make myself," Liliana said at her elbow.

Willa swallowed a startled curse. Liliana had appeared so quietly, she hadn't had time to make a lame excuse to be somewhere else. Having a mother with a Hunter's stealthy abilities could prove to be very inconvenient.

Liliana's hair was down today, the soft waves flowing over her bare shoulders. Small chips of emerald glinted in her earlobes, a match for the ones that encrusted the sword at her hip. Impractical for a battle and also somehow defiant, as if she'd dressed for her own funeral.

It occurred to Willa that she might have liked this woman if there had been more time. She attempted a smile. "It's a reasonable question. I'm not even sure what okay looks like anymore."

They should probably have a moment. One of those tear-jerker goodbyes you saw in the movies. But her mother just reached out and squeezed her wrist, the gesture down low and hidden from prying eyes.

"Be safe," Liliana said but her eyes were on Caspian, her words sounding suspiciously like a command. He nodded curtly, avoiding Willa's annoyed glare as he called for everyone to gather. She wasn't used to having anyone take care of her.

Mae spun away from the edge of the platform, the wind catching the purple scarf that bound her curls. Zara scrambled to her feet. Another unfortunate blemish had erupted on her forehead overnight, and she kept touching it nervously as she glanced at Caspian.

Willa raised an eyebrow. The Hunter *was* looking particularly delicious this morning, twin knives strapped across his broad chest. Oblivious, Caspian crossed his arms, biceps flexing. "As the newest Trinities, we have been assigned to go in as the second wave."

He grimaced while he said it, and Willa knew he hated not being on the front lines. "Zara?"

"Yup!" she saluted with one finger.

Caspian suppressed a sigh. "We will position our teams behind the battle lines and wait for Lyra's signal to engage."

"And then what?" she asked, waving at the enormous rift hovering above them. "IF we do. Then what?"

Zara popped a piece of gum in her mouth. "Well, then we patch up those nasty rifts with our magical needle and thread and live like heroes for the rest of our days." She patted at her pockets, eyes widening. "Oh shit, I must have forgotten my sewing kit"

"That is not helpful darling," Mae said mildly. Zara blew her a kiss.

Caspian scowled. "Let's deal with one problem at a time."

Eden twirled an arrow between his fingers, silver flashing. "What about the humans?"

Willa frowned, hoping her friends were far away from this mess. There had been no time to warn Asher.

"They're armed but..." Caspian said, glancing over at Lyra before lowering his voice. "Nearly useless. Think of them like extras in a movie—townspeople with a pickax and misdirected zeal who are going to die before you even think about getting a popcorn refill."

Mae lifted a manicured eyebrow. "Tactless."

"Any idea how many Skotos we're facing?" Zara asked, smacking her gum.

Caspian grimaced, whether it was from the gum chewing or the question, Willa couldn't tell. "The reports aren't good."

"Trevor was one of the scouts," Beckett interjected. "He said the number was...substantial. Hundreds"

Eden's spinning arrow dropped into his palm. "Well, if *Trevor* said it..."

The group lapsed into awkward silence. The platform swayed. Trinity started to disappear around them, winking out like fireflies on a summer night.

"Hundreds," Mae said softly, staring into the distance.

Willa thought of Asher then. Thought of the pocket in his bag where he kept extra food and medicine. He'd distribute them when no one was looking, slipping relief into the hands of the starving and hopeless. He thought she didn't know about that pocket. But she did. She knew.

The tremor in her hand stilled. Today was about Asher and the dead child at the bottom of her apartment stairs. It was about Donut and the park with the twinkling Christmas lights and the tiny scraps of life the Darkness hadn't managed to steal.

Willa lifted her chin. "Let's go see, shall we?"

Caspian unsheathed his blade and nodded. "Yes. Let's go see."

· · · ● · ● · · · ·

A scream drifted through the air, punctuated by the sharp clash of swords and the high whistle of Travelers' wings. Willa glanced at Caspian. He was crouched just outside the covered bodega door, watching the empty street. She hadn't seen him move since they'd arrived in a swirl of Eden's frost and wind.

Zara's team was positioned across the street in an abandoned laundromat and she could see CJ and April playing catch with a balled-up t-shirt through the broken plate glass. Zara leaned against the doorframe, blowing bubbles with her gum.

This is not what she expected the end of times to look like.

It felt like hours had passed, but Eden was only on his second cigarette. Willa had never seen him smoke while sober but she supposed it didn't matter much now. His long legs were stretched beside hers, and he was busy tracing the letters of a faded old lottery poster with one finger.

Willa fiddled with the gun on her lap, listening to the sound of battle just streets away. "Maybe we should just go?"

Caspian didn't turn from his post. "Lyra's instructions were clear."

Eden stubbed his cigarette out on the chipped linoleum. "Maybe there's no one left to give the signal. Maybe they're all—"

Someone was running toward them.

It was Lyra, her long white ponytail trailing behind her, the tip red as if she'd dragged it through blood. They scrambled to their feet as she stopped in front of them.

"Ambush," she gasped, wings scraping the blacktop. One hand was pressed to her side, the gold bangles on her wrist jangling quietly as blood squeezed between her fingers. "The humans were compromised. The Skotos were waiting for us—an army of them. They knew."

Her words were cut off by another scream, this time guttural and wet and filled with triumph. Caspian raised his sword.

"We need you," Lyra managed, before hurtling into the sky, blood pattering to the pavement in bright red drops.

They followed her—running toward the battle instead of away. Willa checked her magazine as they ran, stray bullets slipping through shaking fingers and clattering behind them. There was no time to stop.

Eden took to the air as they burst from the jungle of buildings and into the battle that raged on 5th Avenue. Willa stumbled, the smell of death hitting her like a wall. It was a war zone.

Skotos poured from the mouth of the museum, blood cascading down the marble stairs after them. The sky was a storm of Travelers, their wings ringing like a thousand swords.

The others barreled into the fray. Zara hacked the arm off a Skotos as she went, gore soaking her purple hair. Willa hesitated on the edge of the chaos. She'd seen her share of death. She'd watched soldiers beat women in the streets and seen the swollen bellies of starving children, but there had never been anything like this.

Her gun was forgotten in her hand. She couldn't do this. Not even for Asher or Donut or a thousand fairy-lit trees.

"Damn it, Willa!" Caspian's hands were rough as he dragged her behind a battered minivan sagging on the curb. She pressed herself against the passenger door and tried to force air into her lungs. Nearby, a girl she recognized from the Triad floor buried her sword into the eye of a Skotos. It shrieked and opened her throat with one swipe.

Willa choked on a scream. There was no honor here—just chaos and death. Everywhere she looked, Trinities were fighting bravely, sword to claw, but just as many were laying down their weapons and stepping silently into their death.

"Darkness help us," Caspian muttered as a Traveler fell from the sky, glancing off the side of the van and landing in a tangle of shattered wings.

She could feel Eden above them, launching arrows into the crowd with deadly precision. Bodies were scattered everywhere, human and Trinity alike. She was no expert in warfare, but it was clear they were losing—that the battle was actually a slaughter.

Caspian must have seen it too because he cursed and stood, exposing himself as a nearby Healer desperately tried to hold his glistening intestines.

Willa felt the truth of things dawn on her—a cold certainty like falling through an icy pond. She grabbed Caspian's arm. "We can't go out there. This battle is already lost."

Caspian's eyes blazed down at her. "I'm no coward, Celadon."

"This is not about your Darkness damned pride," she hissed. "It is about surviving to fight another day. It is about the *future*."

In her peripheral, a human boy's skull disappeared inside a Skotos' rotting maw. Willa heard bones crack. Her stomach lurched.

Caspian wrenched his arm away with a snarl, plunging into the fight, sword flashing. Willa swore, her hand tightening around her gun. She had a split second to decide—live like a coward or die pointlessly?

A woman lay nearby, wings twisted grotesquely underneath her as a Skotos feasted on what was left of her face. The Traveler's limp arm was outstretched toward her, three gold bangles glinting on a blood-soaked wrist.

Willa pressed a hand to her mouth. The tide was tipping. She turned to flee, but suddenly a line of sight cleared through the grotesque turmoil. And she saw him.

Asher stood at the top of the stairs, an oasis of calm in the middle of a massacre. Willa would have noticed him even if the line of his shoulders hadn't been achingly familiar. She would have noticed because he was the only one without a weapon. It should have been the most disturbing about seeing him on the bloody battlefield, but it wasn't.

Asher's aura was gone.

The absence of his familiar blue flame was as disturbing to her as a lost limb. Without thought, she was moving, her gun already in hand as she plunged into the melee. She aimed and shot on instinct, reloading quickly as she dodged through a storm of arrows and claws, vaguely aware that Caspian was following her, screaming her name.

Ahead, a Skotos crouched over a corpse at the bottom of the grand stairs, lifting its head as she approached. Willa shot it in the face, not hesitating as gray matter sprayed into the air, and vaulted over its falling body.

Terror pulsed down the bond from both of the boys. Caspian's sword was a blur at her back and the wind from Eden's wings lifted her hair as she raced up the stairs, skidding to a stop a few steps below Asher.

Her heart thundering. He turned and something broke inside her.

There was no humanity in his eyes. From a distance, she had thought he was wearing gloves, the long kind designed for prom dresses and ball gowns, but it was blood, coating his arms up to his elbows, as if he had reached inside a fresh corpse and pulled out warm entrails.

He grinned, blood caught in his teeth, and Willa understood.

"Asher," she breathed.

She should run. Should leave him in the middle of this lost battle with his blood-covered hands. Caspian's back pressed against hers, his sword a flurry as he held death at bay. Overhead, Eden unloaded a barrage of arrows. A Skotos crawled toward her through the gore, quivers sticking from its ravaged spine like quills.

Somehow, her Healing shield was up—controlled by the part of her brain that could still hear Caspian begging her to run. Telling her Asher was already dead. And he was. Willa could see it in the horrible emptiness where his aura should be and his feral grin.

But also. Asher was wearing that damn shirt he loved; the one from Al's Garage that was black with grease and soft with time. The one he had been wearing the day he'd saved her life.

So Willa raised her gun, willing her shaking hands to steady. Behind her, the screams of battle were fading into sobs. It was almost over. The thing-that-was-not-Asher leered and Willa pulled the trigger.

The bullet screamed past not-Asher's ear. He flinched.

Willa lunged, grabbing his wrist and funneling the full breadth of her newfound power into his skin. It poured into him, searing and white, filling her vision. She cried out. Or maybe he did.

The shield around Caspian and Eden flickered and vanished, but she didn't see it, too busy wadding through Asher's darkness. Somewhere Caspian was screaming her name and—

A blue ember guttered in the black ocean inside Asher.

Willa hesitated. She'd healed flesh before. Had knit together bone and muscle, but this was different. There was no margin for error. She closed her eyes and remembered Asher's smile in the back of that cop car a hundred years ago—remembered the flash of the key gripped between his teeth. Remembered hope.

The warm power inside of her became a supernova.

Asher made a ragged noise and collapsed against her. He smelled sour, like sickness and sweat, but his hand found hers, their fingers knitting as they knelt on the bloody steps.

The blue of his aura flared, luminous, and bright as she touched the back of his neck, ignoring the gore caught in his eyelashes. There was only devastation in his eyes, the nightmare he'd escaped still real and raging around them. There was nothing she could do about this new pain. It would require a different sort of healing.

""Just go easy Ash. I'll—"

"Caspian!" It was Eden's voice, high above them, that wrenched her back to the present. All around them, a thin brown haze hovered over the quieting battlefield; the aura of dying settling between the bodies of the fallen. Caspian knelt a few steps below them, head bowed, his bloody sword forgotten at his side. His hands were empty.

A Skotos loomed above him, red-tinged spittle dripping from its shattered jaw. A dagger was buried to the hilt in the side of its neck as someone had tried to saw through the sinew and failed. The monster lifted one gnarled hand, bone finger claws spread.

Eden screamed again, wings tight against his body as he dove out of the sky toward them. Time slowed. The Skotos lifted the Hunter's limp body from the step. Caspian didn't fight but his eyes were open, meeting hers, his aura charred black.

Her stomach hollowed. She'd sacrificed one boy's life for another.

The Skotos grinned as if it knew, its teeth etched in blood, and pierced Caspian's chest with a single claw. Willa felt it slide like a surgeon's knife between the chambers of his heart the same as if it were her own flesh. His body jerked.

Eden tumbled from the sky, landing on the hard marble steps in a snarl of wings as Willa sunk to her knees. The Skotos turned away still clutching Caspian's body, trod over corpses as it descended the stairs, bones crunching.

She knew the exact second he died—felt the bond between them snap, as if someone had reached inside her chest and yanked out her heart, leaving only arteries and veins dangling in the hollow it left behind.

Willa pressed her forehead to the cold marble, barely aware that Asher was still holding her. She'd never fully understood the Fractured before. Now she clutched her chest, curling around the frayed emptiness as if she could mute the agony by collapsing around it.

A few yards away, Eden groaned. She tried to crawl toward him as the sun burned her skin, blisters bubbling wherever the light touched her.

They were Fractured now—her and Eden—doomed to the stench of the Umbra forever. She sent out a childish plea to the universe to *leave her be* as her skin burned—to give her something in this hard life that wasn't wrecked and ruined and broken.

Asher's hands were on her face, but the only thing she could see was Eden and their devastated future.

"Help us," Eden begged her, his hand outstretched on the cold marble, but there was nothing to do. No amount of healing could fix death.

· · · · ● · ● · · · ·

Willa thought about joining Caspian. It would be easier that way. So much easier to just press her cheek against the blood-soaked ground and let one last sunrise burn itself onto her retinas.

Sores erupted on her hands and the back of Eden's bowed neck, the pain dim compared to the anguish inside of her, but Asher grabbed her chin. "Willa."

She squinted at him through the harsh light. Horror was etched into his face, blood caked in the scruff of his beard. His fingers dug into her shoulder. "I won't let you die."

It seemed like a curious thing to say. She touched his cheek, desperate for some sort of anchor—looking, in a way, for *him* to heal *her*. Asher's aura thrummed under her palm, warm and luminous.

So she kissed him, brushing their lips together as the sun burned a path across her skin. He made a startled sound against her mouth, but she wound her arms around his neck—pressing closer—desperate for something solid and good and true.

Asher's breath caught in her own. She angled her head, sinking deeper, wrapping the luminous blue of his aura around her like a funeral shroud. His mouth moved against hers, soft and wanting, a question she answered with the deepest part of her heart.

It was broken that heart. The frayed ends of Caspian's severed tether bleeding into her chest, but Asher's hand pressed between her shoulder blades, and she sighed against his lips, and—without quite knowing what she was doing—healed them all.

Asher ripped himself away from her, his bruised eyes wild. "What did you do just do?"

"Willa?" Eden was on his knees, clutching at his chest, his voice filled with wonder.

Willa didn't answer—she didn't have to. The connection between them hummed, a tether reforged, a Trinity born.

Her skin pricked as each blister faded into healthy skin. An army lay dying around them, but somehow—at the end of the last battle—she had stumbled up to the door of prophecy and turned the key.

THE END

Coming Soon

B ook 2 of the Umbra Duology coming soon!
Follow rdbarto.com to stay updated.

Acknowledgements

Thank you to my youngest son, Taro, for all the brainstorming sessions at Joey's Pancake House. If it weren't for you and hashbrown casserole, this story would have much bigger plot holes.

I'd also like to thank my husband, Joel, for making space in our lives for my creativity. I haven't been satisfied with a traditional career path and you've been so patient with me (and publishing) for the ten years it took to make this book happen. Thank you to my oldest, Caden, for his enthusiastically believing in me even when I wasn't so sure.

If it weren't for my best friend, Noel, I would never have picked up a pen. Thank you for dragging my introverted butt to the first (and last) writing club meeting. You've been there for me the whole way.

Thanks to my mom, Sheila, for never setting a book limit during our *many* trips to the library, and my dad, Ed, for all those times he fell asleep during story time.

About the Author

Rebecca Barto is a former library kid who successfully used headphones, hoodies, and Stephen King novels to survive high school. As a result, she believes in stories that weave magic into everyday life. She tried out being a 4th-grade teacher and professional chef before settling on writing as her second (and hopefully final) midlife crisis. Rebecca lives in the mountains of North Carolina with her husband and two kids who refuse to acknowledge her on Tiktok. Find her at rdbarto.com.